A MATHEMATICAL STATE OF GRACE BOOK 1 AND 2 COMPLETE SERIES

FRAGMENT: FINALE FUSION

Cathy McGough

Stratford Living Publishing

WHAT READERS ARE SAYING

US:

"Brilliant! This is a highly creative young adult novel. This is a story of wild imagination, fantastic adventure, and mind-bending concepts about the nature of the universe."

"Grace is a different kind of heroine and this is a different kind of YA dystopian tale. At first glance Grace is rather unremarkable, aside from being a math prodigy. After an accident, it starts to become apparent that things might not be what they seem at the surface. I enjoyed the layered aspects of this story. A unique tale a joy to read."

"The first part reads like a mystery novel, which makes you want to keep turning the pages. There are lots of romance scenes. I also enjoyed the humor scattered throughout. Overall, there is a lot to enjoy including great characters, cool fantasy elements and great descriptive writing."

"There is a floating quality to the story that bends the mind to open possibilities."

UK:

"Excellent writing and a cracking plot keep this novel moving along at a superb pace."

"A geeky girl, a sporty boy - thrown into the chaotic world of strange winds, earthquakes and faced with being the only living beings left in the world. A story of survival and love."

TABLE OF CONTENTS

QUOTE

"I think while we were still approaching,
before we made contact,
we were in a state of mathematical grace."
Ian McEwan, ENDLESS LOVE

FOR MABEL AND MICHAEL WITH LOVE

BOOK ONE:
FRAGMENT

CHAPTER 1

Sixteen-year-old Grace Greenway liked to sleep in, especially on school days.

Her mother, Helen Greenway heaved the door open and marched inside. The two heads on her koala slippers led the way. The heads shhhh'd as they whispered their way across the cool hardwood floor.

When Helen reached the other side of the room, she let her guard down. She removed the perfume-filled handkerchief she had been covering her nose with. The air in the room was ripe due to last night's experiments, which by the smell of it had something to do with Sulphur.

Once she arrived at the window, Helen lifted the glass wide open. She stuck her head outside, filling her lungs with pure outdoor oxygen. Refreshed, she drew back the curtains. Helen pointed herself and her slippers in the direction of the lump on the bed: her daughter, Grace.

Across the room, Grace's computer made its presence known as an alarm sounded. It began flashing random numbers on the screen. It read them aloud in a voice not unlike Stephen Hawking's.

Helen considered the significance of said numbers. They made little sense to her non-mathematically oriented brain. Her koala headed slippers leaned in, feigning comprehension. Helen crossed the room, while the koala heads nodded and whispered to each other. Helen herself was clueless in matters of mathematics. She had no idea from whom her daughter had inherited her numeric genes. Helen considered this genetic transference as she studied her daughter's cocooned form.

"It's time to wake up, love!" Helen said.

Grace moved a little and threw the covers back. Stalling she stretched and yawned without opening her eyes.

"Good morning, sleepyhead," Helen said as she kissed her daughter on the forehead.

"Morning, Mum," Grace answered, finally opening her eyes.

"Bus will be here in fifteen! You've got to get a move on. I'll put something together for you to eat on the run."

"Okay, Mum," Grace said as she unfolded herself from the covers. She sat up, only to fall back down against her pillow again. She so wanted to get back into her dream state—back to the Vincente Marino state of mind.

"Come on, Grace!" Helen reiterated as she made her way toward the door, "Be downstairs in five!"

Grace whispered Vincente's name out loud, quietly, softly, almost as if she imagined he might hear her. She imagined him climbing up the lattice outside the window. Tap-tap-tapping.

The sound of her computer made her wake up. She rubbed the sleep out of her eyes. She looked down at the nightgown she was wearing. She hated this thing, with its white lace and red ribbon tie-up. It was absolutely virginal.

Grace ran her finger over the red tie, and it sliced into her flesh. It hurt like hell, like a paper cut would, but the ribbon was fabric. She unfastened it from her nightgown. Watched as it drifted towards the floor, followed a few seconds later by crimson drops of blood.

Grace sucked her bleeding finger, but it continued to drip onto the floor. It blended in with the red ribbon, which twisted like a snake. She closed her eyes and fell back onto her pillow. She thought about Vincente Marino. She couldn't wait to see him today.

Grace moved to the edge of the bed where the blood drops had been, but now they were gone. Shrugging, she picked up the red ribbon. Grace reattached it to the lace collar of her nightgown and made her way into the bathroom.

Helen bellowed another reminder from downstairs, but Grace did not acknowledge it. Instead, she closed the door behind her and with a yawn, let her white nightgown fall onto the cold tile floor.

Grace leaned into the shower cubicle and turned the hot water on full force. She let the steam rise while she glanced back over her shoulder. Her nightgown in a pile on the floor, looked almost like a spirit which had come and gone.

Then she stepped into the steaming hot water. Only hot, never cold. She washed her hair, her face, and the rest of her body, then let the hot water fall over her.

When she was as hot as a buttered crumpet, she turned the water off and stepped back. She turned the cold water on full blast, counted to three, and stepped into it. The jolt to her system was like a chemical reaction, an electric shock. In this moment, she felt the most alive. All her senses were attuned. It was almost like she had been reborn.

Grace contemplated the water as it travelled on its journey down the drain. She noticed the red tie had somehow fallen into the drain. Caught in the swirl, it went around and around and around.

She reached in and caught the red ribbon, crumpling it up into a ball in the palm of her hand, to drain away the excess water. When she opened her fist, it sprung to life and formed itself into a shape.

Intrigued, she repeated this process: Crumple the ribbon, make a fist, open the fist. See the result again. And again. And again.

It always happened.

Time and time again, it cast itself into the same form: the shape of a heart.

CHAPTER 2

G RACE TOSSED THE NIGHTGOWN into the dirty laundry basket. She began to dress in her school uniform, hiking the skirt up as high as she could get away with. All the girls at school did that to make it shorter than it was supposed to be. When her uniform was acceptable, she returned to her room and began to blow dry and brush her long, auburn hair.

She glanced over her shoulder at the computer screen: Still searching. Grace hoped it would find the answer overnight. She had programmed it with one goal: To find the next Fibonacci sequence. If successful, Grace Greenway's name would be recorded in the history books. Her discovery would rival The Golden Mean.

Grace smiled and set her hair into place. She remembered her nickname for Vincente Marino. She called him her Golden Mean. It was her little secret.

To finish things off, she reached far back into the drawer where she hid her makeup and brush. She put on some foundation and a little bit of blush. Grace sprayed a tiny splodge of perfume onto her neck before she made her way downstairs. She hoped to zip past her mum. Hoped her mom wouldn't notice the shortened skirt or any of her other accentuations this morning. Otherwise, there would be drama.

The bus driver honked at the curb, and Grace broke into a run. She grabbed her books and a piece of toast as she flew by her mum. She made her way out the door past her mother's I-Spy eyes, up the stairs and onto the bus.

Helen watched her daughter climb aboard, knowing full well that her skirt was shorter than it ought to be.

Helen continued to watch as her daughter ambled her way towards the back of the bus. She remembered the first time she had stood there and watched as her daughter boarded the bus. Helen had wanted to walk to the bus with her daughter. Grace was so excited and determined to be a big girl she wanted do it on her own. Helen remembered it like it was yesterday: how her daughter was ready to cut the cord. For Helen had been unprepared for the overwhelming pain wrenching at her heart. She followed the bus on its journey with her eyes until she could no longer see it. A tear rolled down her cheek. Helen brushed it away.

On the bus, Grace found her usual seat and then opened her book. She hid behind the textbook like it was a wall, a disguise. There, she could await the arrival of Vincente Marino, incognito.

As the bus groaned along the road, Grace lost track of where she was for a second. She came back to reality when Vincente Marino climbed aboard.

Grace sat up straight then, like a jolt of adrenalin had gone through her. She held a textbook in front of her like a shield. Inside, her heart was thumping and thumping so hard it was almost as if it had grown wings and was about to take flight. Her pulse pounded, and she had to think about taking each breath.

Vincente moved from seat to seat, high-fiving, and helloing, until the bus driver told him to take a pew. After whistling a whistle so high that every dog in the neighbourhood must have heard it, Vincente slid into his seat alongside his girlfriend, Missy Malone.

Grace was in love with Vincente Marino, but she only loved him from afar. She knew that he was totally out of her league, but at the same time, she had hope. She believed that love was a mathematical equation. She believed true love was predetermined.

It was like any other mathematical formula: you just had to search. Seeking it out until you found the perfect Golden Mean. With all the numbers from the correct sequence in place, the universe would conspire for two people to fall in love. Grace Greenway was waiting for her Golden Mean to click into sequence. Then she and Vincente Marino would be in the perfect state of love.

Grace looked up from behind the textbook. Vincente's voice floated toward her. She watched his blond hair shimmer as it caught the sunlight. His golden locks brushed across his shoulders. He laughed and whispered something into Missy's ear, and then he turned in the direction of the back of the bus.

Grace's heart stopped when their eyes locked for a split second. Her cheeks turned crimson. She covered her face with the textbook once again, like a curtain. Grace could still see her feet, her shoes. Then athletic running shoes Vincente Marino's shoes touched hers. She lowered the book, and his cobalt eyes locked with her hazel eyes. She coughed when she finally remembered to breathe.

"Hey, Grace," Vincente said. "I was wondering if you could save my life?"

She nodded.

"The game last night went late, and then we had to go out and celebrate, I mean, we won! You know how it is."

"Yeah, I know," she whispered.

"And then this morning, I realized I didn't do my math homework, and you know old Mr. Dense has it in for me. He would love to get me kicked off the team."

"Yes, I know."

"Grace?" She took in a deep breath when he said her name, as he continued. "If you could find it in your heart to lend me your homework, I'd be forever in your debt. You would absolutely save my life."

She reached into her bag without hesitation.

"I'll have it back to you before class." Then he did the motion of crossing his heart and hoping to die. He beamed a smile in her direction. "Thanks babe," he said, blowing a kiss her way as he stuffed her book into his backpack. Vincente returned to his seat, where Missy Malone was keeping an eye on their interaction.

Grace and Missy's eyes locked for a second over Vincente's shoulder. The two of them were not rivals. Missy knew that Grace wasn't a threat, but she could see that the poor idiot was smitten with her Vincente. Everyone knew that she followed him around like a stray puppy.

Grace put the textbook barrier back up and smiled to herself. In fact, she wore the biggest and most stupid grin possible. She was so excited she would be speaking with Vincente again. Even the thought of Fibonacci could not distract her.

Then she realized that the bus had stopped, and all the passengers were clambering into the aisle. She too made her, burrowing herself in until she was standing directly behind Vincente. He let Missy out in front of him. The scent of Vincente's cologne wafted in her direction. Grace breathed it in, breathed him in.

Once he stepped out into the sunlight, the rays kissed the blood gold ring on his finger, and for a moment, blinded her. She bumped into him, but he didn't seem to mind. He laughed and beamed a toothy smile in her direction.

Grace forgot to breathe.

Missy Malone hooted, put her arm through Vincente's, and led him away.

Grace arrived at her locker. She took a deep breath and then threw her backpack inside. She looked over her morning schedule: Aboriginal Indigenous Studies, Math, Art, then Lunch, followed by more Art, English, Spare. She could go to see the game. The bell rang. She slammed her locker shut. She ran along the corridor and took her seat alongside the windows.

Her teacher Miss Smart took attendance, and then introduced a special guest to the class. The guest speaker was a woman from The Stolen Generation.

She told the class about how she was taken. Then adopted into a white family. How she was not allowed to practice or follow the traditions of The Gadigal people.

Grace felt sorry for her. After all, no child should be abandoned, let alone stolen. No child should be excluded from her own history. It was preposterous.

Grace could not understand why the woman's parents had allowed it to happen. Grace imagined the situation unfolding at her house. Strangers showing up. Demanding to take her away. Grace's parents would have hired every lawyer in town and stopped things before they even started. She thought about asking the woman this question. Another classmate beat her to it.

The woman remembered how the white man had brought weapons with him, including guns. Her parents knew that blood would be spilled if they resisted, so they did not. She said there was no point in fighting, because taking the children away had been sanctioned by law.

"It didn't only happen in Australia," the woman explained to the class. "It happened to Aboriginal Canadians and to Native Americans, to Indigenous New Zealanders, and to many other peoples in different places all over the world. Each instance was different, but these terrible things changed our families forever."

Although Grace felt empathetic, she believed the woman should forget the past and move forward. She believed that life was like a mathematical formula. You had to keep searching and moving always. Reconfiguring. Making progress.

Grace made her way to Math class, where Vincente passed her homework across just in time to hand it in. Mr. Dense was the kind of teacher who did everything by the book. He appeared to be pleased when Vincente Marino was the first person in line to hand his homework in.

Fibonacci was being reviewed in class today. As sixteen-year-old Grace Greenway was a recognized child prodigy, her teacher dismissed her early. Grace passed the free time studying at the library. She went to her other classes, lunch, English. Then back to the library for her free period until game time.

After reading and choosing an armful of textbooks to borrow, she made her way onto the field. to view the cricket match. Just then, Vincente Marino, stepped up to bat. The high school crowd erupted into tumultuous applause.

Grace, distracted by Vincente's white cricket uniform as it reflected the late afternoon sunlight, lost control of her bundle of books. She cradled the volumes and juggled them as you do in the hope of a successful recovery. Yet her sheer determination to remain upright cradling the complete works of mathematical role models: Sophie Germain, Hypatia, Lise Meitner and Mary Somerville was not meant to be. As the books hit the ground, she too was bowled over in more ways than one.

✳✳✳

W HEN GRACE CAME TO everything was fuzzy and cloudy. She was dizzy, and she felt like throwing up. Her head hurt something awful. It was like her brain was trying to find a way out of her head. "Everyone stand back!" someone shouted, "Grace? Grace! Are you okay? Speak to me, Grace! Can you hear me?"

When she opened her eyes and looked skyward, an angel was calling her name. Grace wondered if she was dead. Could she have died and moved on to another dimension? Refusing to believe it to be true, she squeezed her eyes closed and opened them again. A boy was floating above her with a halo as big as the sun.

"I'm so, so sorry Grace," he said, taking one of her hands into his.

A crowd had gathered around, pushing, shoving, and shouting. Creating general teenaged mayhem.

Grace could see them bending over her—some with their laughing faces upside down. In her head, was a constant humming. If it weren't for one familiar face, that of the young man, she would have felt or frightened.

She tried to be brave and to stand up. Her legs would not cooperate. They jiggled and wobbled like overcooked spaghetti. In her ears, the sound of the ocean was prevalent.

She sat back down again and rested her head against the young man's chest. He did not seem to mind.

CHAPTER 3

THE BOY'S FACE MOVED closer to Grace's, so that the sun's rays dispelled the shape of his halo. She could feel his sweet, cinnamon-y breath upon her neck. Grace knew what he wanted. She turned her bare neck toward him. Giving him permission to bite her. To taste her.

"Someone call Triple Zero!" the boy shouted as he lifted Grace and held her body.

Grace felt bad. She had meant to go on a weight loss program. She wasn't exactly light as a feather. She leaned her head into his chest in anticipation of hearing his heartbeat. All she could hear was the roaring of the ocean.

Grace looked up at his handsome face. He looked so worried.

Together, they moved amongst the murmurs and whispers of the crowd. Into a quiet place. Finally, up some stairs and through a swinging door. Then Grace Greenway was set down upon a soft cot in a room that smelled like antiseptic and gym socks. She pushed her face back into him, trying to repossess his cinnamon-y-ness.

"This is the nurses' station. Wait here. I'll get help."

"Don't leave me," she said. "Please don't leave me."

"She's not breathing!" someone shouted in time to remind her to.

Soon, Grace felt like herself again. She only wished that the waves would stop crashing upon the shores of her mind.

"Can you hear me?" a woman asked. Grace nodded. "I'm Nurse Hands."

"Nurse, 5. Hands, 5—amazing!" Grace exclaimed.

"She's delirious!" Nurse Hands said. She felt Grace's pulse and her forehead, and then she looked up at Vincente and shook her head.

"No, she's thinking about math class. Mr. Dense let her go early. We were doing Fibonacci," Vincente explained.

"Do you know her name?"

"Yes, she's Grace. Grace Greenway."

Grace scrunched Vincente's shirt into the palm of her hand.

"I really need to get back to the game."

"Grace," Nurse Hands said, "we are waiting for the ambulance. Vincente needs to get back to the game. Please let go of his shirt."

Grace screamed, "Don't leave me!"

Vincente knelt back down beside her and looked into her eyes.

He stayed.

She sighed.

And then everything faded to black.

CHAPTER 4

A T THE HOSPITAL, THE nurse stopped at Grace's bedside and checked her vital statistics. She was stable for now. The nurse pulled the covers back over Grace's arms. She retrieved the tray of unused water glasses, stopping momentarily to glance at the young man in the cricket uniform, He was sound asleep in the chair under the window.

Vincente hadn't left Grace's side since her unconscious arrival. As she exited, she looked at her watch and calculated that there were six more hours left on her shift. She loved her job, but this was going to be a long day.

Back in Grace's room, the patient began to stir and move about. She soon discovered that she was fettered to the bed by an array of noisy machines.

She was in a hospital room. Why was she here? How had she gotten here? She closed her eyes and tried to focus. She tried to remember, but no memories came.

Anxious to break free from the beep-beep-beeping and drip-drip-dripping, Grace attempted to sit up. When she couldn't fulfil this simple desire, she flung herself back onto the pillow. She had an intense desire to bolt.

Why am I here? Grace thought. And why has everyone abandoned me?

Grace noticed a boy who was sound asleep in the chair beside her bed. She wasn't alone after all, and she hugged herself as best as she could with the machines fastened to her body.

She felt happier now, knowing that someone was there. That someone cared.

Although she couldn't see his face, she watched as his blond hair moved in and out with each breath. He was sleeping soundly. Grace continued to stare at him, and at the white uniform he was wearing. She wondered if he worked at the hospital. It seemed odd for a staff member to fall asleep by a patient's side.

Grace felt strange when she looked at the boy's folded arms and his freefalling head of blond hair.

Moments passed, and she continued staring. Then, almost like he had felt her eyes on him, the boy awoke with a start. He whipped his hair back, revealing the face of an angel.

Grace covered her mouth with her hand. He was stunning. The boy stood up and moved toward her.

Grace couldn't breathe. As he moved closer, his dark blue eyes made her heartbeat faster and faster. She thought she was going to faint. And then he spoke. "You're awake, Gracie! Thank God! I was so worried. We've been so worried."

"Yes," she said, not knowing what else to say. He wasn't a staff member. He meant something more to her, she could feel it in her heart, and she knew it deep in her mind. But who on earth was he?

She extended her hand to him, expecting him to take it. He didn't. Instead, he moved back a step. She somewhat reluctantly rescinded her hand.

The boy kept staring at Grace, like he was waiting for something. After the I wanna hold your hand miscue, he protected himself. He shoved his hands deep in his pockets. After a few seconds, he pulled them out again.

Grace felt hot and cold, simultaneously.

"Are you okay?" he asked. "Do you hurt anywhere?"

Grace waited and thought before replying. She wanted her answer to be succinct, but not sharp. How she felt didn't matter! What she wanted to know was, why she was here? What she wanted to know was, who was he?

"My head hurts the most. It's like everything hurts at the same time if that makes sense. And you?"

He beamed a smile revealing glaringly perfect white teeth. Grace thought his teeth should come with a warning: SUNGLASSES REQUIRED. He ran his fingers through his hair, and their eyes connected.

Grace felt an energy from him that hit her straight in the chest first, and then seemed to bounce off the walls. If she weren't already lying down, it would have knocked her off her feet. She was in love. Of this she was certain. But he was acting strange. As if he didn't know what to say or what to do. It was like he wanted to reach out but didn't know how. "I'm okay, thanks," he said. He looked like Winnie the Pooh with his hand caught in the Honeypot.

Grace fell backwards onto the pillow once again, never breaking eye contact with the boy. She wanted to ask him questions, lots of questions, but where to start? Should she blurt them out? He looked so uncomfortable. Why?

She adjusted her position on the bed. Now kind of leaning in toward him, with her head resting on one arm—as much resting as you can do when you are connected to machines—and beckoned him closer.

He paused and looked at his shoes. Then he shuffled forwards. She knew he wasn't going to offer any information, she sensed it, felt it, but she had to know. Time was wasting. "What happened to me?" she finally blurted out.

The boy stepped back a bit, began to say something, and then stopped. He opened his mouth, and then closed it again, like a fish.

Grace tried to help with more blunt questions. "What am I doing in this hospital? How did I get here?"

He remained silent, running his fingers through his hair.

Grace continued, undeterred, "And who are you?"

CHAPTER 5

T HE BOY LOOKED DISTRESSED at question number one and worried about two and three. Question number four caused the most astonishing reaction.

Everyone knew who Vincente Marino was, and Grace Greenway especially knew. He saw her making puppy eyes at him. Sometimes, when she thought he wasn't looking, she followed him around school. She even did it sometimes when he was with his girlfriend, Missy Malone. So, was she kidding him? Vincente was fairly sure she was messing with his head.

He stepped toward her and gazed into her hazel eyes, looking all the way into her soul. He needed to know what she was up to. To see if she was playing a game or a trick on him, but Grace didn't blink or give anything away.

Grace had no idea who he was.

When the boy gazed into her eyes, Grace wondered if she had the wrong end of the stick. Maybe he didn't know who he was, either? After all, he was blond.

"I'm Vincente," he said, all the while looking into Grace's face for a sign of recognition. When it didn't come, he repeated his name again. In fact, he almost sang it, "Vincente Marino."

Goosebumps made their way up Grace's arms and she shivered. She didn't recognize his name, but something deep inside of her stirred. Perhaps it was the tone of his voice.

She repeated his name aloud. Nothing tweaked any memories. The goosebumps began to fade. She tried spelling his name, rolling each letter on her tongue like she was feeling her way in the dark:

"V- I-N-C-E-N-T."

"I spell mine with an e at the end," Vincente said. He explained how he was named after one of Christopher Columbus's navigators. His parents originally wanted to name him Christopher. When his mum told his aunt, not knowing that she was also pregnant, his aunt stole the name. His parents chose another name for him, Vicente, after Vicente Pinzon. When they saw him, they changed their minds and called him Vincente instead.

"That's interesting," she said. "But really, who are you to me?"

"You're not kidding?" Vincente asked. "You really don't remember me?"

"I'm not sure. I sense something about you, but...I don't even remember my own name."

"It's Grace. You are Grace."

"But a while ago, you called me Gracie."

"Yeah, I did."

"Why? If my name is Grace…, why did you call me Gracie? I don't like it."

"Whoa, okay then, I won't call you Gracie ever again."

He backed away, dragging his fingers through his blond locks again. He kept on doing that. Probably a nervous habit. Grace wanted to run her fingers through his hair, too. Why was she thinking thoughts like that? She was trying to understand what she was feeling. The hot and the cold bursts. Trying to make sense of it all. To find a memory stored somewhere inside her head. Yet every time he did that, ran his fingers through his hair, it distracted her, made her knees tremble like jelly.

"Come on Grace! You must remember me! If you don't, to prove it, cross your heart and hope to die."

"I think that is an odd choice of words. Considering I'm in the hospital and all."

"Ah, I'm sorry. Didn't think. Please try to remember who I am, okay? You're worrying me. Maybe I ought to go out and get someone?"

"You're worried? I'm frightened! If you say I ought to know you, then there must be a memory of you stored somewhere back here." She knocked on her head with a closed fist. "Why can't I find you in here?"

He grabbed her hand, stopping her from hitting herself again. He pulled a chair up beside the bed and sat down. He had decided to tell her everything. To explain why she was here, how it was all because of him. How he had injured her, and then brought her to the hospital.

How he sat by her side for days while she was out. Waiting. Praying. "I am the reason you are here."

"You hurt me?"

"Yes, I hurt you."

She grimaced. "You hurt me!"

"Yes, but it was an accident. I play cricket. You were at the match.

Three days ago."

"Three days ago?"

"Yes. Three days ago, I hit a ball and it hit you in the head. You have been here ever since. I have been at your side. Waiting."

"You hit me? In the head? And now I've lost my memory?"

"It appears so."

"And then what?"

"I carried you to the nurses' station at school. An ambulance brought you here."

Grace examined her body. In her shape, she could not imagine him carrying her. He was fit, wearing a uniform, yes, but to carry her? Not possible. "You carried me?"

"Yes."

She had the overwhelming urge to hit him and to hug him at the exact same time. But her head hurt even more.

"I'm so, so sorry," he said.

The hugging impulse overrode the hitting impulse. "It was an accident, so, you have nothing to be sorry for."

"Thank you," he said as he bowed his head. Grace reached out to pat him like he was a good dog.

A strange woman pushed her way into the room through the swinging doors like a whirlwind. She barrelled toward them. Small in stature but forceful in energy, she moved toward them. Her skin-tight blue jeans shushed, and her boot heels clicked on the antiseptic hospital floors.

The woman, glared at Vincente like he was a boil waiting to be lanced.

He spoke in a noticeably quiet voice. Offered to leave the two of them alone. Before they had time to reply, he picked himself up and exited.

"Don't go," Grace pleaded, but it was too late. Grace watched the door for a moment, hoping he might return. He didn't. She turned her attention toward the strange woman. She wondered what kind of a hospital she was in that would allow its staff members to be dressed in jeans and boots.

"And how are you, my love?" the woman asked, and then she bent over and put her lips to Grace's forehead.

Grace deemed this to be a gesture of over-familiarity and said so. "Don't do that!" she exclaimed, "Who do you think you are?" she demanded as she proceeded to wipe the germs away from the place the woman had touched her with her lips.

"Whatever do you mean, who am I?"

"Don't you know either?" Grace asked, offended at the woman's lack of decorum and professionalism.

"Who am I?"

"Is there an echo in here?" Grace asked.

"Then you really, truly, don't know who I am?"

Grace shrugged. The woman turned and darted out of the room. She could run fast for a short lady wearing high-heeled boots.

As she was going out, Vincente was coming in. She nearly knocked him over. Grace was appalled as she heard the woman shrieking like a banshee in the corridor.

Grace thought the doors should be revolving and said so.

Vincente beamed a smile her way, which once again sent her heart fluttering.

Grace wondered what kind of a hospital she was in. A psych ward?

"Who was that crazy woman?"

"That was no crazy woman. That was your mum."

✳✳✳

"MY MUM? HOW COULD she possibly be?" Grace paused and stared at her hands. She couldn't stop looking at them. What was it? There was something lurking there. Something important. She had to remember it whatever it was, as she could sense it was profoundly serious.

Then it happened. She was s flying through the air, going fast in the arms of an angel. She looked up, at the face above her, and the sun streamed in behind the angel, creating a natural halo. She strained her eyes to reveal its identity, but the face was blurry. She wondered if it were possible to ascertain the features of an angel. She thought an angel's features might not be distinguishable to the living. That was it! Grace decided that she must have had a near-death experience.

She held something in her fist as she flew forward, and they ducked into a tunnel. For a second, it was dark, or she had closed her eyes. Then she looked up, and the identity of her angel was revealed. In fact, it wasn't an angel at all—it was the boy standing beside her. She whispered his name repeatedly. It was like music, humming. Drumming a beat inside of her head.

"Are you okay?" Vincente asked.

Grace smiled.

He asked again, "Are you all right, Grace? Do you want me to get someone?"

"I'm grateful," she said. "What for?"

"Why, for you, of course. For you, my angel."

Vincente looked at his feet. Proceeded to jam his fists into his pockets. He looked very worried, like he thought she had really lost it now.

He thought he had witnessed her leaving him before—not in body exactly, but in spirit. She had travelled far away in her mind. You could tell when someone was 'away,' because the eyes would become glassy and dreamy.

Vincente wished Grace Greenway's mum would return, so he could get the hell out of there. She was beginning to give him the creeps.

Then, out of the blue, Grace blurted, "Vincente, are you my boyfriend?"

"No!" he exclaimed, in a tone of voice that could not be misinterpreted. Just in case it was, he backed away even further, until his back was up against the wall.

He looked absolutely, completely mortified. Grace was confused. His denial, that one word, hit her with full force in the chest. The exclamation point felt like a raven's beak puncturing her heart. She felt wounded, but her confusion was overwhelming. She watched him and waited for him to do something, say something. Anything.

"Look, Grace, you have to know that I am not your boyfriend. I only brought you here because I was the one who hurt you."

"So, you're usually too cool to talk to me?"

"Grace, you've helped me with my math homework, and you've helped me to stay on the team. I'm grateful for your help, but—"

"Grateful..." She leaned back upon the pillow and closed her eyes.

She wanted to disappear into the feathery pillow.

He wanted to disappear from the room.

They remained together, sharing the same space, although each of them felt like an island.

"I'm going to get your mum, okay? I think you ought to be with family." He turned and left the room.

Grace felt like a fool. She didn't know who he was, but somewhere in her heart she knew that she loved him. How silly of her, to have blurted it out like that. Perhaps she had loved him from afar? Perhaps he was in love with someone else, and now she had gone and embarrassed herself by telling him how she felt.

She turned her face into the pillow and sobbed.

✳✳✳

G RACE WANTED TO RUN after Vincente Marino. She tugged at the machines in a vain attempt to unfasten them when the cavalry arrived.

"What on earth are you doing, Grace?" Helen Greenway demanded.

"You nearly ripped these off, you silly, silly girl," the nurse scolded.

Vincente having returned said nothing. He shuffled his feet and dug his fists in and out of his pockets as if he were looking for loose change.

"I was —" Grace began.

She was unable to finish because the nurse began to tilt and adjust the bed. Grace lost her balance and fell sideways, about to hit the floor. Would have hit the floor, if Vincente hadn't taken his fists out of his pockets and caught her.

He held her in his arms once again, like in her memory. He was a gift, a gift from somewhere above, and once again, Grace's memories returned. Memories came pouring in like flashbacks. Vincente on the school bus. Vincente playing cricket on the field.

Vincente smiling at her, taking his homework from her. Vincente, Vincente, Vincente. Floods of memories inundated her, and from them, Grace knew two things for certain.

Number one: she loved Vincente Marino. Number two: he did not love her.

She looked into his eyes. They were empty pools of light, bending towards her, wanting to save her from harm, to be a hero. But behind those dark blue eyes there was no love. No love for her.

Grace was the sun, reaching out her rays, feeling for the moon: the dark side of the moon. They were on opposite sides, spinning away from each other.

"Ahem," Helen cleared her throat, causing Grace and Vincente to blink them apart.

"You see, Nurse, she is completely out of hand. She doesn't realize how serious her situation is. How ill she really is." Helen began to cry. Not little tears. No, a near flash flood of body wracking sobs.

"It's okay, Mum," Grace said, as she reached out to take her mum's hand.

"You remember me?"

"Of course," Grace said, lying. She didn't know her or have any memory of her; any more than of the nurse who was still standing with her mouth wide open.

"The doctor is on the way," the nurse announced. She lifted Grace's arm and proceeded to take her pulse. "Your vital signs are excellent, but you need to rest. Perhaps it's time for your friend to go home. He needs his rest, too."

She glanced at Vincente.

The subtlety of her apprehension did not get by him.

"Yeah, I think I should go." Vincente said. He moved a few steps away from the bed. He ran his fingers through his hair. He walked back towards the bed, like he was waiting for Grace's approval. "Or I could stay, if you wanted me to."

"Only if you want to," Grace said with a glimmer of hope in her voice. She realized he was only staying because of guilt, but she decided that she would take him any way he would consent. "Maybe just until I fall asleep?"

Helen chitchatted with the nurse as if they were long-lost friends as they made their way out of the room.

"She'll be out in minutes," the nurse said. "I gave her enough sedatives to ensure that she'll get a good night's sleep."

Helen glanced back at the two of them and then blew a kiss to her daughter.

Grace thought it was difficult for her mum to leave her there alone with a virtual stranger. Her mum didn't complain. She wore it like a battle scar.

✳✳✳

IT DIDN'T TAKE LONG for Grace to fall asleep.

Vincente took the opportunity to turn on his mobile phone and ring his mum. He'd been texting her with updates about Grace's condition. He refused to leave her side until he was certain that she was out of danger. He needed to go home and take a shower, not to mention to finally change out of his cricket uniform.

Soon, Grace was in a deep, deep sleep, one in which she imagined voices all around her. Whispering voices. Then the voices grew louder and louder. They filled her mind with laughter. Devilishly loud laughter followed by screaming and scratching, as if someone had been buried alive. The voices were trapped. They were screaming and scratching, screaming, and scratching.

Grace awoke with a start, perspiration streaming down her forehead. Her bedclothes were damp and cold. She was disoriented. Too afraid to open her eyes. She wondered if whatever it was that she heard in her dreams was in the room with her now. If she opened her eyes, she would see it, and if she saw it, she would need to get away. She listened intently. The only sounds were the tick-tick-tocking and the slip-slop-slopping of medical equipment.

She opened her eyes, all the while repeating one slip, two slop, three tick, four tock, to herself. Grace was alone. She began to shiver in the cold room. She needed to change clothing. She couldn't get to where she needed to go, so she pushed the panic button. Within seconds, the nurse arrived and helped her to change into a clean gown.

"Do you have to...go?" the nurse asked. This one was smaller and friendlier than other one had been, and she smiled kindly. Grace flushed scarlet as the nurse put the bedpan under her.

Afterwards, Grace asked if she could move nearer to the window. The nurse pushed the bed forward, keeping the equipment intact. She pulled back the curtains, letting the daylight in. It blinded Grace with its sudden intensity. She gazed down at the wispy grasses bending with the breeze. She looked upward into the deep blue, cloudless sky. After so long in the hospital, she felt alive.

"If you need anything else, let me know," the nurse said.

Grace took her hand into hers and said, "Thank you."

Once again, she alone, but this time she looked further along the pathway. She spotted a little flower garden, and just beyond it, a tree. Beside it, she saw a piece of paper floating upwards, mocking as it went. Past the stationary flowers, almost like it was saying, Look at me! You may have pretty petals and vibrant colour, but I can do something you cannot do. You are fettered, but I can fly. Watch me fly!

The piece of paper continued its journey. Grace followed it as it flew high, higher, and higher still until she could no longer see it. Grace laughed. It was like watching magic.

"What are you doing?" Grace's mum exclaimed when she saw her daughter in a near-standing position. Helen Greenway shooed her daughter back onto her pillow and pushed the bed back against the wall. She then tucked her daughter into bed. Grace appreciated the pampering. She thought it might evoke a memory—a memory of this woman standing in front of her. But once again, no memories came.

CHAPTER 6

"**I** HOPE YOU'RE FEELING up to a visit from Dr. Christiansson," Helen said. "He'll be coming in soon to talk about your condition."

"I have a condition?" Grace said.

"You do, indeed Grace."

Grace was worried when the doctor made his way inside. He acknowledged them and pulled up a chair. He sat down for a moment and then stood up. He took Grace's pulse. He felt Grace's forehead. "Hmmm. How are you feeling, Gracie?"

"Please call me Grace."

"Oh sorry. Grace it is then. How are you feeling today?"

"I'm feeling better. The headache isn't so bad now, but Doctor, I can't remember anything."

"Nothing?"

Grace looked embarrassed. She didn't want her mum to know she didn't remember her. She hesitated. "I have flashes of memories."

"Flashes?"

"Yes."

"Tell me more," he said while scratching notes onto a clipboard.

"Flashes, mostly about a boy. Vincente Marino," Grace said.

The doctor looked at Helen with a raised eyebrow.

"The boy. The one who hit her with the ball," Helen said.

"Oh, yes. That's normal, since he was the last person you saw before you lost consciousness." He hesitated, scribbled something down. Then You do remember your, mum, correct?"

Grace had hoped and prayed that he wasn't going to ask her this. Should she continue to lie, to keep her mum happy? She knew that she had to tell her doctor the truth, the whole truth, and nothing but the truth for him to be able to help her. She shook her head. Helen began to sob.

The doctor patted Helen's hand, and then he focused his attention on the patient. "Grace, you have suffered what we call a Traumatic Brain Injury. What do you think that means?"

"I don't know."

"Well, let me try to explain it to you then," the doctor said. "You were hit with a cricket ball." He hesitated and then looked over at Helen. She was sobbing so much that her chest was shuddering. It was evident she was attempting to take control of her emotions.

Grace wanted him to get to the point.

"The initial impact from ball hitting you, the sheer force of it, was enough to cause the injury. There are complications. Serious complications."

First a condition. Now complications. What else was going on here? Was her life in danger?

"Yes, complications in the form of blood clots or aneurysms near the brain. The pressure from the aneurysms could be causing your memory loss. We hope this will only be a temporary condition."

"Temporary?"

"Yes. If we go in and remove them, we hope all your memories will return. But the operation is extremely dangerous."

"You mean I could die?"

Helen's sobbing became louder.

"To put it bluntly, yes. You could die if we operate, Grace. But here's the thing: You could also die if we don't operate."

"Huh?"

"The clots are growing, causing you pain and memory loss. They are dangerous. More may form, though we don't know when. Unfortunately, they won't go away, unless they burst, break up, and get into your bloodstream."

"So, how do I get rid of them?" Grace asked, trying not to cry.

"We give you blood thinners. Eventually we operate. Today. Or tomorrow. As soon as you give consent. We'll take our best shot to get rid of them all. We have the experts here at your disposal. Surgery is your best chance for survival and complete recovery."

"And if I say no?"

"You are sixteen, so your mum can sign the papers for you. We really think that you ought to make the decision and be on board with it. It'll be better all around. That's why I'm telling you the truth, straight up."

"Do I really have a choice?"

"If you say no, the clots will still break apart when they are ready to do so. The result could be fatal, and without warning."

"Why can't we wait and operate later? If we need to."

"We can. It's up to you. You can wait. You will more than likely grow stronger every day, get healthier. But we would be taking a chance. If you relapse, get weaker, your chances of a full recovery may also diminish."

"So, the sooner the better then?"

"Grace, you are taking this very calmly," Helen said, still sobbing. "My strong little girl. So brave." She hugged her.

"I don't want to die. I'm only sixteen."

"We'll do everything in our power to get you through this," the doctor said.

"How will we know when things become more urgent?" Grace asked.

"When the clots burst, you move onto our critical list. We will get you into the operating room immediately. It will become a life-or-death situation at that point."

Grace was fighting back tears. She wanted to live. She didn't want to die, not like this. She needed time, but time wasn't on her side. She wanted to be alone. She wanted time to herself. Time to reflect. Time to think.

"I have given you much to think about, Grace. It's a lot for an adult to deal with, let alone a teenager. Talk to your family and your friends. You will need their support and love. Oh, and one more thing. Your condition, the clots, may have been this way for some time. Perhaps dormant for months, even years. They may have been affecting you emotionally. Making you feel tired, giving you headaches. Until that boy hit you with the ball, we didn't know about it. Now that we know, we have to consider that accident to be a lucky catalyst for helping you to get well again."

Grace hadn't thought of it that way. She nodded.

"You understand—taking action, is imperative?"

"You've made it perfectly clear, Doc."

"Good girl," he said. "Talk to your mum. She loves you very much. Then get some rest. Think on it. I'll be back tomorrow to answer any questions you may have."

Grace nodded. Helen moved closer to her daughter. "And you, Helen, get yourself some rest. Grace will need your strength. When did you sleep last?"

"I'm not sleeping very well these days," Helen admitted.

"I'll get one of the nurses to give you something to help you sleep. You have to rest and eat and take care of yourself, not just for your own sake, but for the sake of Grace."

"Yes, I understand. Thank you, Dr. Christiansson," Helen said.

He turned and left. Grace's mum stood by the bed, lost in her own thoughts.

"Mum, I'd like to be alone for a little while, to be able to think."

"But you're not alone. You don't have to make this decision all by yourself."

"I know, Mum, and thank you."

Helen kissed her daughter on the forehead and left the room.

Finally, alone, Grace's tears overflowed. She hugged herself tightly. Let herself sob it out.

✳✳✳

T HE NIGHT AIR WAS freezing cold. Whipping around her. Slicing through her nightgown, which billowed behind her like a veil. Grace hid her face in Vincente's chest. They continued to fly upward. Higher and higher. Into the darkness. Leaving everything behind.

Grace shivered.

Vincente pulled her in close. His arms folded around her. He held her. She felt safe.

It was now. Now or never.

She pulled the high-collared nightgown away from her neck and undid the red lace tie. She leaned back and waited for him. Waited for the pain, and for the pleasure.

Vincente bared his teeth and then she began to fall. Drifting. Down. Crashing. Down.

She could feel him deep, deep under her skin as she plummeted towards the waiting pavement.

She opened her eyes and screamed.

CHAPTER 7

WHEN GRACE CAME TO, someone was tucking the covers in around her neck. She felt a cool hand brush against her cheek. The man asked, "Are you awake?"

Grace blinked her eyes open, trying to focus. She could make out his eyes—deep, hazel. His cheeks attracted her attention, because when he smiled, they spread like a child's. She attempted to rub her own eyes, but man had tucked her arms in. She couldn't get them out from under the blankets. She felt trapped. She did not feel frightened.

"Grace," he said.

"Uh, I can't get my arms out."

"Oh, I'm so sorry. I tucked you in too tightly," he said as he pulled the covers down, allowing Grace to rub her eyes and focus. Now she noticed a second younger man step closer to her. He had his arms crossed over his chest.

"Thanks."

"Grace, would you like a drink of water?"

"Yes, that would be lovely," she said, as the man poured some and placed the cup into her shaking hand. He held it, like a parent holding a child's hand when she learned to drink by herself for the very first time. After she drained its contents, he took it from her and placed it upon the night table. He waited.

Grace looked around the room, knowing full well that she ought to know who these two people were. They expected her to know.

"I'm your dad," the smiling man said, "and this is your big brother Daryl."

Grace could see it now: the family resemblance, the hazel eyes.

Yes, she had her father's eyes.

"Your mum mentioned you might not remember us," he said. He patted his daughter's hand. Daryl moved in closer, along the side of the bed. He extended his hand to Grace.

"You are looking well, my girl," Benjamin Greenway said.

Grace felt both uncomfortable and comforted at the same time. "Thank you."

"We were so worried about you, when we heard." Her father wiped a tear away. "I'm sorry I wasn't able to get here sooner. Away on business, you know."

"I understand."

"Nothing is too good for my little girl, though, and we'll get the best experts in here. We'll do everything we can to make you normal again."

"Normal?"

"As you were, you know...before."

"Uh, thanks," Grace said, and then she shuffled her feet under the covers, waking them from a deep sleep. It was like that lately. Part of her body was awake while other parts were sound asleep.

"We want you back to the way you were before," her brother said. He leaned in and kissed her on the forehead. His lips felt cool, like he had recently finished drinking a soft drink.

"I'm okay," Grace said. "Just tired...and of course there's the whole no-memory thing."

"Yeah, it's a bummer, not being able to remember anyone or anything." Daryl replied. Then he hummed a little and laughed. Awkward.

Grace closed her eyes for a second and then opened them up again.

Her dad and brother looked kind of cagey. She again tried to evoke a memory, any memory, but was unsuccessful.

"Have you decided to go ahead with the surgery, then?" Dad asked.

"I haven't decided on anything yet."

"All in good time my dear, all in good time," he said. He reached over to touch Grace's hand. When their skin met, she expected to feel warmth, but his skin was cool.

"I spoke with the doctor yesterday," her dad said. "I told him to pull out all the stops. I told him money was no object. I told him to bring in the big guns. To do anything to bring my little girl back."

"I'm right here, Dad," she said, as Vincente poked his head inside the door to her room.

"Come in, Vincente," she invited, "you're not interrupting."

He looked around the room and walked towards her. Ran his fingers through his hair. Shoved his hands deep into his black Levi's pockets.

"I'd like to introduce you to my dad and my brother, Daryl."

"Your dad and your brother?"

"Yes."

"Uh, that's why I didn't come straight in. I, uh, I thought I heard you talking to someone."

Grace thought he was acting very strangely, almost to the point of being rude.

"Would you like me to, uh, call someone? Your doctor? One of the nurses? Do you need help?"

"What do you mean?" Grace felt really cross at him, but she smiled. "Dad, this is Vincente Marino, the boy who brought me to the hospital. Daryl, this is Vincente Marino. Vincente, my dad, and my brother."

Vincente looked around him. There was no one in the room. Not a single soul. But poor deluded Grace thought there was. Should he go along with her delusions? Pretend? Extend his hand? Shake an imaginary hand in return? Vincente wasn't a medical professional. He had no idea where to look or what to do. He didn't want to take responsibility for pushing Grace Greenway over the edge. He'd done enough to her already.

"I'll go and get the doc for you, okay?" Vincente said as he ran his fingers through his hair.

"Why? Because I am introducing you to my family? It's not as if I'm asking you to marry me or anything!"

"Grace? What if I told you..."

"Yes?"

"What if I told you there was no one here in this room but you and me?"

Grace looked into the eyes of her father then her brother. They acknowledged her with a nod.

"What do you mean? They are standing right here!"

"Grace, now listen to me. Please. Your dad and your brother were killed, in a car accident. It was a head-on collision. There was a memorial service at school."

"They couldn't have been killed," Grace said. "Unless, unless...I'm seeing dead people!"

"I'm sure there is a perfectly innocent explanation, Grace. Probably just a side effect to the pain medication. Please let me call for help."

Grace reached out for her father. He backed away. She reached for Daryl. He also retreated.

"Sweetheart, we really ought to go now...now that Vincente is here. We will come back another time. Another time when you are alone," her dad said. He and Darryl backed up against the wall. They disappeared.

Grace covered her eyes and began screaming. And screaming and screaming.

 ✳✳✳

WHEN THE MEDICAL STAFF finally arrived, it was too late. Grace had already pulled out some of the tubes.

After they gave her a sedative, she calmed right down. She soon fell asleep.

Vincente remained at Grace's side until Helen arrived. He explained what had happened.

Helen was upset because she hadn't been there. She wondered what it all meant. Was her daughter losing her mind? Did she need to speak to the doctor about putting her into a different kind of hospital? One where she would be monitored 24/7? She shivered at the thought.

Vincente attempted to reassure her that Grace was not crazy. At the same time, he was also trying to convince himself.

He looked out the window at a plastic bag sailing in the wind like a daytime ghost. He thought about books he'd read about dead people coming back to reclaim the living. Could there be a supernatural explanation?

Helen contemplated her daughter's sleeping form. She looked like such an innocent soul resting there. Helen folded her arms around herself. It had been such a long time since they talked, really talked. She glanced at the boy standing beside her, and she wondered if he might know her daughter more than she did. She hated the thought that one day, she and her daughter might grow apart.

Grace stirred in her sleep. Then she began counting aloud.

Helen listened until Grace was nearly at one hundred. Then her daughter stopped counting. She had always fallen by the number one hundred. Grace had been in love with numbers for her entire life. She found comfort in numbers.

Helen considered this. Although her daughter had lost her memory, she was still doing normal things like counting in her sleep. Helen believed this was a good sign. She nearly shared it with the Marino boy. He was busy looking out the window, so she decided to get a cup of tea.

Vincente assured Helen that he would remain in the room until she returned. Helen was grateful for his assistance.

Vincente flipped through a magazine and continued staring out the window.

Grace shouted, "Please don't take me. Please don't!"

Vincente lifted her up and held her. She was still fast asleep, just having a nightmare. When her body relaxed, he placed her head onto the pillow.

"Please don't die," Vincente whispered. He opened the door and looked outside for Helen. He seriously wanted to be rescued from this situation. Where was Helen Greenway? He glanced back at Grace who stirred in her sleep again. Sighing, he closed the door and returned to his post.

CHAPTER 8

GRACE AWOKE FEELING TOTALLY disoriented. She had a night filled with terrifying dreams.

She dreamed that she had two visitors: her dead father and brother. The room was pitch black, and when she opened her eyes, there was the distinct scent of soap and antiseptic in the air. She wondered how long she had been sleeping.

Grace felt her forehead, and it was extremely hot. She was burning up with fever, and she needed a change of nightclothes again. She reached across the bed, pushed the buzzer, and waited. Nothing.

She tried to pour herself a glass of water but found the pitcher to be empty. She waited for the nurse to come to the room, but no one came. She pushed the buzzer again. Her thirst was growing. She felt her forehead again and leaned on the buzzer.

She sat upright and spotted Vincente. He was sound asleep, lounging on two chairs just under the window. His feet and legs were on one chair. His upper body was on the other. Problem was, his middle was sagging downward, drooping. He was going to hit the floor soon. The only way to stop it was to wake him up.

Grace called out his name. Startled, his body moved the chairs apart. His middle hit the floor.

He jumped up. "What? Where?"

Grace couldn't help but laugh.

He glanced in her direction for a moment, and then he brushed his clothes down with his hands. Finally, he finger-combed his hair. He looked at her for a second or two more and then rubbed his eyes and realized where he was. He ran his hands through his hair once more and then moved toward Grace and said, "Whoa, sorry. I must have drifted off."

"That's okay. I was hoping to stop you from falling, but sorry, I only made it worse."

"No harm done." Vincente said. He did some jumping jacks, trying to wake himself up.

"It's really late! Why didn't they get me? Your mum was supposed to take over. Family-only guests allowed after ten now. Hospital rules."

"I've been buzzing for a nurse for quite some time," Grace said, "But so far, nothing. Here, let me try again." She hit the buzzer and just held on.

Vincente could hear the sound reverberating throughout the corridor. Strange. He decided to go and look. Where the heck was Helen? Vincente had specifically mentioned the need for him to be out of there by ten on the dot to Helen Greenway. She had promised to wake him up. His mum was picking him up, and he had a cricket match the next day. He needed a good night's sleep.

She was taking him for granted. Treating him like family. What the—?

Vincente was becoming more and more annoyed as he wandered around. At first, everything seemed to be normal, but the absence of all hospital staff alarmed him. He reached into his pocket and pulled out his mobile phone. He turned it on and waited for 4G to kick in, but the signal was weak, only one bar. He checked for text messages and emails, but there weren't any. He glanced at the clock at the end of the corridor. It read 2:30 a.m. What the heck?

Curious, he opened one of the hospital rooms, prepared to apologize for intruding, but it was empty. He continued opening door after door, and the result was the same each time: empty.

He stepped into the elevator. Rode down a floor: same as above. Where had everyone gone? This was starting to get weird. He took the elevator down to the ground floor. It was the same story there. Even the receptionist's desk was empty. There were no patients or family members in the waiting room or in the emergency bay.

He stepped outside and breathed in deeply. The air had a strange smell, a blend of car fumes and eucalyptus. All he could hear was an incessant humming.

In the distance, his eyes connected with the full moon, whose brightness lit up the night sky. The stars were out in full force. He dwelled upon these things for a few moments because they were what he expected to see, i.e., normal.

A few seconds later, the humming brought him back to reality, and his eyes scanned the parking lot. He coughed as he moved toward the closest vehicle, which had exhaust pouring out of its tailpipe.

The car had its front driver's side door wide open, so he leaned in, only to find it empty. He checked in the back seat and found it to be empty, too. He turned off the ignition, but it immediately started up again. He finally removed the key, and that seemed to do the trick.

He went to the next car, also empty with the engine still running. He stood in the middle of the parking lot. Each vehicle was running, but there wasn't a driver or passenger in sight. Vincente shivered and ran back inside to find Grace.

***

G RACE WAS STILL SITTING where he'd left her. He was never so happy to see anyone in his life. He bit his upper lip as he entered the room, wondering if he should tell her what was going on. Then again, he didn't know what was going on, anyway. He ran the facts through his mind:

Fact: The hospital deserted.

Fact: The car park deserted.

Those were the cold, hard facts.

Vincente wondered how he should convey the situation. Should he sugar-coat it for her? Or should he tell Grace everything? He couldn't help wondering about her current mental health. She had seemed so close to the edge only a short while ago. He didn't want to be the one to push her over. He'd done enough damage to her already.

Vincente noticed that Grace was perspiring a lot. She already seemed worried and anxious, and he hadn't even told her anything...yet. He asked if she wanted a drink of cold water, and she said that she did.

He filled up the small pitcher of water and poured out a glassful. Grace, thinking it was for her, reached out her hand for it. But Vincente seemed to be in a world of his own and, instead of handing it to her, he drained the glass himself. He then repeated the entire process and drained every drop out of the second glass as well.

When he came back to reality, Grace was beginning to get more and more frightened. Something was definitely wrong. Vincente had seen something, and he was afraid to tell her about it. It was that bad.

Vincente's eyes met Grace's. He poured a glass of water, placing it into her waiting hand. She drank, watching Vincente's facial expressions change from one moment to the next.

Grace couldn't take it anymore. She wanted Vincente to snap out of it. "I, uh, really need to go to the little girls' room." She leaned on the buzzer again. She hoped one of the nurses would be in the room in a second.

Vincente was running out of time. He observed Grace. She was waiting for a nurse to come and help her, though there weren't any nurses around. What on earth was he going to do? She was in a serious health crisis, and she needed meds. He wasn't a doctor and had no idea how he was going to take care of her.

Then he got an idea: he was going to take her to another hospital.

Yes, that's what he'd do.

"Sorry about yesterday. I mean about the seeing dead people thing," Grace said.

"That's okay."

He was going to have to tell her. The sooner the better.

✳✳✳

"**T**HAT NURSE SHOULD BE fired!" Grace exclaimed. She really needed to go to the bathroom!

"When did you last get your meds?" Vincente asked.

"I don't know. I'm sleeping so much, it's difficult to know whether it's day or night sometimes."

"It's night-time now. Way past visiting hours."

"So, they let you stay late again?"

"I don't think so. Your mum was supposed to wake me up. She was going to spend the night with you. Considering—"

"Considering what? She thinks I'm losing my mind?"

"Uh, kind of, sort of. I mean, she just wants to keep an eye on you."

"Well, she should make sure I'm getting my meds, then," Grace said.

"To keep the blood from clotting, you need your medication."

"I know," Grace said, annoyed, "They always record things on the chart at the end of the bed. Have a look. It should tell you everything you need to know."

"Good idea," Vincente said, as he lifted the clipboard. It had abbreviations resembling a secret code. He managed to catch the drift of it.

Grace hadn't seen anyone—nurse or doctor for over twenty-four hours.

She really had to go to the loo. The drip-drip-dripping of the machine beside her wasn't helping. She tried not to think about it. She tried not to think about the vampire version of Vincente Marino. And she tried not to think about seeing dead people, but it was difficult not to think about any of that. Especially when her bladder was full.

Vincente decided it was now or never. He had to tell her. He had to tell her the truth. He had to get them out of this hospital, get them somewhere else. To a place where Grace could get the care that she needed.

He walked to the window and drew back the curtains. He decided he couldn't stall a moment more. He had to tell her…now.

$$* * *$$

"GRACE, YOU AND I are alone here in the hospital," Vincente blurted out. Brutal, he thought. Absolutely brutal.

"What?"

"They're all...gone."

"That's impossible! Nurse! Nurse!" she shouted, while bearing down on the emergency button again.

"I checked around a few minutes ago, and this hospital is deserted. Totally."

"Are you trying to freak me out?"

"Yes. I mean, no, but I think we should get out of here."

"But outside...I mean, outside of the hospital, did you see people?" Grace asked.

"No. I couldn't find anyone inside here, or outside of the building. We need to go. Get out of here. Go to the city. I saw cars out there, with the engines running, but there aren't any people behind the wheels. No passengers. Lots of empty cars."

"But I can't leave the hospital. What about my condition?" Grace exclaimed. She looked at Vincente, and for a moment she wondered if she was dreaming again. She closed her eyes and then opened them. No, she was wide-awake. Perhaps it was Vincente who was asleep, and she was in his dream? Or worse: maybe whatever she had was contagious? Maybe they were losing their minds?

"If we leave now, we can find our families. They will know what to do."

"But I'm connected to these," she pointed to the machines and the wires.

"No problem, I will disconnect you," Vincente said.

"Do you know what to do?"

"It seems obvious, but you will have to trust me."

CHAPTER 9

GRACE CONSIDERED HER OPTIONS. If Vincente were correct and why would he lie? Then everyone in and around the hospital had vanished into thin air. Even after acknowledging this, Grace still questioned her own sanity. First, she believed Vincente could be a vampire. Then she believed her brother and father had visited, even though they were dead. And now, there was this.

"Of course, I trust you, Vincente. But I'm frightened. I don't understand what's happening to me."

"This isn't only happening to you. It's happening to me. You and I are in this together. There is no one else here but you and me."

"But am I dreaming? Are you certain this isn't a dream, Vincente? Tell me it's not a dream! I think I'm losing my mind!"

Vincente pulled Grace close to him and held her. His warm breath tickled her ear. He whispered, "You are not losing your mind. This is real. You and I are in this together...and we have got to get out of here."

"What if the clot bursts? What if?" Grace began.

"Then we'll deal with it. I'll take you to another hospital. In another place."

Grace nodded, as Vincente detached the heart monitor. "I'm afraid," she confessed.

"And I'm afraid of what will happen if we stay here," Vincente said. He removed the last Velcro attachment, causing the machine to violently flat line. The machine screamed and flashed until Vincente pulled the plug out of the wall.

Then there was silence in the room.

"Now this is the tough bit," Vincente said. "I need to remove the needle from your hand, and it's going to hurt."

"Talk to me. Distract me."

"Okay. Did I tell you that I had a big game to play? I was so looking forward to playing. It seems like it has been a long while since my last game." Vincente hesitated. "All finished."

"It didn't hurt me a bit. Thank you," Grace said as she swung her legs across the bed. They were naked legs, which had been hiding under the covers up until now.

Vincente looked away as she stepped down onto the cold linoleum floor. The coolness caused an involuntary shiver to take control of her weakened body. Vincente held her up and supported her. She eyed the bathroom door. She moved towards it. He supported her until she was safely inside.

Grace emptied her bladder. She flushed and went to the basin to wash her hands. She looked at her reflection in the mirror, she gasped. Her hair was a disarrayed mess, and her complexion was pasty. She looked very sick—which she was. Grace brushed her teeth, combed her hair. She opened the door and saw Vincente ransacking the place.

Before she had the chance to say anything, he asked, "Where are your clothes?"

"I have no idea. Maybe Mum took them home to wash?" She made her way back to bed. "I was thinking, maybe we should just stay here and wait for them to come back? Surely, they will come back. Or maybe I might just wake up, or you might wake up, and then everything will be back to normal again?"

"No, Grace. We need to get out of here...now. You are not dreaming, and you're not losing your mind—not unless I'm losing mine, too! Don't worry about clothes. Your hospital gown will do fine until we can find you something else."

She shivered again. Vincente wrapped a blanket around her shoulders.

"Come on, Grace. Let's stop talking about what was and think about us here and now. We need to get our butts out of here."

"Maybe you should just leave me. I'll only slow you down."

"I'm not leaving you, Grace. We must stick together. We're in this together now. Come on."

"But Vincente, maybe if I just lie back here on the bed and sleep for a while, you can find help on your own. I feel really tired." She moved toward the bed and started to climb onto it.

Vincente reached out and pulled her towards him. He put his hands onto her shoulders. "Grace, don't you trust me?"

"I do, but—" Grace stood there shivering, all the while looking into Vincente's dark eyes. She was afraid. She was afraid of being awake. She was afraid of being asleep. She wanted distraction, and she wanted to know more about him, more about his life. She wanted to hold back, to make sure he was the real Vincente Marino. She had begun to question everything.

"Where did you live before you moved here?"

"My family moved around a lot," Vincente said. "We've been here in Sydney for nearly five years now, and five years is a long time for my family to stay in one place."

Grace surprisingly remembered the very first time Vincente came to school. It was a memory gift. She let it flow into her consciousness, and she relived the scene. She watched it repeatedly in her mind.

"Are you okay, Grace?"

She was so involved in remembering. She forgot the real Vincente was standing right there in front of her. Grace was hesitant about revealing the dream to him. She wanted it to be for herself, and herself only. But she finally decided there was nothing to fear.

"I was remembering the first day you came to our school. It was like a shaft of light went right through my heart, piercing my soul. I couldn't breathe."

Vincente didn't know what to say to this admission, so he said nothing.

Grace was certain that he did not remember seeing her on his first day at school. Why would he?

"I remember you," he said.

"You're just saying that to get me to go with you," Grace said.

"Why would I lie? It was on the grass, in front of the school. You were sitting down. Reading a book. You were under a tree, all alone."

"Yes. I was reading Wuthering Heights."

"And I walked by and pretended to trip. I dropped a pen near you."

"I picked it up and returned it to you."

"Yes, but Grace, you looked at me like I was a creature from another planet."

"Yeah, that whole awakening of my heart and soul thing. I was speechless."

"But you didn't even know me."

"I knew you, Vincente. I always knew you."

"Grace, think about what you just said to me. You have specific memories stored in your brain, about me. I think that's an incredibly positive sign. A sign that you are getting better."

She thought about it then beamed a smile from ear to ear. "Okay," she said, "now let's get out of here."

"I won't leave you, Grace. We have to stick together. We're in this together. Come on."

The phone beside Grace's bed began to ring. Grace reached out for the receiver. Vincente stopped her from answering because another phone in the room also began to ring. Then another one rang in the room next door. Then another one rang, and then another. The ringing of telephones was echoing up and down the corridors. The sound was deafening.

"Let's go!" Vincente shouted as they went into the hall. The ringing reverberated and grew louder and louder.

They covered their ears and arrived at the elevator. The doors opened and shut, then opened and shut. It was too risky to get in. They headed toward the stairwell.

The ringing sound lessened while they were climbing down the stairs. When they arrived at the ground floor and opened the door, the sound was louder than ever.

"Come on!" Vincente shouted as they made their way out the front door. They found a car. He buckled Grace into the passenger seat.

He pushed the gas pedal to the floor, and they sped away into the still, inky night.

✳✳✳

VINCENTE SANG A SONG about driving to an unknown destination. They passed through Sydney's Inner West. He noticed Grace was quiet and had fallen asleep. He thought that was probably a good thing, since he needed time to think. To make a plan.

The cars were lined up bumper to bumper everywhere, blocking the main roadway. He had to weave in and out. At times he had to drive up on the sidewalk to get through.

Along the way he saw many abandoned and running vehicles. There were also transport trucks, taxis, police cruisers, and ambulances. All were idling in the street—even planes and helicopters. The air was thick with fumes. It was like something out of a Stephen King novel, an absolute apocalypse.

At first, Vincente stopped at crosswalks, keeping his eye out for children, adults and even dogs crossing. Seeing nothing he gave this up.

It seemed like no one was left. Still, Vincente hoped to find his family and friend waiting in the suburbs. He tried to ring his mum on his mobile, but there was no answer. He left a message. He did the same thing at his grandparents' place.

Grace awoke and asked, "Where are we?"

"We're just cruising around Sydney now. Sussing things out. While you were asleep, I went to the Royal Hospital and checked it out."

"You should have woken me up."

"No, there was no need. I could hear the phones ringing there as well. I knew the hospital was empty without even going inside." Vincente made his way into an intersection. Grace grabbed his arm and told him to stop.

He slammed on the brakes. They waited, as it was a pedestrian crossing but there was no one to cross.

Grace mentioned laundry flapping in the breeze, laundry which had been left out for who knows how long. She noticed there were no birds visible in the sky. No dogs barking. She saw that businesses were still open, but there was no staff working, and no customers around to buy anything.

There were also burned-out vehicles.

"The city is totally deserted," Vincente said.

"It's hopeless," Grace grumbled.

"Never give up hope."

✳✳✳

"Everything is going to be okay," Vincente assured as he reached across and touched Grace's hand. She felt a jolt as his skin connected with hers.

"What are we going to do?" Grace asked.

"Well, we are going to continue with Plan A," Vincente said.

"We have a Plan A?"

"While you were sleeping, Grace, I devised Plan A. It involves checking out the other hospital and familiar suburbs. I thought if anyone needed our help, we'd more than likely find them."

"It was a good plan."

"So far, nothing has been sighted either dead or alive."

"Where have the birds gone?" Grace asked.

"Probably out towards the water. They'd want to get away from the noisy cars polluting the air," Vincente said.

He noticed the tank was nearly empty. He filled it up at a petrol station. Then grabbed a few things at the convenience store. Vincente threw a chocolate bar across to Grace, and he opened a Mars Bar. "I left the money on the counter."

"You left money?" Grace was really surprised.

"Yes. I can't just take petrol without paying. It would be the end of civilization as we know it if we just took whatever we wanted! Besides, the owner of that station has known my family since we first moved here. He has helped Mum a few times when she was in trouble with the car, and Dad was out of town."

"I like your logic there."

"Yeah, we don't want anarchy now, do we?" he laughed.

Grace was more in awe of Vincente now than she had been before. She admired his take-charge attitude. His honesty. For whatever reason, fate had thrown them together. She and Vincente were on an adventure. It was exciting and scary and strange all at the same time.

Vincente made a quick turn into a gingerbread-like house. "Here we are," he said.

CHAPTER 10

"THIS IS MY GRANDPARENTS' house. I always stay here during school holidays and when my parents are away on business. Since my family moved around a lot, this has always been my second home."

As she took in the scent of eucalyptus in the air Grace said, "It's really early in the morning. Do you think they'll mind?"

"I tried to ring last night, but there wasn't any answer. I left a message. If they are sleeping, they won't mind. We can just go in though as I have my own key. Besides, this is kind of an emergency here."

Vincente pulled open the door.

Grace was still looking at the garden, focusing on a huge tree in the middle of the yard. The tree was leaning over and had most of its roots exposed. She shivered and wrapped her arms around herself.

Vincente, already inside, shouted, "Come on in!"

Now inside, Grace tried to make herself at home. Suddenly, a gust of wind came in through the open door and caught the back of her hospital gown. She was chilled right through to the bone, and she shivered again.

Vincente reached across the back of the sofa and pulled off a hand-crocheted, multi-coloured blanket his grandmother made. He draped it around her shoulders.

Grace snuggled into it and breathed in the lovely fragrance.

"Wait here," Vincente said. "I'll go upstairs and check on them."

"Okay," Grace watched Vincente climb the stairs and round the top of the hallway.

When he was out of sight, Grace went to the window and peeked through the curtains. The roots of the tree seemed to shift. The branches began to sway. She shivered again then closed the curtains.

She looked around without being too nosy. The home was a shrine to Vincente. There were photos of him everywhere. Vincente as a baby. Vincente as a small boy. Vincente in his sports uniforms. Vincente with his parents. Vincente with his trophies. The photos went on and on. She took note of a particular kind of photo that she did not see among the others, i.e., Vincente and a girlfriend. That was a good sign.

Vincente returned downstairs. She could tell by his expression and haste his grandparents were not in the house.

"They're not here, and there's no sign that they were here last night at all. The bed hasn't been slept in, and there's nothing in the laundry basket. Gran was always a stickler for putting dirty wash into the basket before we went to bed."

He sat down and ran his fingers through his hair and then put his hands on his head with his fingers interlocked. Sitting in this position helped him to concentrate. He did this often when he needed to block out the crowd at one of his games.

Grace stood nearby, quiet as a mouse.

Vincente snapped out of it and said, "Ah!" before jumping up and moving rapidly through the house.

Grace followed him along the hallway past the kitchen and bathroom into a tiny room at the end of the hall. It was an office.

He checked to see if the computer was up and running. It wasn't—the plug had been pulled out of the wall. "Granddad must've been saving on electricity again," he said. "It'll take a few minutes to reboot, so we might as well get a snack and some coffee in the meantime. Come on."

Grace and Vincente made their way into the kitchen, which had avocado-green appliances. The tea towels had decals of fruits and vegetables. In the centre of the table bunny-rabbit salt and peppershakers grinned mischievously at them.

"Gran always keeps the fridge well stocked," Vincente said as he pulled open the door. He tossed a chicken leg to Grace and began munching on the other one himself as he set the kettle on to boil. Next, he grabbed some coffee and sugar, the whitener, and two mugs. When the water was hot, he poured for them, and then they made their way back down the hall towards the computer room.

Once inside, Vincente sat down and began clicking away on the keyboard. When Facebook popped up, he went into his profile to update it, and then checked it to see if any of his friends were online. None were.

He clicked a few times and checked out the newsfeed. No posts or updates had been made by any of his friends in well over twenty-four hours.

"I can't believe anyone has been on here. Not even Liz, my cousin in the USA, who updates her profile at least five times a day. I'm afraid that it might not just be happening to us here in Sydney. It might be everywhere."

Grace covered her mouth, trying to hold in a gasp, but it escaped and filled the quiet room. "Maybe they are all together somewhere? Underground or somewhere safe, somewhere without computers, waiting."

"The entire world, underground and waiting? Now that would really be something," Vincente said as he logged himself out of Facebook. "I'm checking my email," he explained.

"You've Got Mail!" the browser greeted. It was a short message from his Gran asking about his cricket match.

"So, what should we do now? Where else should we check?" Grace asked.

"I-I don't know," Vincente said, and again, he placed his hands on his head and put his head between his knees.

Grace reached out and put her hand on his shoulder. He took her hand into his, accepting her comfort gratefully. "I know it's early morning and all," she said, "but I'm exhausted. Maybe we should take a nap, rest here a little. When we wake up, things may have changed, or we might dream up a great idea about what to do next."

"Yes, I'm exhausted too, and you're right, maybe an email will have come through, or someone might go onto Facebook between now and then. Who knows? We don't have anything to lose.

"Just let me try one more thing," Vincente said as he took out his mobile. He sent a group text to everyone in his address book. "There," he said. "If anyone has their phone, they'll reply. Now we can get some rest. They won't reply if we're just sitting around, watching the computer and the phone." He plugged his mobile in to recharge and then walked toward the stairs.

"Where should I sleep?" Grace asked.

"Come on upstairs, I'll show you around."

Vincente and Grace climbed the stairs and entered a bedroom with a four-poster bed. "This is my grandparents' room, and you can sleep here. I have my own room down the hall. A couple of doors down."

To be honest, Grace felt a little frightened and didn't want to be in the room all on her own. But what could she do? Ask Vincente to sleep on the chair beside the bed or share the same bed with her? She nodded and then, grateful for the soft bed in front of her, fell in and went straight to sleep.

Vincente realized how tired Grace was, but he wasn't tired enough to go right to sleep himself. To remedy this, he meandered around the house, ate a few Vegemite sandwiches. He returned to the computer, hoping things had changed. They hadn't.

He clicked on the television, hoping for a little distraction. Every channel was off the air and filled with snowy white static. Same story when he tried the radio: only static. He began to think that the world had ended, for everyone—everyone except for himself, and Grace Greenway.

How strange for this to happen, for two people who hardly even knew each other. To be put into such an odd arrangement. She was a sweet kid and all, and he liked her, but she wasn't his type. He wondered if, knowing how she felt about him, he might cause her more damage by leading her on. He had known that Grace had a crush on him for some time. Although they were the same age in years, they were worlds apart in their social circles and experiences.

Vincente thought about their math class. Grace was always ahead of everyone including the teacher. She was destined to be a Mathematician—of this there was no doubt. He was destined to be a professional Athlete—there was no doubt about that, either. What would the two of them do, or be, if they were the only ones left on the planet? What would the future hold for them?

He shook his head and condemned himself for such negative thoughts. He made his way up the stairs, looked in on Grace. She was sound asleep. He headed to his own room.

He went to the dresser to find his clothes, but his pyjamas were not there. Strange. He had slept in his clothing all night, and he was ready to wear something else. He checked the other drawer, finding a pair of black underwear and a pair of socks. He put both on and fell into bed. He was soon sound asleep.

✳✳✳

"Vincente! Vincente!" Grace called out and moments later, he was back at her side.

"Are you okay?" he asked.

"I forgot where I was," Grace said. She moved away from the bed and threw her arms around him. Soon they were in an unexpected, forceful embrace. Upon realizing she pulled back and apologized.

"You don't have to be sorry," he said. He looked down, realised he was practically naked.

She noticed it too, then. She flushed deep red. "I'm going to get dressed now, if you're, okay?"

As Vincente began to walk away, the lights above them started to shake. The light fixtures affixed to the ceiling began to tremble, blinking on and off. His grandparents' room resembled a seedy motel room with a strobe light.

Thing on the dresser began to shudder and shake in a rhythmic dance – then the floor joined in.

"I think it's an earthquake!" Vincente shouted. "Come on! It's not safe up here."

The pair stepped onto the staircase, and all at once it began to come alive. It shifted from side to side in a rhythmic two-step. Grace tried to hold onto the banister, but she was having difficulty moving forward. Vincente grabbed hold of her hand, and she moved down the stairs.

As soon as they arrived on the ground floor, the shaking stopped. The staircase was out of alignment now, and its demise was imminent.

"There's bound to be an aftershock," Vincente said. "Let's stay close to the front door, just in case."

A second tremor struck. Only, this time around, it was more critical. The staircase turned into an escalator. The steps crashed down to the ground floor in a massive heap.

Vases and pictures flew around the room. Chairs began to rock. A mirror broke, making a deafening crack. Grace screamed.

They raced toward the front door.

✳✳✳

Before Vincente was able to pull the front door open, under the power of a strong gust of wind it opened itself.

The teenagers held onto each other as they made their way out onto the veranda.

Straight in front of them the giant tree, the one that Grace had noticed before, was twisting, and turning. Its branches were reaching out like old, arthritic fingers. It held an eerie pose as it stretched out in all directions. Its roots shifted like snakes.

In front of them, inanimate objects formerly not meant to fly zipped past. Umbrellas, rubbish bins, BBQs, and laundry trees were whipping around. Crashing into everything. A flying shovel hit the side of the tree, and an almost humanlike moan filled the air.

"It's just the wind," Vincente soothed as he pulled Grace back indoors. "We can't go out there—it's too dangerous. It's like a hailstorm of Home Depot objects!"

With the wind pushing on the back of the door, it took their combined weight to get the door closed. They stood with their backs firmly against it. It shifted and pushed at their backs. Vincente and Grace stood their ground.

"So, what do we do now?" Grace asked. She was shaking. Her knees would no longer hold her up. Still, she held her ground side by side with Vincente.

"Well, I've read about earthquakes, and they usually get worse before they get better. There are generally some warning tremors, and then one big one hits. I guess we have to decide if that was the big one, or if we should get the hell out of here while the going is good."

"I think it's going to get worse."

"Then let's go with our gut feelings, because mine is telling me the exact same thing. First, grab the phone book so we can check out your home address and phone number. You can give your mum a ring once we have that information. Okay, now let's get out of here!" Vincente shouted, as another tremor hit.

This one displayed phenomenal power. It was followed by a crash, a snap, and a crunch. Then the large tree fell onto the house, pushing straight through the roof. The pair stood looking up at the tree, now implanted firmly in the living room. It seemed ironic that the door they were protecting was still intact, while the ceiling was now the sky.

"Come on!" Vincente shouted as they ran out the front door.

The blowing objects were flying all around them as they made their way towards the safety of their car. As Vincente moved to open the door, Grace noticed that the ring on his finger glinted and glowed like a third eye. It seemed to be drawing in light from the sky.

Strange thoughts were flying around in Grace's head, as items were scattered and crashed around her. She looked at Vincente and considered that if he were a vampire, then he was immortal. He could make her into a vampire, too. If that happened, then neither of them would ever be alone again. The thought was crazy, she knew.

Then something strange but distinct flashed in her mind. A distant memory about killing vampires with wooden stakes. She eyed Vincente as a tree branch sailed toward them. It would puncture Vincente's back if she didn't do something.

"Get in!" she shouted. "Watch your back!"

He jumped inside just in time, as the piece of wood impacted and dented the car.

"Thanks! That was a close one!" Vincente exclaimed.

Once inside, a whirling dervish in the form of a metal umbrella sailed past, right before their eyes.

A rip-roaring crack. So loud they had to cover their ears. Another crack followed. The earth began to open before them like a broken coconut. The fissure in the earth was moving along the road, coming perilously towards them. Things were falling into it, like whole houses and trees and cars.

"Go!" Grace screamed as the devastating crack snaked its way closer to them.

Vincente backed up, and then floored it. Their necks flew back like elastic bands as they peeled away in a cloud of dust.

"Don't look back!" Vincente shouted.

He drove as he had never driven before. He dodged deserted cars and debris like a professional race car driver. He kept on going; he kept them safe and out of the earthquake's deadly path of destruction.

They drove and they drove, and they drove, without looking back.

✳✳✳

I T WAS QUITE SOME time before they stopped. Before their breathing patterns returned to normal.

"We can go back, when it's safe," Grace said.

"I'm afraid there's no point," Vincente said, as he took a deep breath. "The house is surely in the hole. It's gone. Everything is gone."

"I'm so sorry, Vincente."

"It's okay, I have some good memories of that house. They are in here." He pointed to his heart. "And in here." He pointed to his head. "No one can take them away from me."

Grace thought about her current situation. How her memories had been taken. A lone tear trickled down her cheek.

"I'm sorry, Grace. I didn't mean—"

"I know you didn't, but it's true. Mine have been taken from me."

"But you'll get them back. I know you will."

"Thanks for saying that, but no one knows for sure if I will or not, especially without any doctors around."

"I know the memories are still there somewhere, inside of you. They aren't completely lost. You just have to find a way to tap into them."

Grace acquiesced. She liked the sound of tapping into her memories.

"And speaking of which," Vincente said. "Why don't you flip through the White Pages and find your family's phone number and address? Then we can give your mum a ring."

Grace smiled and began walking with her fingers through the pages, stopping when she found Greenway. Vincente gave her his mobile, and she began dialling. When she heard a voice on the other end—her mum's voice—she smiled. She began to speak to it but was instructed to leave a message at the sound of the beep.

"It's just a machine."

"It was the same at my place. It's okay. We have the address, so now we can go there and check it out."

"Sounds like we have a Plan C."

CHAPTER 11

"**O**H MY!" GRACE EXCLAIMED. "Look out!"

Vincente turned his attention to the road. Grace reached across and grabbed the steering wheel. The vehicle veered sharply to the right. Vincente tried to keep control of the car, but with Grace's hands clamped upon his, he was unable to.

"Look out!" she cried again.

Vincente struggled with Grace. He regained control of the car. By then it was too late to stop it—the course had been set. The tires began to fishtail, and soon the car came to a full stop as it careened into the trunk of a tree.

"Are you crazy?" Vincente bellowed.

"I—" Grace said.

"What the hell do you think you're doing?" He shook his head from side to side, like he had just stepped out of a shower. "We just barely got out of the other situation alive and now, goddamn it, Grace! What the—?"

"I—" Grace said.

"Why would you do that?"

"Would you like me to answer you now?" Grace said, very calmly.

"Bloody well right, I would." Vincente said. "You nearly got us killed. K-I-L-L-E-D!"

"I know how to spell killed, thank you very much. Do you want me to explain myself or not?"

"Yes," Vincente said, exasperated. He was trying to calm himself down by taking deep breaths.

"First," she said, "I need to go back there and see if I can find her. Then I'll explain."

"Her?"

"The little girl," she explained.

And soon she was running. Her hospital gown flapped in the wind, but she didn't care. All she cared about was the little girl.

Vincente ran after her. He was on her heels. He thought she had lost her mind. A little girl? He hadn't seen anyone. Grace must've imagined her.

Grace stopped. She turned around and around in circles, looking for the little girl in every bush, in every possible hiding space. Grace out of breath, and unable to find her, stopped. Stock still she listened intently.

"She was a child, dressed in a white nightgown with lace all around the edges and a red tie-up on the collar. She had long, dark hair that flowed over her shoulders, and the biggest olive green, almond- shaped eyes."

Vincente was standing alongside her, listening to her description. He was paying attention to her and trying to understand but not understanding.

"She was right here. We—you—nearly hit her."

"A little girl?"

"Yes."

"Grace, there wasn't a little girl here."

"She was there! I saw her! Standing right there in the middle of the road. She was beautiful."

"Grace, I didn't see her. She wasn't real."

"She was real, as real as you are to me standing here now."

"Are you saying she only appeared to you?" Vincente asked hoping to snap her out of it.

"I don't know. I hadn't thought of that."

Vincente didn't want to do it, but he had to get them back on track again. He hesitated. "Real—like your dad and your brother were?"

"That's a low blow and you know it!" Grace said, as she ran across the road, through the trees. Away.

Vincente was more certain she was losing her mind.

Grace tried to save a little girl from harm. She saw the little girl as plain as day, standing there. What was she supposed to do—let him hit her? She so wanted to hit him and hard. Instead, she kept on running. Running to anywhere. Anywhere away.

✳✳✳

WHEN HE EVENTUALLY CAUGHT up with her, Grace was on the grass in a field, watching the clouds going overhead.

"May I join you?" he asked.

"Sure."

He felt the soft grass and took in its scent. They were silent for a moment.

"Tell me again, what you saw on the road with the little girl."

She remained silent.

"I promise I will listen to what you have to say."

"Look at the clouds up there, continuing like nothing is happening. They are so beautiful, high in the sky, floating weightlessly."

"Grace, tell me."

She took in a deep breath, glanced at Vincente, and then looking back up at the sky said, "There was a little girl. She saw me. She acknowledged me. She made a sign like this to me." She held her hand up, making it into the sign language stop sign.

"When did you learn sign language?" Vincente frowned, realizing that she wouldn't remember when or why she had learned it. "Sorry, dumb question."

Grace was silent, watching the clouds, giving them her full attention.

"Wait a minute, you can't remember your phone number, but you can remember sign language?"

"I guess so."

"Don't you realize what this means, Grace?"

She remained silent.

"It means I was right. You can access, tap into your memories when you want to," Vincente said with excitement in his voice.

"I guess I did kind of do that with my dad and my brother."

"And now, this little girl. Who was she? What was she to you?"

"I don't know, but now I'm thinking about how I put us into such danger. We could have died when we crashed into that tree."

"Yeah."

Grace stood, feeling hopeful again. Wondering if the child was hiding, afraid. She called out, "Little girl, wherever you are, come on out and talk to me. We won't hurt you. You'll be safe. We can help you."

Only the sound of stirring leaves and the whistle of the wind filled the air. Grace put her hands on her hips. She felt strongly that the little girl couldn't have disappeared into thin air. She had to be there somewhere.

Vincente was still dubious. He tried to touch Grace, but she swatted him away like an insect.

She continued calling for the little girl to come out. Grace was singularly focused on the task, crying out until her voice was hoarse.

✳✳✳

ALL GRACE'S ENERGY WAS now spent. Still no sign of the little girl. It was time to give up, so she made her way back to the car. Vincente followed behind her in silence. Her body language told all there was to say: she understood the truth now. The little girl had been an illusion. The question was, why?

Vincente kicked the tire of the car and then looked up at Grace. She was exhausted and embarrassed. She couldn't even make eye contact with him. Yet, somehow despite that, he found her to be extremely attractive standing there. She looked so drained of hope, and so all alone. Like she needed to be saved.

He walked towards her and took a lock of her hair between his fingers. He wrapped it around and around, drawing Grace nearer and nearer to him. Then he kissed her. Gently, softly. A little kiss, enough to leave her wanting more. She responded at first, and then he stepped away. "I'm sorry."

"I'm not," Grace said, smiling both inside and out. "But next time I tell you to stop the car, just stop, okay?"

"I will, I promise."

"Even if you can't see anyone?"

"Even if I can't see anyone."

"Okay."

"Okay."

"I think maybe we should stay here for a little while longer, in case she comes back."

"Grace, she's not coming back. Please, just get in the car."

The engine fired up straight away. Off they went. Grace tried not to look back, but the impulse was overpowering.

CHAPTER 12

A S THE CAR CONTINUED speeding along, Grace focused on the present. She rolled down the window and held her arm out. She let the breeze tickle the hair on her forearm, causing goosebumps. She felt alive. Like maybe she and Vincente now had a chance to be what she dreamed they might be. Still, she was afraid to think about it too much, to focus on it too much, because she didn't want to jinx it.

Grace laughed as the wind ran through her fingers. For a second, she flashed back to that moment. The moment of the kiss: their first kiss. It had been nice, gentle, warm, sticky, and she could feel his desire for her pushing up against her.

It was strange, driving along a wave of unmoving vehicles. No horns blowing. No sirens blaring. No one shouting. She didn't miss those sounds. The sounds, which she only had a vague memory of, were generally irritating. However, she did miss the birds singing. She missed their activity, the songs, the flittering from tree to tree. She missed the buzzing of the bees. She wondered how Nature would provide, how pollination would occur now.

Nature was adaptable to many changes. Mother Nature would find a way to survive.

Grace looked over at Vincente. He was concentrating on driving.

He seemed deep in thought.

Vincente was worried, and angry with himself. First, he told himself not to lead her on. He knew she wasn't his type. Not his type at all. She was Grace Greenway: brainy mathematical phenomenon. She thought in numbers.

Hell, she probably dreamed in numbers.

He tried not to think about the kiss, their first kiss. He decided their first kiss was their last. Even though it had been unexpectedly nice. Sweet. Innocent. She hadn't expected it, and then there was...Ugh, he didn't want to think about how he felt when she kissed him. How he had become aroused so quickly, at just one simple kiss. It was probably because he was out in the world, wandering around in his underwear. His desire for her was likely just an uncontrollable urge, a natural reaction. Not something he wanted to happen.

He paused for a moment, feeling her eyes on him, and adjusted his grip on the steering wheel. He tried to think about other things to distract himself from thinking about her. He thought about movies. Video games. Food.

Meanwhile, Grace thought about the world. The big world out there, which was theirs, hers, and Vincente's alone to share. She thought about her past, how she felt incomplete without all her memories at her disposal. She also thought about it being a good thing, instead of a negative. It was a way that she could recreate herself. At the same time, she knew she wouldn't ever be whole without the biggest part of herself restored. The part that was her mathematical nature: the mathematical state of Grace.

She tried to remember everything she once knew about Pythagoras. She used to know everything about his life and his mathematical theories. Now the facts and numbers were all blurred together in her mind. She tried to remember Fibonacci numbers, but they were no longer clear in her mind either. She resolved to go to a library and read up on these two, plus others including Einstein and Galileo. She would teach herself everything she used to know, and by doing so, she hoped to open up her memory bank, to tap into it.

"I saw this movie a long time ago, "Vincente said. "It was about aliens who came down to Earth and attacked in their spaceships."

Grace was startled. She had grown used to the comfortable silence they shared. She encouraged him to tell her more about the movie. "Sounds intriguing."

"It was just that. But I haven't told you the most fascinating bit yet."

"Well, don't keep me in suspense."

"In the movie, there were only two survivors left, a man and a woman."

"No way!"

"And why didn't the aliens kill them?" Vincente asked? Grace shrugged. "Because they wanted to observe them. To study them." He stopped and waited, watching Grace out of the corner of his eye. "And then, they put the two humans in a cage, like in a zoo. To watch them procreate."

"What if they didn't want to procreate?" Grace said, her voice quivering.

"They made them."

"How could they force them to do that?"

"They didn't want to die, and they needed food to survive. So, they did what they had to do, and the aliens watched them, observing what made humans tick."

"Disgusting."

"Well, if you think about it, humans have been putting animals into cages for centuries. Watching them procreate. Studying them, even sometimes using them for experiments, to advance medicine and whatnot. So would they really be any worse?"

"No, I guess not, not when you put it that way. But you and I, we have an opportunity here to change things. We can't change the past."

"True. If we are the last two survivors," Vincente surmised, "then we can live the way we want to."

"What happened...I mean, at the end of the movie?"

"I never saw the ending. I was at a sleepover at a friend's place. We were kids and shouldn't have been up so late. When we were found out by his parents, we ran to his bedroom. I never did find that movie again."

"What did the aliens do to all the other Earth inhabitants if they were the only two left?"

"That I do know. They zapped them! Kind of ironic really, when you think about it, because in the movie, the aliens phaser-gunned them all down—poof! —and then they just disappeared. Nothing was left behind, no remains at all. I mean, no bones, no bodies, and no ashes. It was like they had never existed at all."

Grace folded her arms around herself, realizing too late it was giving her the creeps. She hoped he was finished now, so she could go back to her lovely thoughts about the future, their future, together.

Vincente interrupted her bliss with more cinema talk. "Another one I remember was about aliens who came to earth and incinerated everyone. All that remained was a pile of dust in the place of each human being. It was the only evidence of those who had lived. Evidence that there once were people." He paused. She didn't comment. She hoped he was now finished. "Then there was another one, where they tapped into all their human minds by planting a chip in their brains and controlling them. These movies became scarier and scarier."

"Don't forget about E.T." Grace said.

"What?" Vincente gasped, fascinated, waiting for Grace to realize she had unknowingly tapped into a memory.

"You know, 'E.T. phone home?'"

"Yeah, I know," he said, and he smiled a smile that was so big that for a moment Grace wondered what he was smiling for.

Then it hit her. She had unlocked a memory. True, it wasn't the most fascinating of information, but it was still a memory, nonetheless. She beamed back at him.

He was so proud that he reached over and took her hand into his for a moment then they were silent again.

✳✳✳

W HEN VINCENTE NEEDED TO turn on a roundabout or a bend, he let go of Grace's hand. Their eyes met for a second, then he concentrated on the road again.

He was proud of her.

Grace was feeling enormously proud of her little memory break. She visualized the inside of her mind as a library. She was walking up and down the aisles, searching for memories. Reaching onto the shelves, she picked them up, examining them individually. She selected a thick, red-covered book, hoping to find something about herself within it, but nothing happened. She wasn't going to give up on this technique. She intended to keep on trying.

Vincente was thinking about advances in technology over the years. So many inventions created, some good and some not so good. Looking around, with only the two of them to cater to, he wondered what all the hard work had really been for.

In the distance, the sound of a bell rang out. It grew louder and louder as they pulled up in front of a building, "Recognize it?" he asked.

Grace read the sign, "Queen Victoria's High School, The School Where You Make Your Dreams Come True." She did not remember.

"It's our high school," he said.

"I thought it might be, but I wasn't sure," Grace said. She looked around the campus and finally found the cricket field in the back: The field where she had been injured on her last day at school. "I wonder what that bell was for?" Grace asked.

"Was just thinking about it myself. Probably just set on a timer. Automatic. But there is a chance that someone might be trapped inside and in need of help, so I'd like to go and check it out. Do you want to stay here?"

"No, I want to come with you."

"Okay, but just stay behind me. We don't know what to expect. It's probably nothing, but you never know," Vincente said. He had envisioned someone stuck inside, too afraid to come out.

Grace had been imagining the aliens, like in the movies, waiting to catch and trap the last two people on Earth. She shivered as Vincente swung the doors open and they stepped into the long corridor. It was very quiet; the only sounds were their feet slapping along the cool linoleum floors.

Vincente remembered how much fun he had within these walls. How he'd always been a bit of a sports—for lack of a better word—hero. He arrived at his locker, opened it, and pulled out his gym bag. He put a pair of cricket shorts on over his black underwear and threw on his jersey. You could still see his black undies through the shorts. Grace laughed.

"It's not like you haven't seen them before," Vincente said, though he laughed, too.

Most of the locker doors were wide open, with contents strewn all over the place. "It was probably from the earthquake," Vincente surmised.

Grace was still shivering.

"Take a deep breath," he said, trying to calm and reassure her.

Grace's heart was beating faster and faster. She had a bad vibe about the place.

Vincente asked loudly, "Hello, is anyone here?"

His voice echoed up and down the corridors, coming back unanswered. Then the school bell rang again. Because they were inside, the sound resonated.

Further along the corridor, Vincente pushed back the doors and entered the gymnasium. It had been left in preparation of a basketball game. The empty bleachers and court felt kind of sad.

"Were you good at basketball, too?" Grace asked.

"I was surprisingly good at most sports. I loved the excitement. The cheering of the crowd. The rush I got when I tossed a basket, or when we won a game. Very heady stuff."

"Yeah, I can see that. It sounds like a powerful drug."

"It felt like a drug sometimes, but this is only high school, getting a break in the big game, you know? Going pro—now, that was just a dream."

"You wanted to go pro?"

"Yeah, but it seems kind of silly now."

"Dreams are never silly," Grace said seriously.

"That's the kind of thing my mum and dad would have said to me."

"I wish I would have met them," Grace said. "You will, one day."

They jumped as the bell sounded once more.

"Let's get out of here, it's giving me the creeps," Grace said.

"No, first we check out the offices, just down the hall. Make sure they are all clear, and then we can go."

Grace followed Vincente out of the gym. The bad feeling in Grace's stomach changed from a rumble to a roar.

✳✳✳

OH NO! OH NO! Oh no! were the words running through Grace's mind. She had no control over it as she continued walking behind Vincente.

"This is the secretary's office. Over there is the counsellor's office." He looked inside, since the door was wide-open, confirming that it was empty. "This is the Vice Principal's office. And this is the principal's office." He tried the door. It was locked. "Hello!" he called.

They heard something. It was a tap-tap-tapping. Faint, yet constant. It was coming from inside the principal's office.

Vincente knocked on the door. "Is anyone there?"

No answer.

"The aliens probably can't speak English, "Grace said.

Vincente pushed against the door with his shoulder, but it didn't budge.

The tapping stopped. They waited, holding their breaths. It started up again.

Whatever it was, it was running out of energy. They had to get in there. It was running out of time.

✳✳✳

"Think! Think!" Vincente said aloud to coach himself while he paced back and forth. A few seconds later he said, "Okay, I've got it. Follow me."

Grace did as she was instructed. Soon they were back inside the gymnasium. Vincente was telling Grace to stand behind the bleachers while he pushed over one of the basketball hoops. They began dragging it along the corridor.

Vincente explained its base was filled with sand. Once they had it back to the office, they could use it to bust the door down.

"What a great plan!" Grace said. "I think it just might work."

"We have to use maximum force. I mean, give it everything we've got."

Just as they were going by the ladies' room, Grace realized that she had needed to go for quite some time and hesitated before attempting to open the door.

"No way!" Vincente shouted, "You're not going in there without me checking it out first."

"It'll be okay."

"You probably don't remember, but most of the bad things in scary movies happen in the girls' bathroom. I'll go and check it out, and if it's okay, you can go in after me. So, you stay here. I mean, don't move an inch."

"Okay, boss," Grace said.

There was a flush, and then Vincente returned, telling Grace it was all clear.

She went in, but now found that she couldn't go after all, though she knew that she needed to. She started running the water in one, two then three taps until her kidneys responded in kind. After she had relieved herself and flushed, she exited the loo.

They carried on, with their athletic weapon in tow. Back outside of the office, they two stopped and reassessed the method of entry.

"First, let's switch ends," Vincente said. He thought it would be best if he had the back end, the heavier part of their weapon, to convey maximum results upon the target: the office door. When they were in position, Vincente continued explaining what he had in mind.

"When I count to three, push it forward with all the strength you can muster. Then stop. I'll count to three again, and we'll push it another time. And so on and so forth, until we break through."

"Sounds like a plan," Grace said, getting a good grip on the front of the apparatus.

Vincente counted, and their first hit was dead on, but didn't budge the door. On the second hit, it shifted in the frame, and they felt one of the hinges at the top pop. They went for it again, gaining strength, and on the fourth time, the door crumbled inward, falling on top of the principal's desk with a crash. The pair was now presented with a new problem: the door was half open, and half closed, vertically. They weren't any further ahead getting inside.

"Anyone in there?" Vincente asked.

Silence was the only reply.

✱✱✱

STANDING SIDE BY SIDE, peering in through the gap, both were hesitant to climb up on the door and go inside.

From the hallway, they spied a tree branch. It had broken through the window and was positioned on top of the principal's desk. They also observed a large amount of broken and shattered glass debris strewn across on the floor.

One thought occurred to both of them simultaneously. Since the window was broken wide open, had anyone been trapped in there, they would have already climbed out. That is unless they were injured. There didn't seem to be any blood around. Perhaps he or she was unconscious, under the desk?

Vincente decided to use the door as a plank. After all, it was anchored at the other end, by the desk.

"I'm coming in," Vincente shouted. He stepped onto the door and inched forward. "No way!" he exclaimed, as he led Grace into the office.

It was a black raven. It was staring them right in the face as it swung to and fro on the end of the branch. Its beak clicked against the desk in a violent tapping pattern.

"How strange," Vincente said. "Very Edgar Allan Poe-ish."

Just then, the wind seemed to pick up. It caused the branch to sway. The bird's head connected with the desk several times, making even louder tapping noises.

Vincente and Grace cringed at the sound.

Grace, wanting to get away, prepared to climb back out of the office. As she moved backwards, Vincente stopped her with his hand on her back.

She turned around.

The branch was lifting itself up, with the help of the wind. Lifting? Yes, strangely, it was rising, higher and higher, nearly level with the open window.

He watched the branch carrying the bird upward. All the sudden, it took the branch completely outside of the window. The gust continued carrying it up into the sky.

"Come here, Grace, you've got to see this!" he whispered.

The branch grazed against the broken window on its journey out. It drew the bird up higher and higher and higher.

The two stared out the window, wondering where the tree was taking the dead raven.

Grace couldn't take her eyes from the dead bird's eyes. They were catching the rays of the sun in them and reflecting it back. It was like a mask—a mask of death.

"We've got to get out of here!" Grace said.

"No, wait. I want to—" Vincente began to say, and then the wind swept around the branch.

The other branches suddenly came to life. They moved upwards on their own volition. Closely following the branch with the dead bird attached to it.

The sound of all the branches, moving together, swaying with the wind, rising upward, created an appalling cacophony. It sounded like crushing bones.

Grace put her arms around herself as goose bumps formed on her exposed skin. When the sound became too loud to take, she covered her ears. Even so, she couldn't turn her eyes away from the raven's dead eyes.

The deceased bird continued to rock backwards and forwards, forwards and backwards in a lullaby. All while remaining skewered on the end of the branch like a shish kebab.

Grace held her breath. With every fibre of her being, she wanted to get away.

And yet, she couldn't stop watching the eyes of the bird. She was transfixed. Engulfed.

As was Vincente.

They stood frozen in time.

Waiting to see what would happen next.

✱✱✱

THE BRANCHES CONTINUED RISING. There was an ominous silence in the office as the bird proceeded with its journey. It was still surrounded by branches, which encircled it and scooped it up like it was weightless. Then using their crone-like, arthritic fingers, the branches began to cradle the bird in it and rock it, back and forth, back, and forth.

The sight was so awful that Grace wanted to scream. Instead, she began to rock to and fro, as did Vincente. It was beauty in motion, the rising. The rocking. The rocking and the rising.

They needed to move forward, closer to the window to see it now. They were careful not to step on the glass shards covering the floor around them as they craned their necks through the broken glass and out of the window. Higher and higher, the bird was still rocking gently, being carried heavenward.

Then everything came to a halt, mid-air.

Silence filled the scene.

The trunk of the tree moved.

It was a small movement at first.

Barely noticeable.

It shook, like someone who had just woken up.

It coughed. It sputtered.

It swayed and convulsed.

And then it yawned out from a grotesque face. A face with an enormous, gaping mouth into which the dead raven dropped.

There were crunching sounds. Appalling noises, like bones breaking, grinding.

It burped. A few black feathers flew out of its mouth. One drifted below, landing upon the windowsill where Grace and Vincente stood, gaping.

Then the branches resumed movement. Changed direction. Pointed downwards.

✳✳✳

"RUN!" VINCENTE EXCLAIMED.

Behind, they could hear the tree moving rapidly. As the branches re-entered through the window, more fragments of glass crashed onto the floor.

Holding hands, Vincente pulled Grace along the corridor. They flew, almost like the spirit of the raven had entered their bodies.

The arthritic, wooden fingers groped their way along the corridor, following, knocking, destroying, and scraping at everything within its reach.

Once Vincente and Grace exited the school, he took the keys out of his pocket and tossed them to her. He told her to open the door, to start the car, and that he'd be back with her in a moment. If not, she should drive away.

"I don't know how to drive."

"You'll learn fast!"

Once inside the car, she watched him remove his shirt. She watched him tie the jersey around the door handles. He weaved it in and out as many times as he possibly could, hoping to buy them some time.

As the branches rounded the corner at the far end of the corridor, Vincente turned and ran. He jumped into the car, slammed the door, and floored it.

The car peeled away when the branches smashed through the doors.

"Wow! That was a little too close for comfort," Grace said, once they were blocks away from the school. She was still breathing loudly, having trouble catching her breath.

"No kidding! Everything about that, that thing was insane!"

"What kind of a tree was that, anyway?" Grace asked.

"I think it was an olive tree. Question is, why was it feeding on birds? Why did it have an almost humanlike mouth, and the need to eat flesh?"

"I've heard of birds nesting in trees, but never trees eating birds!"

"Yeah, well, we're in an entirely different world now Grace and I'm thinking that maybe we ought to make a point of getting us some weapons. Who knows what else is out there? We need to think about protecting ourselves. The sooner the better."

"Where would we get weapons?"

"I know a place in the city where we can try out guns, knives, whatever we need. In fact, there's no time like the present. I'm shaken up enough to get the weapons now."

"I'm exhausted, but I don't think I'll be falling asleep any time soon," Grace said as she crossed her arms across her chest.

As they drove along the tree-lined streets, they now had a fear in their hearts, which had never been there before: trees! Flesh-eating trees.

"I always thought olive trees were symbolic, for peace. And I remember stories of olive trees in the Bible and in mythology," Vincente said.

"Are they native to Australia?"

"Definitely not. But why would that matter?"

Neither knew for certain. Nor did they know why the carnivorous tree had taken on such an uncharacteristic trait.

They tried not to think about it as they made their way towards the gun shop in the heart of Sydney.

CHAPTER 13

A FLASHING SIGN OUT front pulsed the words: *'Guns! Guns! Guns!'* In the small print it read: Permit Required by NSW State Law.

Since they were living in a brand-new world, those rules of law were no longer the law of the land.

Vincente Marino and Grace Greenway didn't have a permit. They weren't 18 years of age. They had no identification, and no money. But it didn't matter. They were here to protect themselves. Nothing was going to stop them.

Vincente pushed the door open, and they went inside. Grace stood behind Vincente, feeling overwhelmed by all the weaponry. She looked around, trying to get into the spirit of things, but it was a stretch beyond her imagination.

"This is a good one," Vincente said. "You can fill it with lots of bullets, so you won't have to reload as much. It would be good to have in a battle. It can easily pierce the trunk of any tree."

"Hmmm," Grace said noncommittally because she couldn't think of anything else to say.

Then Vincente moved on and he picked up another weapon. "Now, this one is also good because it is small and easy to hide. See, I can put it right in the front of my pants, and no one would even know I was wearing it."

"But isn't that dangerous? For you, I mean. Couldn't it, uh, go off accidentally?"

Vincente smiled, "I'd leave the safety on. I wouldn't want to shoot anything off."

Grace smiled and blushed. She couldn't believe they were having this conversation as Vincente put the gun into the palm of her hand. "It's also small enough for you to put into your purse."

She felt the gun. It had no weight at all, and it did fit nicely into the palm of her hand. She was surprised that it didn't feel more alien to her, but it wasn't too scary, probably because it felt like a toy.

"It isn't loaded," Vincente said. "In fact, none of the weapons are loaded. Don't be afraid to pick them up and take a closer look."

"Try before we buy?"

"Yeah, very funny. Let's keep looking."

He watched as Grace opened her mind, accepting the fact that their new reality required weaponry.

Grace picked up a plastic basket and began perusing the knives. They were made in all sizes and shapes, and there were swords too. Intrigued, she grabbed a few knives in metal cases and popped them into the basket. She could always use them to chop carrots and onions, if worse came to worst.

"Wow, that baby," Vincente pointed to one of the knives Grace had in her basket, "could probably chop a log in half. Great choice."

Grace beamed. Vincente had piled quite a few guns into a military-looking trunk. He was carrying several large portable targets under his arm.

"I'll teach you how to use the guns once we're out of the city. I'll have to do a refresher course too with real weapons, since all my weapons experience is from playing computer games."

"We could fire a shot straight down George Street and no one would hear it," Grace said.

"True, true, but it would just feel too weird. Uncivilized, if you know what I mean?"

"Yeah, I do," Grace said. "After all, Sydney is our home. We have to treat it with the respect it deserves."

"Yeah, it's our city, our Sydney, and I can't think of a more beautiful city to be stranded in with you, Grace."

She blushed as he came towards her. He took the plastic container of knives and made his way towards the car. She had never loved him more. The more he took charge, the more he oozed sensuality and testosterone. She wished she could just run up to him and openly kiss him. He would probably think she was too forward and had lost her mind—again.

Vincente was thinking how sexy Grace looked, holding the gun in the palm of her hand. He thought she would be even sexier if he taught her to shoot. He stopped himself. Grace wasn't his type. She had been very brave back at the principal's office. She remained cool when many others would have totally lost it. Still, he was worried, mostly because he was thinking about her too much. Why? They were already spending 24/7 together. Why wasn't he longing for some alone time?

With Missy Malone, after a couple of hours—if they weren't making out—he got bored. He wanted to do sports or go and hang out with the guys. She was his type: pretty and popular. She wasn't the brightest spark, but that didn't matter as long as they were a good fit.

The reality was, Missy was probably gone now, just like all the others. He missed her, and wondered if they were the last ones left, would things be different. Different than they were now between him and Grace. He felt comfortable with Grace, and she wasn't demanding.

"Are we ready to go NOW?" Grace demanded causing him to snap back to reality.

"Yeah, sorry. I just drifted off for a second."

"It's getting dark. Maybe we ought to find somewhere to crash for the night?"

"Yeah. I know just the place. Let's go and stay in Sydney Harbour. We can relax there and pretend we're tourists."

"Sounds perfect."

They drove towards The Quay and stopped just outside the Marriott. They went inside, and after making themselves some food in the empty hotel kitchen, continued upstairs into the penthouse suite with multiple bedrooms.

In their separate rooms, they fell asleep and dreamed about flesh-eating trees.

And kissing each other.

CHAPTER 14

The next morning, Vincente stood on his balcony. He looked out at the Sydney Harbour Bridge then scanned the horizon, taking in the Opera House. Everything appeared to be normal, the same as before. Most of the ferryboats in the harbour were anchored to the quay, being buffeted back and forth by the waves. Waiting for passengers. Close up, it all looked like he remembered it to be. Then he widened his scope and realized that a few ferries had crashed into the shore. They were half in the water and half on land.

Grace called out to him. When he called back, she came in through his room and joined him on the balcony. He made them both a cup of coffee. They sat outside.

Grace had already showered. "I think we really need to get ourselves some new clothes today."

"Yeah, I agree. Should have thought about that yesterday."

"Let's go for a walk, get a few things, and then we can try to enjoy the day and the sunshine a little."

"That's a good plan for the morning. Then in the afternoon I'll drop you back here and you can maybe get a book, or we can find you a laptop."

"Think I'd rather stay with you."

"Ah, then you must be feeling a lot better this morning," Vincente observed.

"Yes, I am. I feel... Well, I feel terrifically happy today."

"Let's go and get something for breakfast and then do a little shopping."

"Let's go!"

✳✳✳

THE TEENAGERS TRIED ON lots of clothes, both fancy and more practical items, but shopping wasn't the same when you could have anything you wanted. After a while, they got bored of it and only took with them what they needed.

Back in the room, Grace slid into a pair of skinny blue jeans, a sky-blue halter, and a pair of Nike runners. She also found some bright red comfy flip-flops.

Vincente wore a pair of black Levi's jeans, with a white t-shirt, and a pair of Reebok Pumps.

In the car, they were noticeably quiet as they drove along the tree-lined streets. They noticed all kinds of dead trees, which seemed to mock them on their journey. The skeletons of the trees, dying or already dead, left them feeling a little less hopeful. The long, bony fingers of the branches reached out, taunted them.

It seemed that nature was turning on them. A flesh-eating tree. The trees dead or dying. No more apples. No oranges. No pears. No lemons. No limes. No olives. No Christmas trees. No majestic oaks swaying in the breeze.

Beside the road, they found the most bent and twisted wooden structure they had ever seen. Its tormented, decaying limbs stretched skyward, like it was reaching for what it couldn't have, for eternity.

Grace shivered and then spotted a single tree in the distance. This tree was different from the others. Its arms swept across its trunk, in the shape of a cross.

Vincente stopped the car. "My mum's an artist," Vincente said. "I think I remember a painting by someone, maybe Delacroix with similar trees and Jacob fighting an angel."

"Do you think it's a sign?"

"If it is, a sign, I don't know how to read it."

"Maybe it just grew out of the ground that way."

"Maybe."

Grace noticed something else. It was a cluster of bushes. Rose bushes. On the end of one branch, there grew a single red rose. It was the last one. Perhaps the last flower ever.

Grace bent down beside it, like she was kneeling to it. Praying to it.

Vincente watched, unsure what to do or say.

Grace smelled its fragrant perfume, cradling it. Sheltering it from the breeze. Grace thought she would like to lie down beside it, to remain there, in sight of this beauteous, single red rose.

"Come on, Grace," Vincente interrupted her thoughts. "It's getting darker and darker now."

"I want to stay here."

"We can't stay here. We can't make time stand still."

"I know that! I'm not crazy. I just want to remain here, holding onto this rose." She cradled it. "I want to be a part of something of real beauty. I want to hold something grown out of the ground; from the earth we once knew. I want to replace the memory of that bloodthirsty tree with the memory of this rose. A thing of beauty—"

"—Is a joy forever," Vincente said. "English class. John Keats."

Grace was still transfixed by the rose.

Vincente was getting worried, as it was so dark now, and they were currently in a field surrounded by all kinds of trees and bushes.

What if one was like that other tree, which they thought was an olive tree? What if they were all like that? He wanted to get out of there, to get them both out of there. Out of imminent danger.

"Grace," he said, bending down beside her, "that flower will fall when it is ready to. You can pluck it now and bring it with you. That way it will remain with you. The beauty will remain with you for a few days. Or you can leave it to fate, to chance, to nature, or to God, if there is one, and just walk away."

The wind was gathering up its strength, and Grace began to shiver.

"There is a storm brewing, Vincente. Look up there at the clouds. They are building up together, almost like they are trying to push each other out of the sky."

He looked up, but all he could see was darkness.

"Can't you feel it?" she asked. She shivered again, and her teeth began to chatter. She put her arms around herself, letting go of the rose.

Together they stood in the field, until the night-like sky began to churn and swirl and coil. Then the rain began to fall in black inky droplets, causing them to hide their faces and to run for cover.

Shafts of light were thrown down from the dark sky in Z-shaped spears towards the earth, striking wherever they were directed in random hits.

All around them lightning bolts struck trees and houses, bursting into flames. The rain fell harder, and the lightning struck once again.

"It had to learn to fight for itself, in order to survive," Grace said. She was referring to the rose, but she knew that they too must fight, and that nature itself was going to put up the fight of its life.

"So much for our new clothes," Vincente said.

They escaped from that place, all the while playing dodgem with the lightning bolts.

CHAPTER 15

WHEN THE NIGHT SKY had finally burned itself out from the lightning and the rain, Grace and Vincente pulled over to the side of the road. Together they watched the sun come up on the horizon.

"It's a brand, new day," Grace said.

"Yeah, and today's the day I think we should take a trip over to your mum's house—your house."

"Really? It's kind of scary. Do you think it's maybe too soon for me to go back there, to experience my home again? What if—?"

"No 'what if's' today. Let's just go, and we'll find what we find when we get there, okay?"

"How far is it?"

"Not far from where we were before, by the school."

Grace thought about her home for a moment. She imagined her mum at the front door, opening it up. Greeting her with a big hug. Glad to see her. Grace felt a tear running down her cheek and she brushed it away with the palm of her hand, hoping Vincente hadn't noticed.

"It's okay, you know, to think about your mum. You shouldn't be afraid to remember."

"It's just...I'm imagining things, making them up, instead of having real memories to live by. It feels like a lie to me."

"Hey, you're not the first person to lie to yourself, and you won't be the last! When I was kid, I used to dream about being an artist, like my Mum, and look at me now: I'm an athlete. And if I were artistic instead of athletic, do you think I would have been popular? Would have been accepted?"

"Why is that so important to you? I mean, being accepted by other people, some of them you probably don't even know?"

"I-I haven't really thought about it before," Vincente said. Now he was lying to himself, and he was also lying to Grace. He couldn't tell her that he was indeed an artist in his own right because he'd never told anyone or showed anyone his work. He always kept it hidden in his room. No one knew, except for his parents and his grandparents.

He looked across at her. Grace Greenway, the girl who once completed his math homework for him. Grace Greenway, the girl whose ability to formulate mathematical equations, was far beyond her years.

And here he was, Vincente Marino, the sporty guy, the one who was revered and adored, the one who relied on her assistance to keep his grades up high enough so he could continue to play. Because if he didn't play sport, he was nothing and he was no one. It was Grace who allowed him to continue to play, and she didn't even ask for his thanks or appreciation in return. In fact, she never once refused him, even when he fell in with the crowd and wasn't always the nicest guy to her. That is, he never openly supported her, even when the other guys made fun of her weight and her superior calculating mind.

He appreciated her now, though, more than she knew, and he was determined not to fall into the same trap as before. He no longer wanted to be the kind of guy who took Grace Greenway for granted.

"This is it," Vincente said, as they pulled into the driveway of 15 Wheat Field Lane.

"Before we go in, I have to say something." Grace hesitated and then continued, "Back there, did you feel like something was suffering? Those black raindrops, I mean black raindrops!? I can still feel it, but it's not as strong. It's as if something is bubbling under the surface, waiting for vengeance—although on whom, I do not know. It's like nature itself is in pain and crying out for help.

"Grace, I think you might be right, and it's something we need to think about. Really think about, and maybe even do some research on those raindrops. They were only temporary and washed right out of our clothes. But for now, let's focus on the present. You are home, and whatever was happening out there before is now calm. Let's enjoy the new day."

"I'll try," Grace said, "but whatever it is out there, I think we need to be ready."

"We are ready. We have weapons. Most of all, we have each other. Neither of us is alone in this. We're a team now."

"A team," Grace echoed as she stepped out of the car and looked at her house for the first time. She ran her hand along the reddish-yellow bricks all the way until she reached the front door.

She stopped for a moment, gazing at its beauty. Expecting to remember such a significant front door, but no memories came.

"It's a..." Grace said, admiring the stained glasswork, which took on the shape of a bird in flight. Grace ran her fingers along the outer edges, hoping to grasp a connection to it.

"Phoenix," Vincente noted. "According to legend, it bursts into flame and then is reborn."

"A combustible bird. My parents have a combustible bird on our front door?"

"Seems like it. I think it is totally cool. It's also a symbol of peace and truth. I guess that's another reason why they could have chosen it."

"Yeah, it does sound like a nice bird to have guarding your house." Grace stepped carefully on the grassy lawn, looking things over.

"Don't try to push yourself too much, Grace. Just open your mind up to the memories. Let them know you are ready to receive them."

"I've been ready to receive them since the day I woke up!" Grace exclaimed, but she totally understood what he meant. She didn't want to reinforce doubts and unnecessary barriers. She wanted to be like a river, a river into which her memories could flow back to her freely.

"Let your feelings guide you," Vincente said. "Let your senses take control."

"Okay, okay," Grace said. "You make it sound so easy, but it's not. I feel like a blank canvas, and I shouldn't feel like this. Not when I am home."

"Give it time. Be patient. Now let's go inside. Maybe inside..." Grace knew exactly what he was thinking. She reached for the handle. It wouldn't budge. She knocked on the door and rang the bell, but it was clear that no one was home.

"Maybe there's a key somewhere out here," Vincente suggested. "Try to think—where would your mum leave a key?"

"I have no idea," Grace said. Although she did have a thought, an inclination her mother might have left it in the mailbox. She followed the impulse, opened the flap, but the search was unsuccessful.

"You're doing great!" Vincente said.

Grace knew he was trying to encourage her. She just felt so out of her depth, it was difficult to appreciate or accept his little supportive messages without feeling like they were condescending.

Grace closed her eyes and tried to envision a key. She thought about it being under a mat, but there wasn't a mat at the front door.

"Vincente, I think it's under a mat."

"That's where my mum always leaves the key for me. Are you sure you're not tapping into my memories?" Vincente joked.

They laughed.

"Maybe around the back?"

They found a mat, and the key. Grace Greenway was finally home.

CHAPTER 16

GRACE HESITATED BEFORE PUTTING the key into the lock. She was thinking about how grateful she was that they found the key. She had been dreading what would happen if they didn't find one. They would have to smash a window or break a door down. She would be entering her own home like an intruder would, and the thought of it made her shiver, even now.

"Nearly there," Vincente said, trying to urge Grace to open the door. Knowing full well how frightened she must be. It was a new world, yes. But, it was still her own world. If she had no memories of it, then what? Surely, those memories would return. In time. For now, they'd deal with whatever came their way together. "Are you ready?" he asked.

"I'm just thinking about how grateful I am that we found the key."

"We didn't find it, you did, and that's a good sign, but we're not in any hurry. Whenever you're ready." He sat on the top stair, giving her the space to open the door in her own time. One thing they had plenty of now was time. It certainly hadn't been like that before, when they had classes to go to, buses to catch, friends to hang out with, homework and exams and school sports, and family stuff, too. The days were always full of things to do.

"Okay, here goes," Grace said. She turned the key in the lock and then pushed the door open. She invited Vincente to join her inside, and a flash went through her mind again, about vampires needing an invitation before they could enter any home.

She smiled, wondering why the vampire theme kept running through her mind at the strangest of times. If he were one, a vampire, how could he possibly be feeding? When they were the only two warm bodies left in the world? Unless, whatever happened had changed his system, so he no longer required blood to survive? Why could she remember all this vampire stuff and nothing else?

Grace shook her head. She tried to make the weird vampire thoughts disappear so she could return to the moment. The moment when she re-entered her own home. Then again, maybe that was exactly what she was trying to avoid thinking about.

The end of the house was an atrium, with lots of plants and cushions. A place where you could sit, look out into the garden, and relax. Grace turned back, noticing a swing set and slide tucked away behind the garden shed.

She imagined for a moment sliding down and swinging as a little girl. She tried to remember her mum or her dad pushing her on the swing, or Daryl and herself running around in the garden. She could imagine it all, but it was just that: her imagination. Not memories of what really happened.

Vincente was standing beside her, watching her, and not watching her at the same time. He thought that she needed to have space, and he didn't want to be in the way or make her feel uncomfortable. At the same time, he wanted her to lead the way. After all, even if she didn't remember, it was her own home, and he was nothing but a stranger here. He quietly watched her, lost in her thoughts, as her eyes perused the garden.

"I-I don't remember it," Grace finally said.

"It'll come." Vincente said. "Let's go inside and try to relax."

"Okay," Grace said, and she made her way along the hallway. She passed by a room with a closed door. Curious, she opened it only to find the laundry room. Further along, she entered the kitchen. It felt like walking into a ray of sunshine. The kitchen was all yellow. Canary yellow, including appliances, curtains, wallpaper, tablecloth, and placemats. Grace moved closer, noticing small imprints of sunflowers on nearly everything. Her mum was clearly a big fan of yellow, and an even bigger fan of sunflowers.

"Sunflowers," Grace said, beaming a smile. She took the dry stems out of the vase, filled it at the sink, and then placed them back into fresh water. They perked up straight away. Grace looked out the window, discovering a row of dead sunflowers running along the side of the house. The ones she had just touched had been plucked by her Mum. Maybe by herself. They brought into the kitchen and placed into this exact vase.

"Your mum sure knew how to bring the sunshine inside," Vincente said, trying to reassure Grace, who was once again lost in her thoughts. He sat down at the dining room table, careful not to make much noise as he pushed the chair back. He looked around the room and thought that it was kind of nice, but a little overdone for his taste. Some sunshine in the house was good, but this was really, well, bright. At this moment, he seriously missed his sunglasses.

Grace ran her hand along the countertop, trying to reconnect. She opened some of the cupboards, finding a coffee mug with her name on it. There was one that said, #1 Dad, and another that said, World's Best Mum, and then a mug that said only one word: Daryl. This was her house. There was evidence. Proof. Why couldn't she remember?

Please let me remember, she thought, Something, anything. Please.

Vincente thought Grace had been lost in her thoughts for long enough and decided that it was time for a distraction. He moved the chair back, not quietly this time, making a scraping noise as he said, "Oops sorry, but my stomach is rumbling so much, I really could use a snack."

Grace flashed back to the vampire thoughts for a second, and then turned and opened the fridge. There wasn't much in it, as her Mum had been spending most of her time at the hospital. She opened the top cupboard, pulled out a jar of coffee and made a brew for each of them. She spooned in some fake creamer. They sipped in silence for a few moments.

"If you could have anything to eat, anything at all, what would you have?" Grace asked. If he answered a bottle of blood, she would faint dead away.

"I would have a big juicy steak—rare, and a baked potato with sour cream and butter slathered and melting all over it, and for dessert, a Lamington."

"Let's make ourselves a feast next time we stay over in a hotel, okay?" Grace said.

"Are you a good cook?"

"I have absolutely no idea! But I'm willing to give it a try."

"I haven't cooked much. Usually mum cooks, and on occasion when she's out, I use the microwave or get takeaway."

They were silent again for a few more moments. Grace was looking down the hall, willing herself to look around the rest of the house. She checked out the clock over the sink, and it told her that it was just after six.

Soon, however, they would be tired, and would need to get some sleep. Soon it would be dark. True, they could turn on the lights, but she preferred to look around the house now, while they still had all this lovely natural light to work with.

"Okay, I'm ready to continue the exploration," Grace said. She stood, rinsed the empty cups in the sink. Then she exited the kitchen and continued along the corridor.

Vincente followed behind her silently, once again giving her time and space to explore freely. He allowed her the opportunity to ease her mind wide open.

✳✳✳

THE CORRIDOR WAS LONG and not as bright as the kitchen had been. Although Grace's mum had side tables, mirrors, and pictures which kept you company as you made your way towards the absolute darkness of the living room. Grace stepped across the carpeted floor and flung the curtains back with one fell swoop. She turned around to see what she had missed. She was hoping by making this sudden movement, it would all come back to her.

Vincente observed, without making it obvious he was doing so. He didn't want to add more pressure to the situation.

Grace put her hands on her hips, and for a few moments, hope appeared in her heart.

She held her breath.

Vincente noticed a glimmer of hope too, and he made a move towards her.

She stopped him with the palm of her hand. She began pacing.

Grace was like a bird, looking for food from above. Around and around the room she pirouetted.

Soon the glimmer of hope went out of her eyes, and she fell into a heap.

She put her hands over her face, and she wept.

CHAPTER 17

Vincente knelt in front of Grace. He searched for the right words. He couldn't find them because his mind was spinning, and his heart was racing. He was out of breath from holding back—holding back the urge to take her into his arms and...

Vincente checked himself. He had a conversation with himself about how she wasn't the kind of girl to whom he was attracted. How it really didn't matter how much he was being swayed by her emotional turmoil. He was an empathetic person sometimes. Not often, but sometimes. When he saw things on the news, about people being hurt, about people being held captive, or war-torn countries, or children or animals being abused, he cried.

Now watching Grace before him here and now, had become like watching the news for him. He wanted to reach out and comfort her in the same way he would a child. Then why was he also feeling something else? Something different? And what was it? He examined his feeling for a moment, and he realized exactly what it was. He was feeling the need to care for Grace. To protect her. Yes, that had to be what it was! It couldn't have been the other thing.

The feeling he had in his loins just then. It couldn't be lust. No, not that.

When Vincente came back to the present, Grace was standing. She was running her fingers along the mantelpiece and the framed photographs. When Grace stopped, Vincente went to stand beside her.

After he saw the photograph, he smiled and picked it up. Together they examined it more closely. It was Grace. She was probably around four or five years old, and she was cradling an abacus.

"It's definitely you," Vincente said. "I can see your eyes in her eyes."

Grace smiled and sifted through the fog in her mind.

"I know that she's me. I can see that she's me. But I can't remember her, or the abacus."

Vincente took her closed fits into his hands, and he opened them up one by one, like opening two roses. He drew her into his arms.

She snuggled there, listening to his heart, feeling a new kind of connection. She pulled away.

"Look here!" she exclaimed. "It's my dad and my brother." Under the photograph, a plaque read: Benjamin Greenway, beloved husband of Helen, dear father of Grace and Daryl. Gone too soon, aged 55.

The other photograph had a plaque, too: Daryl Greenway, beloved son of Helen and Benjamin Greenway. Gone to rest with his father, aged twenty-one.

Grace took in a big gulp of air, remembering them at the hospital. She shook her head. They hadn't visited her, she corrected herself, because they were both dead. She must've been imagining it.

"It's so sad," Grace said. "Two people who meant the world to me, and I don't feel anything. Except sadness for myself, that I can't remember them. I'm such a selfish person!"

"You're not selfish! It's just that you can't remember right now, and it's not your fault."

"I so want to remember something. Anything!"

"And you will, just be patient. Give it time."

"I don't think it's going to happen, Vincente. I don't think I ever will remember."

Vincente put his hands on his hips. "They came back to visit you, in the hospital, for a reason. Maybe they came back to help you."

"How? By making me think I was losing my mind?"

"No, to prove that you still knew them, even though they had crossed over to the other side. You spoke with them. Had a conversation with them."

"Yes, but it was meaningless."

"Because I interrupted. Maybe they hadn't told you yet what they needed to say."

"It would be interesting if it were true, Vincente. But I don't think it sounds very believable. Thank you, though," Grace said. She crossed the room and stood at the bottom of the stairs.

"Maybe," Vincente said. Grace turned back toward him. "Maybe they were giving you a message. Taking you back to a time in your life when you had both with you: a happier time. A time when you had a past to remember, a present to live in, and a future to look forward to."

"Two out of three, then," Grace said.

Vincente laughed and began to sing and dance.

"Keep going," Grace coaxed.

Vincente slid across the floor, using a vase as a microphone and on one knee serenaded Grace, who applauded enthusiastically.

Her cheeks were flushed deep red as she moved towards him and kissed him hard on the mouth.

He kissed her back. His hands wandered, and her hands wandered, and their tongues explored.

They both became aware of what was happening at the same time and simultaneously backed away.

"What are you trying to do to me?" Grace asked. "I'm sorry, so sorry," Vincente said.

"It was both of us—"

"Yes, it was the moment. I agree we both—"

"Let's just forget it ever happened," Grace said.

"Good idea," Vincente agreed. He watched Grace make her way up the stairs.

When she reached the top, she turned around and smiled over her shoulder. "See you soon. I'm just going to find my room and get freshened up a little."

"Great!" Vincente exclaimed, as he finger-combed his hair. When she was out of his sight, he returned to the loo and splashed water over his face. He looked at himself in the mirror and wondered who that person was who was looking back at him? Who was that person? Who had feelings, real feelings, for someone who only days ago wouldn't have meant anything to him, other than a girl who could help him with his math homework so he could remain on the team? Now, he had led her on big time, and she had responded, opened up to him. He was so ashamed of himself for taking advantage of Grace, especially during this time when she was so vulnerable.

Then he thought about her soft lips, about how they had hesitated and then opened up to him. She kissed him like no other girl had kissed him before. She was falling even more deeply for him, and he knew it.

Problem was, he was falling for her too.

CHAPTER 18

Upstairs, Grace also splashed cold water onto her face. She was glowing, both inside and outside. for a moment, she didn't care if she remembered her past at all, because she thought her future was more important. Vincente was more important to her now than any memory ever could be.

She walked along the hallway, passing by rooms with closed doors. Her mind flashed back to the kiss and the fever that had rushed through her body like fire, until she found her bedroom. It had to be hers, because there was a computer ticking away, and pictures of Einstein and Fibonacci, textbooks an abacus and...well, it just had to be her room.

On the dresser, she discovered a little jewellery box. When she opened it, a song began to play.

"Need any help?" Vincente called.

Grace returned to the top of the stairs with a small pillow in her hand. She tossed it at him. It was a pillow in the shape of a heart.

Back in her room, she turned over the jewellery box that identified the song as a famous love song. She left the box open, listening as it played the tune over and over again while she made her way towards the shower.

She stopped for a moment, hearing a strange sound. A murmur. A whisper. She listened. She closed the jewellery box's lid. Listened again. Thought it must be inside her head. Took another step. Heard it again. Stopped. Listened.

The volume was increasing but only slightly.

"Are you all right up there?" Vincente asked, seeing Grace standing still, staring vacantly down the corridor.

Grace nodded. She returned to her room. She changed her clothes just in time, as Vincente arrived at the top of the landing.

"I'm fine," Grace said. "I just—" she hesitated. "Uh, did you hear anything?" She averted her head, waiting to hear the noise again.

"I heard some music," Vincente said.

"Yeah, that was my jewellery box, it plays music. But anything else?"

"Like what?" Vincente said, looking down at his feet.

Grace thought he had heard something, but he didn't want to say it to her, in case she hadn't heard it. He was worried about it though, she could tell. "Like a whisper," Grace said.

"Yeah, I heard something."

"I thought it was in my head," Grace confessed. "At first. But now—"

"No, I can hear it, too. It's like—" Vincente paused, standing statuesque.

"Shhhhh," Grace said, as it had started again. A little bit louder still.

Almost like a moan.

It was whispering her name, Grace, repeatedly like it was the chorus of a song. "Maybe it's my mum?" Grace suggested.

"Maybe."

"Maybe she's hurt."

"Maybe."

"Shhhh."

A strong gust of wind seemed to blow in through the front door and push its way up the stairs towards Grace and Vincente. Its sheer power was so great that it forced them flat against the wall. The contents of the house shook, and the foundations groaned.

Another earthquake?

They decided being on the top floor wasn't the best place to be. They grabbed a hold of the other's hand, making their way towards the staircase.

"Let's get out of here!" Vincente exclaimed.

Grace knew they needed to do so, and straight away. However, she was worried about her mum being trapped in the house. What if she was hurt?

When they reached the staircase, they grasped the wooden bannisters as the stairs rocked from side to side. The house began to shake and twist, almost like it intended to take flight. The stairs began to play like keys on a piano, breaking apart, causing them to abandon their plan to return down to Terra Firma.

Once again, the voice called, "Grace."

***

G RACE STUMBLED ALONG THE corridor, seeming to follow the sound of the voice. It was coming from a room with a closed door at the end of the hall.

"I think it's my mum," Grace said as they passed by a bedroom with its door slightly ajar.

It was Daryl's room she discerned by the array of musical instruments, CDs, the unmade bed, and the empty wicker chair sitting. The chair was sitting directly under the window, almost like it was waiting for her brother to return. The window was wide open, and a new gust of wind breathed in. They stopped it from pushing them over the top of the rail by slamming the bedroom door shut just in time.

The voice whispered the teenager's name over and over again.

The teenagers trembled and held hands. Together they made their way along the corridor. Towards the closed door at the end of the hall, while the house screamed and roared around them.

✳✳✳

THE MOANING SOUND WAS growing louder and louder.

The whisper was no longer a whisper.

It was clearly a woman's voice.

It was the voice of Helen Greenway, calling for her daughter.

"Perhaps you should answer?" Vincente suggested.

"Mum!"

"Grace!"

"Mum!"

"Grace, Grace!"

They arrived just outside the door. It felt warm to touch, and it was intact. Still on its hinges.

The house had stopped shaking and roaring.

They pushed it open.

Something slipped past them, entering the room before them.

It was like an icy breeze.

They shivered as the door closed behind them and then the locking mechanism clicked into place all by itself.

✳✳✳

T HEIR TEETH CHATTERED AS their eyes adjusted to the light, and they could look around. Grace was certain that they weren't alone, but she couldn't see her mother, and the voice was no longer calling or whispering her name.

It felt cold. Cold like death.

"Can you see anything, anything at all?" Vincente asked.

"I can see cold breath. In the shape of Fibonacci snowflakes."

"What?"

"See, there? Snowflakes."

The snowflakes were falling around them. They shivered more and put their arms around themselves as their skin felt the wet melting flakes turn from crystal white to tears.

"I can feel something, a presence here with us. Maybe that's why I remembered the Fibonacci stuff."

"Yeah, well done, but is it dangerous?" Vincente asked, "I mean, is it going to try to hurt us?"

"No, I don't feel like it wants to hurt us. But I feel like it wants to know me."

"What?"

"It wants me to comfort it."

"Stay here, beside me. Don't move," Vincente said.

"It is trying to reach me, in my mind. It thought that if it brought me here, us here, then it would be able to get what it wanted from us, but now that we are here, it doesn't know what to do." Grace stopped speaking, her hands flying to her head in pain.

"You are talking to it? It's hurting you?" Vincente asked. Grace's entire body shook in reply.

"It's using a kind of ESP to communicate with me. Scanning my brain, my body. Listening to my thoughts and emotions."

"Get away from her!" Vincente shouted as he picked up a chair and threw it against the wall.

Grace cried out in pain while Vincente was lifted into the air and thrown down violently onto the bed.

CHAPTER 19

G RACE CONTINUED TO WATCH in horror as Vincente was shaken back and forth like a demon had possessed him. She couldn't help but wonder, through the veiled level of pain that riveted her body every now and then, what was causing this. Was it a creature from another dimension? A werewolf? A vampire? A ghost? A demon? Grace scanned the room, looking for a weapon. Not seeing one, she waited as Vincente's body calmed. His feet and arms were then bound by an unseen, unknown being.

Vincente remained still now. Grace tried to run to his side, but it was as though her feet had suddenly been cemented into a slab in the floor. Her upper body shifted forwards, like she was circus freak, but her legs were simply unmovable.

"Are you okay, Vincente?"

"I'm not in pain anymore."

"That's good."

"How about you?

"I feel normal again, but I'm really scared, Vincente. I can't move my feet."

"Not to mention, it's going to get dark in here soon. Can you reach the light?"

Grace struggled to bend her upper body in the direction of the switch on the wall. She stretched and stretched, imagining that she was in fact a circus freak made of rubber, touched it, and heard the click, but nothing happened. The power had been cut off.

"It doesn't work, Vincente. It'll be pitch black in here soon!" Grace put her arms around herself and tried to stop the trembling.

"Can you still feel it, the presence around you?"

Grace tried to throw her feelings out, imagining them to be tentacles searching for something unseen and unknown.

"It's quiet now, Vincente. Maybe it got what it wanted from us and now it has moved on. Or maybe we weren't what it hoped we would be."

"Yeah, for the first time in my life, I wouldn't mind being a disappointment to this thing. But let's try to think. What could it want from us? What could it be?"

"A werewolf?" Grace suggested.

"It's not a full moon, not for a few days, anyway. But hey, I don't think they can be invisible."

"What about a vampire?"

"Yeah, they only come out at night, don't they?" Vincente said, chuckling under his breath. The rope was tied very tightly around his limbs, and the need to move about was overwhelming. Problem was when he did move, the bounds tightened up even more, and then they cut through his skin. He could see drops of blood collecting on the bed sheet from his ankles.

Grace noticed the blood dripping onto the sheets, too. She watched the red bleeding onto the white, spreading. She was befuddled by movements coming towards her from underneath the carpet. Definitely movement. Snakelike. Slow. Slithering. Coming for her.

"Vincente!" she screamed, as the thing inched its way over to her. Her upper body backed away. Back, back, as far as it could go. Unfortunately for Grace, it was not far enough.

✳✳✳

"VINCENTE!" GRACE SCREAMED WITH her eyeballs nearly jumping out of her head.

He could see that she was terrified but had no idea why. He tried to loosen the ropes, but there was nothing he could do. Any struggle only caused them to tighten and bite even deeper into his flesh.

The thing continued to clear a path to Grace.

Vincente was able to discern the existence of a moving thing under the rug. He saw Grace's legs turn to jelly, as it closed the gap between them.

Grace stood firm, trying to control herself. She wanted to scream and scream but instead she focused on breathing. As it drew nearer and nearer, she could feel it beginning to probe her.

A sense of calm overcame her, overwhelmed her senses. She felt intrinsically that it did not want to hurt her.

"Grace!" Vincente shouted, and the ropes cut into his skin. He bent at the middle, now resembling a new-born calf. Then a gag came out of nowhere. It fastened upon Vincente's mouth.

Under it, Grace could tell that he was screaming, screaming louder than he had ever screamed before. But all that came from his direction was a pained silence. Silent screams are the scariest screams of all.

They held each other's gaze. Reaching out to each other with all they had, they locked eyes as the thing arrived at Grace's feet.

It began moving upwards beginning at her toes, inching its way further and further up.

It was then that Grace's voice filled the house with an electrifying shriek.

✳✳✳

DON'T FIGHT IT, GRACE said to herself, knowing very well that Vincente would be saying those exact same words to her, if only he could.

Relax, she thought, let it do what it needs to do and then maybe it will go away.

She tried to block it out, to block out everything except for Vincente on the bed with his eyes open wider than wide. From where she was, she could see a small collection of blood, which was pooling from his right ankle. She watched his chest heave up and down.

The thing turned her and twisted her until it made her feel like she wasn't herself anymore.

Its power had been building. At first, the pain was bearable like a slight burning sensation. Almost like a hot kiss. It was addictive; she wanted another kiss, and then another, and then another. Then it turned into something different. A more definitive burning. Like a branding. Hot. Hotter. Sizzling.

Her face was flushed, and she held her fists tight. Her will to fight was pushing itself forth, but the pain was too great to bear.

Once it reached her pelvic area, the sizzling spiked, and the temperature climbed higher. It was like she was on fire. Burning at the stake. She couldn't think. She was like one big nerve—a raw nerve. The pain was beyond excruciating. She couldn't take it any longer, and yet it rose.

Grace managed to hold onto consciousness while it made its way up towards her breasts. They too were on fire, as the heat moved on, synchronizing the pain so that it was pulsing throughout her body.

Until everything faded to black.

CHAPTER 20

WHEN SHE CAME TO, Grace was no longer inside her body. She slowly understood what had happened. The pain had caused her mind to fragment.

From somewhere above the scene, she could still see herself writhing, spinning in an imaginary cocoon-like case, as the whirlwind of pain tossed her, turned her, and twisted her body, still moving within her. Holding her captive in its burning grasp.

Feeling the burn, smelling her own flesh sizzling, Grace could no longer bear to watch herself, so instead she turned her attention toward Vincente.

He was writhing too. His body was surging from side to side, and he was shaking almost like he was in the midst of an epileptic fit. She moved towards him, floating. She touched his searing forehead with her lips.

His eyes flew open, almost like he sensed her presence. She screamed out to him, trying to break through the barriers, but his muffled screams were not heard. The intensity of her screams, through the body, which she was no longer a part of, chilled the hot room and caused him even more distress.

Grace wanted to murder the thing. Whatever it was, she wanted to take it and strangle the life out of it, cutting off the spirit. She wanted it to end. Then she knew what she had to do. She had to return to her body, to face the awful creature head-on. She had to go back. She had nowhere else to go.

Yes, the thing had her body, but it did not have her mind, and it did not have her spirit. The same was true for Vincente. Yes, they were both being tortured, for reasons unknown. Perhaps, because they were the last two human beings on Earth. Just like in the old movie Vincente had mentioned, with the aliens trying to discover what made humans tick. Or maybe they were trying to kill them!

Whatever the reason, Grace was not going to let them have what they wanted. To let them take their lives without a fight.

For a split second, she imagined flying out the window. Leaving herself and Vincente behind. But she couldn't do it. She loved that body, even though it had its flaws. While there were many, it was still hers and only hers. And then there was Vincente. She loved him, of that fact there was no doubt. She had to return to herself. She had to save him. Perhaps save them both.

Outside of the room, the tall trees blew forwards and back, forwards, and back, in the magnetic power of the breeze. She and Vincente were like those trees, moving with the pain like they moved with the wind.

She took a deep breath and then re-entered her body. The pain sliced through her like a knife. She instantly wanted to break away, but soon realized that it had weakened her, lessened her control and power. Her essence had been altered. She now understood that by fragmenting, she had given the thing additional power over her physical self. She was now determined to take the power back!

Once inside her body, her home, she gathered all her positive thoughts and energy, plus all the love that she could find in her heart. She summoned these things from the memory bank, stored far beyond her reach.

Pushing back the will to detach again, she concentrated all her energy not on the sizzling, relentless pain, but on creating a powerful light source of her own.

Once she envisioned it, she moved it like a ball of sunshine. She held it in the palm of her hand until the ball of light was like a heart: the combined hearts of Grace and Vincente.

She projected all the energy from the ball towards Vincente. It drifted across the room, shining gallantly. For a few seconds, Vincente's body no longer writhed. She pulled the heart back when the searing pain once again overpowered her and held it. It allowed her the strength to bear what she needed to.

And somewhere inside her soul, a song began to play, a song that she did not recognize. A song that was totally unfamiliar to her. As it played, and as she sang it, her lips no longer burned, and her eyes reached out to Vincente. Her heart told his to join in with the song, to sing it with her.

Together they sang in their minds and their souls, and the ball of light became stronger and stronger and stronger.

"I never invited you here, spirit, or whatever you are. You have no right to invade my body. To invade my friend's body. Now, get out!"

And it did. It went.

Grace crumbled to the floor.

CHAPTER 21

Hours later, Grace felt out of sorts which wasn't surprising since she had NO IDEA where she was.

When she tried to move, every single part of her body ached. Her arms and legs were twisted into unnatural positions like dead or disjointed tree limbs. She tried to gather her body into herself, but every movement made her writhe in pain.

She attempted to stand—the operative word being attempt—but only collapsed once again. Grace looked at the carpet. Tried to think, to remember. What was it about that carpet? She glanced around the room. Found the bed. Found Vincente.

Everything about their spine-chilling ordeal came back to her.

She willed herself upward, walking like a toddler, as she had to teach her body the motions all over again. She eventually reached Vincente and gazed down at his unmoving body. At the bloodstains, now brown. No longer spreading.

Her eyes fell upon his lips. His oh so kissable lips. She leaned in, but stopped when his eyes opened wide, then wider. He wasn't pleased to see her. He was terrified.

"What is it Vincente? Whatever it was, it's gone now. We're safe. We're okay. It's going to be okay."

Although Grace continued purring these positive words to him, Vincente's terrified expression only seemed to escalate. His eyes darted back and forth, back, and forth. He was telling her something. Warning her?

She whispered, asking was there something behind her? He nodded.

She thought for a moment, reached out, and felt for the thing, but she could not find it. She wanted to run, to escape, but she knew the thing was there for her. It had returned for her.

Or was it something else? A different thing? She dreaded the thought that this thing could be stronger, more powerful, could break her. Destroy her.

Vincente's eyes remained frozen, staring just over her shoulder. His fear was contagious, and she trembled and shook. Then she realized the only way they were going to beat this thing was together.

Grace bent over and began to untie the ropes that were holding him with one hand, while the other hand searched in the bedside table for any kind of a weapon. Something she could use. She hoped her Mum might have had something there, a tool that could help her in these grave circumstances.

Vincente's eyes screamed. His eyes became her eyes.

In the drawer, a pair of tweezers was the only useful tool to be found, and Grace began to cut away the ropes. It would take ages to free Vincente at this rate, though. She bent over and began biting the ropes with her teeth, making nice headway, until Vincente began to shake and writhe once again. His eyes met hers, and then he closed them.

She whirled around and shouted, "What are you and what do you want from me? From us? We mean no harm to you. Tell us what you want, and we will give it to you! We will try to help you, but please, stop hurting us. Stop hurting my Vincente. I will give you anything!"

Vincente stopped writhing.

His eyes popped open as Grace was lifted off her feet and into the air.

The force slammed her into the ceiling. Then banged her against the walls. Bump. Thump. Bump.

Finally, it dropped her onto the floor, where she remained lifeless as a ragdoll.

✳✳✳

B REAKING GLASS. SHATTERING. FLYING everywhere. Hitting her skin. Puncturing her skin.

Grace shielded herself as best as she could with her arms and her hands.

Something picked her up and carried her out of the window. She was upon a flying creature's back smelling its smelly smells. She held on. It felt soft. Not feathered, but hairy, furry.

It was very dark, so dark that she could not make out any shape of the thing on which she was being transported.

They glided in and out and over things: black, shapeless, shadowy earthly dwellings and towers and bridges. She sensed that they were gaining height, going higher and higher up, until there was nothing for them to avoid running into. They were up in the clouds.

Perhaps she was dead?

✳✳✳

GRACE AND THE UNFRAGRANT creature flew in the night sky. When the creature veered to the right suddenly, she nearly lost her grip. The thing let out a reassuring "Gwap-Gwap." It flung her back to safety. She threw her arms around it.

Gliding. Drifting in and out of consciousness, Grace was still unsure if she was dead or dreaming. They continued, further and further deeper and deeper into the blackness of the night.

Grace opened her eyes, and for a few seconds imagined they were enveloped in a tunnel made of metal.

She sniffed the air, smelled the sea, and then lost consciousness.

It seemed like they had been travelling for a lifetime and now the sun had begun to rise. It reflected light like a mirrored spaceship as they began to drift downward.

Her stomach dropped as they ricocheted off the strangely solid clouds. Bouncing, falling. Grace did not experience fear at this moment. She felt safe. Grateful to be alive.

Then the creature dropped her.

She fought the wind on the way down.

The sun was up high in the sky, which was normal. Where Grace was, wasn't.

She was cradled in the arms of a gigantic tree, and just looking down made her stomach flip. She was glad to be touching something. She ran her hand along the sturdy branch upon which she had been set down.

The sun was throwing its rays across her shoulders. She picked splinters of glass out of her skin and avoided looking down.

With nothing to distract her, she followed the line of the trunk of the tree. It went on and on and on. The tree was very tall, in the in the vicinity of 145 meters at least.

Grace examined her surroundings, running her eyes around a circle. A circle of trees. She knew instinctively, and for no logical reason at all, that her tree was the King tree. The others were Knights. She searched for a Queen tree but could not discern it.

She tried to remember what she could about trees. Tree of Knowledge. Factor Trees. Binary Trees. Tree of Good and Evil. Wishing Tree. Christmas Tree. Tree of Wisdom.

She wondered about the godliness of trees. She imagined, if she were a little girl once again, this would be a tree that she would be in awe of. It was much more than magnificent. This tree was so tall; it was almost as if it could reach all the way up to Heaven if it existed.

Grace shook her head. She was distracted by its magnificence when she needed a way to get down.

Not to mention, the flesh-eating tree. What kind of tree was this one?

The thought plagued her for only a moment because she leaned back and watched the clouds rolling on by. She felt their presence within her, like she was drifting across the sky on top of one of them. She forgot everything else that she was supposed to remember as she imagined herself stepping onto a marshmallow-like, pillow-y shape.

She was inside one, floating, when she drifted off to sleep again.

***

T HE SUN HAD NEARLY disappeared, and dusk was on the horizon. She stretched and yawned, feeling comforted. Totally forgetting where she was, but only for a second.

Below her, the circle of trees—the Knights—stood with their limbs at their sides. They were all dead trees. However, the tree she was in had some leaves, and was very much alive.

She followed the trunk of her tree all the way to the ground. She noticed that the earth had been shaken at the bottom. There were fresh paths leading away from the tree. Paths, which led to the other trees, the Knights. It seemed clear that the other trees had once been alive but had rerouted their sources of food and energy to save the King. They had died for the King tree. Made the ultimate sacrifice.

But why?

To this question, Grace had no answers.

She looked up into the face of the moon. Albert Einstein's face reflected at her. She smiled at him, almost expecting him to spew forth some formulaic scientific and mathematical answers.

She was surrounded by symmetry, in the branches and in every other life form. It was comforting, to feel the familiarity of the symmetry.

Although it presented no answers, nor did the Einstein moon.

✳✳✳

E INSTEIN WAS FRAMED WITH twinkling stars. They blinked in recognition of his genius. She felt comforted that he was watching over her.

Opening her mind to anything and everything all at once.

Not feeling tired, she searched the skies for answers. If she tried to climb down, she might fall. Or she might make it to the bottom. She could inch her way down. Slowly.

She would undoubtedly break her neck if she jumped. She wasn't so anxious to be on terra firma again as to be on it dead.

She thought about shouting for help, but who could help her? Vincente? No, he was still bound to the bed, as far as she knew.

Or she could wait. Perhaps the thing that had delivered her to the tree intended to return for her? Perhaps it would fly her back to Vincente? Then again, perhaps it would finish her off.

She examined the symmetry of the tree; it was a beautiful piece of art. It would take time, but she could use it like a ladder.

She breathed in the scent of the tree. She shuddered when she considered it might be an olive tree that could eat a dead bird. A tree that could skewer live prey with its branches. She decided she would rather fall to the ground and meet her end, rather than be skewered and eaten.

It was too dark to begin climbing down. Grace was certain she would have better luck in the daytime, although she appreciated the irony of Einstein being there to guide her.

She reclined in the arms of the branches and thought about Vincente. She missed him. They had spent every moment of every day together for the past week, and he had grown to be an important part of her life.

She rested her eyes, used her hands as a pillow, and dreamed up a plan: One that involved a really big axe.

CHAPTER 22

A S A NEW DAY dawned, Grace sat very still watching it rise like she'd never seen it before. Transfixed from her unvoluntary perspective, she was like an angel on top of a rather humungous tree, which was in no way Christmas-like.

She had been awake for hours, tired of sitting still, waiting for a bright idea to form, or new plan of escape to pop into her mind. All through the night, she had sent telepathic messages to every mathematician and scientist who had passed beyond the earth into another dimension. She urged them to send or transmit an idea her way from wherever they were, but nothing came.

Dejected, Grace realised she was totally alone. No one to rely on but herself.

She looked down, down, down. She teetered as far as she could on the branch, which had shown its ability to hold all her weight. She drew back.

It was a long way down, an awfully long way down. Her imagination ran away from her at that moment. She imagined Vincente, coming by in a helicopter to rescue her. He climbed down on a big ladder in the sky, and together they got back into the buzzing machine. They kissed passionately, and then they rose into the Heavens, where they could live happily ever after.

Grace was annoyed at herself for thinking up such childish fantasies. Vincente was in no position to rescue her. He wasn't in control now! The thing, whatever it was, was holding him on bed back there, like he was a sex slave.

She grew more and more furious and waved her fists in the air, for all the good that it did. There was no one to see her brandishing her fists.

Still, somewhere in the back of her mind, a part of her still believed that Vincente could and would rescue her. All she had to do was wait. She knew it was idiotic, and she knew that only she had the power to make it back to the ground, and yet she couldn't motivate herself enough to begin the climb down.

All day, she watched the sun playing games with shadows, dancing in and out of the branches. The leaves laughed, almost like they were being tickled, and she wasted an entire day doing absolutely nothing to help herself.

The stars twinkled all around her as she drifted off to sleep. In her mind a song played,

"Rock a bye Gracie, on the treetop,

When the wind, blows the cradle will rock,

When the bough breaks, the cradle will fall,

And down will come Gracie, cradle, and all."

She awoke with a start, discovering that she had moved to the very edge of the safe spot in which she had been placed. She grasped the trunk with all her might and shifted herself back into position, as the leaves around her seemed to whisper all the tree gossip that she had missed.

She had hoped it all been a bad dream. Trying to convince herself Vincente would ride in and rescue her.

CHAPTER 23

P OOR GRACE CRIED UNTIL she was all cried out. She imagined what it would be like if she had a pair of wings. She could fly right on out of the tree. She could safely get away. She could rescue Vincente, and together, they could escape.

As the sun once again made its presence known, Grace made the decision to begin climbing straight away. The tree seemed to reach out towards the sun with its gangly branches, and for a moment Grace imagined that it was indeed reaching out to her with wooden fingers.

The view from the perch where she sat still took her breath away. It reached as far as the eye could see. All still. Nothing moved, except by the help of the breeze.

Grace felt warm and safe, resting there in the sun's safety net of light. Almost like she imagined it would feel if one returned to the womb. She felt like she was one with the world: one with the universe. And yet, she was more alone than she had ever been in her entire life. How could that be?

Grace felt paralyzed by her deep desire to believe in a power greater than herself, and all at once she knew why. Before there was physics, science and symmetry, there must have been the need for a soul. The need for the survival of the soul: a single soul. One.

She hugged her knees deep into her chest and she let her spirit take over all her senses. She knew, without a shadow of a doubt, that she would once again touch the grass at the bottom of this tree, and she also knew that she would walk away from all this.

One more thing she knew for certain was that Vincente was just a boy. He didn't have any special powers or abilities which one would have if he were immortal. He felt pain. He could be hurt. And most of all, Grace understood that men were sometimes in need of help. Yes, a guy as athletic and strong as Vincente even needed the help of a girl sometimes.

The help of a girl, at a time such as this.

The help of a girl such as Grace Greenway.

***

S HE BRACED HERSELF EASING downwards, all the while hoping the branches below could manage her weight. The branch bent with her and even creaked a little, but it held firm.

She eased onto it a little bit further, noticing how alien climbing down a tree felt to her. She was certain that as a little girl, she had never been a tree climber by nature. Note to self, Grace thought, if you ever have a daughter, be sure to build her a treehouse when she is a little girl so that she can learn how to climb properly.

Grace imagined herself as a professional tree climber. Someone who had been up and down many trees and did so with ease. She realized she was probably not climbing like a professional tree climber would climb. No, she thought, he or she would use the trunk. The thick part of the tree, for stability.

And that is exactly what she did. On went her descent, little by little. Inch by inch.

She was centred. She had slivers stuck into her jeans, and her hands were bleeding from holding her weight on the rough bark.

When she was too tired to keep moving downward, she flung her arms and legs around the tree trunk and rested. Then the pain and the throbbing blood rang out in her brain, but she was too tired to listen, and so she slept.

✳✳✳

"JUST LET GO," A quiet little voice said as she drifted in and out of sleep. "It's time, Grace, for you to just let go."

She held on tightly, even more so than before. She turned her head, muffling the voice with her arms.

"Let go, Grace," it said.

She was growing more and more tired of holding on. Her arms and legs were pulsing. She avoided looking down.

She slipped. And she tumbled.

And a huge sliver embedded itself into her hand and blood poured out, dripping down the tree.

She looked at the blood pouring out and moved down again, undeterred.

CONTINUING ON HER ONE-WAY mission downward, she swept along the blood, which was mopped up by her clothes. She paused to catch her breath. Began moving again. No sooner had she returned to her dripping red descent than more blood was flowing, assisted by gravity to make its way downward.

Grace's blood droplets shimmered and danced in the sunlight, like sapphires.

She couldn't go down anymore. She longed for the safety of the space above where she could rest. She realized that she had made quite a bit of progress in moving down the tree. Yes, it was still a long way down, but she had a renewed hope in her heart.

She would make it.

She spread herself out along the trunk as much as she could. She rested her legs by wrapping them around nearby branches. She looked like a pretzel, but she was holding her own, and she was proud of her progress.

Her mind began to wander, and she realized how thirsty she was, and how hungry. She held on for dear life and tried to focus her mind on other things. She imagined Vincente, how he looked when he first woke up. How he always ran his fingers through his hair. How his face lit up when he smiled. How his cobalt blue eyes seemed to look deep into her soul.

"Vincente!" She called out, "Vincente!"

She was delirious—or nearly there—when she called out to no one, "When I get out of this tree, I am going to eat only a diet of tree bark— Yum, yum!" She laughed like a mad woman.

The constant sun exposure had cooked her brain. She held on, laughing recklessly until something strange happened to the trunk of the tree: it breathed.

She wanted to let go. She was walking a fine line. Certainly, she was losing her mind. She thought perhaps she had misinterpreted its actions. She reassessed things and decided it was more like a sigh. The tree had sighed.

Trees that served other trees. Trees with meat-eating requirements.

The tree sneezed.

It was a short and quick sneeze, not too loud and not too long. Grace wondered if a tree's heart stopped when it sneezed. She reined herself in, coming to the full realization that trees do not have hearts.

Hugging the trunk for dear life, she passed out.

G RACE WASN'T SURE WHAT happened to her before she woke up. She could feel the tree throbbing. She could feel its heart beating and beating and beating through the thick wood. She understood the need to locate its mouth to prevent herself from becoming a tree snack.

She imagined the mouth into which the dead bird had been dropped. It was an exceptionally large mouth, considering the size of that tree in comparison with this one. Its mouth had to be a crater.

Then she had an idea. Without considering the implications, she pulled a large sliver out of the tree, and she stuck it into her upper arm. Blood flowed, descending along the trunk of the tree. At first it was just a few lone drips, but soon the droplets joined together into a large clot.

She watched it as it made its way down, down, down the tree, and then what she'd hoped—and feared—might happen, did.

A huge, black tongue-like thing protruded from a gaping hole, and with the eloquence of an asp's tongue. It flickered and twisted, all the while licking and feeding on Grace's blood.

When there was no more blood left, the tongue reached up higher and higher on the trunk, searching. It was still hungry.

Grace held on with all her might. She didn't want to drop now, not while it was waiting there for her.

She needed a Plan B.

CHAPTER 24

CLINGING TO THE TREE trunk for dear life, she centred herself, quietening her own breath as its breath became more and more shallow. She was desperate to descend. To get out of danger. And she was desperate to relieve herself.

"Grace."

This time she looked up when she heard her name being called.

Don't tell me, she thought, that the tree can also speak and that it knows my name. Don't tell me that!

She was dehydrated. She was hungry and exhausted. Although she had slept some, it was not the kind of sleep she needed.

"You always were a stubborn child," the voice said.

It was a man's voice. The voice of the man who had come to visit her in the hospital. The voice of the man who died in a car crash years ago. Her father's voice.

She was losing her mind. There was no doubt about it this time. She was definitely losing her mind.

"Grace," he whispered.

When she did not acknowledge his presence, he whispered her name, over and over again. Or maybe it was the wind. Was it just the wind calling her name?

"Just let go," her father said. "This isn't right for you and that boy. He isn't right for you, either."

The reference to Vincente caught her attention.

Her father laughed. "Grace, listen to me. You and Vincente are not meant for each other. He is on another path. Just let go. Let go of the here and now."

"Don't talk about Vincente. You don't even know him."

"Grace, I cannot tell you what I know or how I know it, but payments must be made, and the price is too high for you. What's more is that you are being manipulated to mend the past."

"What?"

"I cannot tell you everything I know. You will find out in due time, but I am advising you to give up now. Say sorry now. Then let go. You are only a child, an innocent. The past is not yours to erase. The restitution is not yours to make."

"I-I don't understand."

"You will, and it will be too late then. Please let go. Let it be done now. It is the only way to release yourself from destiny."

She held onto the tree trunk even more tightly. It didn't make any sense.

"Just let go," he whispered.

She was still holding on. Giving it everything she had. She couldn't take much more of his coercive, manipulative words.

She gathered all her strength together as she began to slowly descend once more, inch by inch. Her survival instincts had kicked in, and she was fighting back.

"Grace, haven't you been listening to me? You are a stupid, stupid girl!"

Something exploded inside of Grace's head, and she mentally told him to shut up. All the while she kept gathering up her strength and moved further and further along the tree trunk.

She was no longer afraid. She was not weak. And she wasn't going down without a fight.

Ignoring her duplicitous father, a plan was forming in Grace's mind. She dragged the lengths of her entire forearms along the razor-like branches, opening wound after wound and letting the blood escape.

The descending blood formed into a large clot, which she knew would reawaken the hungry mouth. She hovered just above the spot where she had seen it before, assessing her options. It was risky, but it would solve two problems at the same time. She had no other choice.

When the salty droplets neared the blackened tongue, it greedily licked them up. And then it began searching upwards for more. It was a very gluttonous tongue, greedy for Grace's blood.

She let a new group of droplets flow out of the wound, watching and waiting for the perfect moment when the tongue was positioned in anticipation of receiving another drop—and then she was going to send a bomb down upon it.

Her dad was still chiding her. Grace continued to ignore him. "He likes your blood, Grace," a voice far above her whispered.

It wasn't her father. It was the voice of a little girl.

Grace looked upwards, recognizing the girl. She was the one who had been standing in the middle of the road the other day. Grace had swerved the car to avoid her. She sat safely in the nest of branches from which Grace had begun this journey, twisting the red ribbon on her white nightgown around and around her fingers.

Grace blinked so the little girl would disappear again, but this time, she remained.

"Help me, Grace," she said.

"Who are you? What's your name?"

She laughed. "You know me, Grace. Don't you remember?"

Grace shook her head. Tried to find a memory.

Then the little girl spoke very softly. "I am the chord."

Grace felt immediate regret and sadness and love for the child somehow.

The little girl teetered on the edge of the branch like a marionette and sang,

"I am the woman-drawer,

I am the cry;

I am the secret voice,

I am the sigh;

I am that which is heard

Low in the dusk;

Birds by a note reply,

The flowers in musk;

I am that dolorous plant,

Uttered where calls

A lone bird wand'ring by

Dim waterfalls;

I am the woman-drawer,

Pass me not by;

I am the secret voice,

Hear ye my cry;

I am the power which night

Loses abroad;

I am the root of life;

I am the chord." *

Grace, mesmerized by the sweetness of the little girl's voice and the beauty of her tone reached out to her.

The little girl finished the song. "Remember, Grace, some are given, and some are taken. Remember." The little girl jumped off the end of the tree branch.

Grace's scream was the only sound to be heard.

Except for the flapping of wings as the little girl shape shifted into a raven and flew away.

CHAPTER 25

U NABLE TO DISCERN FACT from fiction, Grace found solace in sleep. Until she woke up, then it all flooded back.

She was barely holding on to the tree and in her state of mind.

To the right, something small and green dangled and swayed. It was an olive nearly within reach.

All she had to do was shift her weight and move over ever so slightly then reach like the rubber woman at the circus would. Her stomach grumbled. She was desperate for sustenance.

As she shifted towards it, for a single moment, she halted. Something deep within her gut felt suspicious of it. Had it suddenly appeared, or had she failed to notice it before? How absurd! It was too much for her to take in. Once again, Grace wondered if she was losing her mind.

Mine, she thought.

She pushed herself towards it, reaching further and further without jeopardizing her safety, until the olive was within her grasp.

She pulled it.

It nearly gave way, and then the tree began to shake, almost like it was having a fit. She looked directly below her, taking notice of a spikey branch that was pointing directly at her. If she went down now, she would be skewered on the branch just like that poor raven had been.

Grace fought to hold on. She clung to the convulsing tree with all the might she could gather into her arms and her legs. She was straddling the tree now.

Suddenly, the convulsions turned into something else. The tree was having a fit. It was in the midst of a giant fury. Or was it in pain? Grace knew pain. She remembered how it made her lose control of everything, even her own humanity.

The tree stilled itself momentarily and then began convulsing even more violently.

Grace thought about the five senses. Wondered since this tree had a mouth to eat, and a tongue to taste, what other human characteristics did it possess? Did it have a beating heart? Did it feel?

She tilted her head forward and took in a deep breath, letting it out upon the trunk of the tree. It seemed to help, even if only for a moment.

She tried something else. She caressed the branch nearest to her. The one that held the olive. While she caressed the branch, she thought about how grateful she was to be alive.

And Grace knew then that the tree had averted her attention from picking its fruit, its child. It was the only thing for which it was living.

It wasn't a King tree after all. The King had sent his rooks, to save this tree, the Queen. She was the hope. She was the future.

And now she too was dying.

Grace moved down carefully, no longer interested in the olive. "I'm so sorry," Grace said audibly. "So sorry."

As the tears rolled down her cheeks, down from her face, they fell onto the waiting branches below. And soon the branch turned downward, no longer a threat to her. Then everything was quiet. Everything was peaceful. And Grace knew for certain that she would be with Vincente again, very soon.

Grace returned to the trunk of the tree and rested. She was exhausted and uncomfortable and hungrier than she had ever been, but she had no regrets.

The tree began to cough. Then the tree began to sputter. Grace began to fall downwards. It was like her fingers had been dipped into butter. She could not hold on.

She looked up into the night stars, into Einstein's moony face, and she was okay with whatever was going to happen. She was resigned to it, because she had done everything she could have possibly done to ensure her survival.

She slipped a little bit closer toward the ground.

She noticed the branches around her were revolving. Swirling. Branches, which were once facing skywards, were now bowing down, gesticulating in her direction.

She dropped further down, knowing full well that the tree was dying, too.

As it writhed in sporadic spasms, Grace slipped and slipped and slipped, all the while watching the endless sky and the swirling clouds above, which moved on without a care in the world.

The nerve-thin branches groaned and ached for the end.

Soon the sun began to rise on the horizon and spread its rays out towards the writhing tree, filling it with a delicate, harmonious light until the branches were warmed and still.

As the sunlight kissed the tree, possibly for the last time, the branches bent, bowed and folded, creating a staircase. A staircase that would lead Grace back down to the ground.

She removed her clammy hands from the trunk of the tree and stepped upon the first step carefully. It easily held her weight. She moved along them quickly, one after the other, steadying herself as she needed to by clinging to the trunk of the tree.

Below her, she could see the grass. She was nearly there. It was a race against the sunrays: would Grace get there before they touched the ground? Who would touch down first?

When Grace stepped down, she and the sunlight kissed the ground simultaneously. She laughed as the grass tickled her feet, and she savoured the earthy, musky perfume.

She stood, positioned under the gigantic tree, and pointed skyward.

She had been an unwelcome guest of that tree at first, and now it was as if she were leaving a long-lost friend. Its branches were bent and twisted, and its spine indicated that it would not be standing up for much longer.

There was a loud creak, and then an earthshattering crack as the stairs began to avalanche downward. They hit the ground, bouncing like a child on a trampoline followed by wooden hail, splinters spraying everywhere, like shrapnel.

Grace stood still, too frightened to move, while the Queen fell to her final resting place at her feet.

One small thing was still in motion. Descending.

She caught the olive in her hand, popped it into her pocket, and went to find Vincente.

✳✳✳

As she made her way towards home, she felt disoriented and exhausted yet lucky to be alive.

It wasn't long before she realized that she wasn't far from the house at all. Once she had her home in her sights, she broke into tears. She could not stop, as she pulled open the front door and made her way up, climbing on what was left of the broken staircase. At the top, she sniffed, realizing she smelled bad. She had a quick shower and changed her clothes, cleaning her wounds.

Then she threw open the bedroom door (it was no longer locked) and saw Vincente still bound to the bed. He was in exactly same position she had left him in. At first, she feared he was dead.

As she leaned her head onto his chest, she could feel his breath on the back of her neck. She could hear his heart beating.

She kissed his eyes, his cheeks, his forehead, and his mouth. She was waking up her handsome prince. Bringing him back to the waking world. Tears rolled down her cheeks.

Vincente opened his eyes. "Am I dreaming?"

Grace didn't answer. She just kissed him on his sweet lips, repeatedly. Then she climbed into bed with him, put her arms around his neck, and fell asleep.

CHAPTER 26

S TILL CLINGING TO THE trunk of the tree for dear life, Grace awoke. It was still pitch black out. Afraid to move, she hung on even tighter. Then she felt hot breath on her forehead. She flinched. Swatted.

The trunk moved.

She heard its heartbeat.

"I could get used to this."

Grace screamed.

"Are you okay, Grace? Wake up!" Vincente said.

She pulled back and looked directly into his bearded face. Although it was dark, she could see that she was with Vincente. She was back home, and they were together once again.

She had a dream within a dream—but this was reality. She hugged him tightly.

"I must look quite a state," Vincente said.

"You look beautiful to me."

"Ah, you probably say that to all the guys you find tied to beds."

"Yeah, I always tell them they are very beautiful, so they let me have my way with them." She laughed.

"We need to talk, about what happened here and about what happened when you were...away."

"I don't want to talk about that now, Vincente. Maybe I won't ever want to talk about it."

"Up to you, Grace, but I hope you will be able to tell me someday."

"It was awful and magnificent at the same time."

"If you untie me, maybe I can shower and change. Then we can catch-up."

She located a pair of scissors in the kitchen and cut Vincente loose. Where the ropes had bound him, there was dried blood, but the cuts looked to be healing.

She helped him up once he was free, but his legs splayed out under him.

"I've got it," Vincente said, as he moved slowly out of the room. She followed, opened the bathroom door for him, and then began to climb through the rubble to get to the ground floor again.

"Mum kept all my brother's clothes. See if you can find anything to fit you." Vincente nodded and then closed the bathroom door behind him. She heard the shower start up and was ready to make some breakfast.

In the kitchen, Grace decided to prepare a picnic. She chose the area in the garden. Then she made a pot of coffee and grabbed some mugs and sugar. Popped some bread from the freezer into the toaster, grabbed marmalade, vegemite, strawberry jam, and butter from the fridge. Then she scrambled up some eggs and carried everything outside.

It was a picnic, but the things that were missing were napkins and a tablecloth. She went through the drawers and found both. She set up everything, so it looked beautiful, and even placed a vase of dried flowers in the centre of the table.

When she saw movement in the kitchen, she called to Vincente, "I'm out here!" And when he walked out, she yelled, "Surprise!"

They ate together in silence at first.

Vincente glanced over at Grace, and for the first time, he saw her in an entirely different light. Up until recently, he had seen her from afar, although she had been right next to him. Possibly because he had been blinded to her before. Since then, she had demonstrated strength and courage, and a passion for life he had never known before. She kissed deeply, like she was kissing with her heart, and he knew—had always known—that she loved him. Yet, he hadn't thought he felt the same way. Until now.

"I never knew coffee could taste so good," Vincente said, trying to change his train of thought. But his deep feelings gave themselves away, and he leaned across the blanket and gently kissed Grace on the lips.

Her body surrendered to him, and together they kissed deeply and unfalteringly. Vincente brushed the hair away from Grace's face and he held her tightly against him. He listened to her heart beating in sync with his, and he was overwhelmed with a kind of love he had never felt before.

Vincente gazed into her eyes as he spoke. "When you were away..."

She tried to interrupt him, wanting to say something. He knew what she was thinking that she didn't want to talk about what happened when they were apart, but that wasn't where he was going.

He put his index finger upon her lips and told her to "Shhhh." He had to tell her now, before he lost his nerve. "When you were away, I realized a few things, the most important of all being that I am in love with you."

She gasped. It was uncontrollable.

He beckoned her to be silent once again.

"Not long ago, I hit you on the head with a cricket ball, and you passed out cold. I was concerned about you, but I thought for a split second, 'who is going to help me with my math homework now?' I was selfish, I know. Totally."

Again, she wanted to interrupt him. "Then I watched you, the silly little girl who always looked at me in a strange way, who sometimes followed me with her eyes. Who was obviously infatuated with me—"

She made a face at this remark, and she felt embarrassed. Wondered why he hadn't just stopped at, 'I am in love with you.' It would have been so perfect.

He continued, "You helped me with my math. You were key to me remaining on the team, but I wasn't grateful to you. Not really. I felt like you owed it to me somehow. I felt like everyone owed me. I was different then. But I have changed. You have changed me. Now, when I look in the mirror, I see a man who would do anything for you. A man who wants to be with you, and I don't mean just today or tomorrow, but always, and forever. And you might be thinking that I'm not your type, and you might be thinking you're not good enough for me, but honestly, I am not good enough for you! In the past, I have just followed what was expected of me, without questioning it. I dated the girl I was expected to date. I have been the stereotypical jock, and I'm not proud to say that. You, Grace, have me thinking about tomorrow, our tomorrow, our future, and I can't wait to share everything with you."

Grace felt tears streaming down her face. She had waited years for Vincente to speak these words to her, and now that she was hearing them, she doubted him and said, "But Vincente, maybe you just feel this way, because we are the only two people left? You know, like we're trapped on a desert island, and even the plainest girl looks good after a while."

Her response to his declaration of love was like a slap in the face. She longed to take the words back, but it was too late. The damage had already been done.

"Look Grace, I know that you are scared, and now you're pushing me away. Well, I'm scared, too, so don't try to push me away from you with that 'plainest girl' stuff. It totally demeans everything that I've just said to you, and no matter what you say and no matter what you do, I will always love you. I love you, Grace."

"I love you too, Vincente."

They fell into each other's arms, and this time the kisses were on fire. They drank each other in, like two alcoholics who hadn't had liquor in months. Their passion filled the air.

Vincente pulled away first. He had no choice, he had to pull away, or they would go too far, too fast.

"Where did you learn to kiss like that?" he asked while caressing her back and feeling the burn of her hot skin on his fingers.

Grace shrugged her shoulders. She was merely responding to his fire. They tried to go back to the food, but the taste on their lips, the taste of each other, made everything else seem bland in comparison.

When night came, they lay down on the blanket and watched the stars twinkling above them, held hands, and kissed. It was a perfect world; a world made for just two.

***

G RACE LOOKED AT VINCENTE sleeping there beside her. Their legs were entangled, and she was unable to break herself free without waking him up. She knew she must have bad breath, but she couldn't do anything about it, so she just watched him sleep. His chest went up and down, and he was peaceful. He looked content.

She felt euphoric. Never in her wildest of dreams had she imagined things would work out the way that they had. Vincente Marino was in love with her, and she was in love with him.

Vincente awoke and yawned. His breath touched Grace. It was sweet, and she hoped that hers was sweet too, because she knew that she tasted of him.

"How long have you been awake?" Vincente asked.

"Not long. It was a beautiful night, and now we have an amazing day ahead of us. What should we do?"

"First, I think we need to talk about us," Vincente began. "About where we want to go, and how fast. Last night, I wanted you, badly, but I wasn't sure how fast you wanted to move. I thought about us a lot while you were away. I have longed to hold you. It's what kept me going, honestly. Dreaming of us, connecting."

"I think we should take it slow."

"I'm for that, as long as you promise to tell me when you're ready."

"When I'm ready, you'll be the first to know!" Grace said with a smile, and they embraced and kissed sweetly.

They tidied up the picnic and moved indoors.

"I think we ought to move on from here today," Vincente said.

"Yes, I think we need a fresh start. But where?"

"Somewhere special, and I think I know the exact place."

"Where? Tell me!"

"No, you'll have to wait until we get there. In the meantime, I am going to pack up a few things. Unless you'd like to, you know..." He smiled as his eyes glanced up the stairs.

She walked towards him, put her hands on his shoulders, and looked directly into his eyes. "'Let's get one thing perfectly clear, Vincente Marino, I am ready, willing, and able. But I don't want it to be here or now. Not in this place. But someday, soon."

He kissed her and began to make his way through the rubble to the upper floor of the house. He turned to her and said, "When you're packing, see if you can find a big axe, just in case we encounter any more crazy trees."

"Will do."

CHAPTER 27

"WHEN DID YOU FIRST know that you loved me?" Vincente asked as they made their way along Parramatta Road towards the Sydney Central Business District.

"I loved you the first time I saw you," she admitted.

"It wasn't real love though, was it? It was a crush. An infatuation. I mean, when did you know you really loved me, as a person? As a real person?"

He couldn't imagine love at first sight being real. He had never felt it. Didn't know of anyone who wasn't in a movie or a play that had expressed that love could be instantaneous.

She put her hand on his, which was resting on the gearbox.

He looked at her strangely. She seemed uncomfortable, but she did have a lovely white, almost ivory neck.

"There is no one else for me, Vincente. There never has been. My heart is so full of you; there just couldn't ever be anyone else in it. I adore you."

He stopped the car and moved towards her bare white neck. His teeth were cool as they touched her, and then they began to burn.

Her heart was beating so fast she thought it was going to jump out of her chest, and she felt hot all over as she felt like devouring him.

After a few moments of this, they regained their composure and began to drive away. The streets were jam-packed with now burnt-out vehicles, with the exception of one Land Rover. Vincente stopped beside it and the two of them had a closer look. It was in nearly new condition with white leather seats, and plenty of room in the back for their weapons and supplies.

Vincente turned the key in the ignition it started right up. "I think this is better than our vehicle, much roomier and more reliable and we should...Take it."

Grace didn't like the idea of stealing a vehicle, but it made sense for them to acquire something bigger and more suited to their needs. "I wonder why this one didn't burn out like the rest?" she asked. Vincente shrugged and the two of them began moving their stuff out of the other car and placing it into the Land Rover.

There was some petrol left, but not much. Vincente made a point of stopping into the next station and filling up.

Grace went inside with Vincente, and they grabbed a case of water and a few other odds and ends to take with them.

"Where are we going?" Grace asked again as they made their way across the Sydney Harbour Bridge.

Vincente grinned. He was so pleased with himself about something. Grace was very curious and excited.

Vincente changed the subject. "We were lucky to have found this vehicle. It's in really good shape, and it should take anywhere we need to go."

"We're even luckier that you have your driver's license."

"Well, technically I don't," Vincente stated, as he looked across at Grace. "But who is going to stop me?"

Grace thought about their situation. She found it difficult to believe there weren't other people out there somewhere, across the country, or in another part of the world. She couldn't believe that they were really the only two people left on Earth.

"Don't you think, there must be others, out there somewhere?" Grace asked.

"I think we're it," Vincente said.

"But if there are others?"

"Then we'll find them, or they'll find us. In the meantime, let's not worry about it, hey? We're nearly there," he said as they rounded the corner and turned onto a road, which was parallel to the beachfront. The scenery was breath-taking. Grace longed to get out of the car and run across the white sand with her bare feet.

Vincente stopped just outside of the waterfront Manly Hotel. Like small children the couple couldn't wait to take their shoes off and run in the hot white sand. It kissed their feet and stirred up like sugar at the bottom of a coffee cup, and when their feet touched the cold water, they shivered and laughed.

"Do you think it's safe?" Grace asked.

"Safe? From?"

"You know, like sharks and jellyfish."

"We haven't seen a living thing in days, no ants or spiders, no mozzies, not a single bird... And you are worried about sharks and jellyfish?"

"Yeah, well, the trees were hungry, so who knows about the..."

Vincente kissed her worries away. Together they played in the water like two children, splashing and chasing each other until they fell asleep, side by side, in the sand.

❋❋❋

IN THE MORNING, GRACE and Vincente awoke covered in sand and feeling very, very hungry.

"I'm ready," she said as she lunged at him, kissing him forcefully on his lips and pushing him back into the imprint they had made in the sand.

"I...think it's too soon," he said, pushing her gently aside, standing up and shaking the sand out of his clothing.

She lunged at him again. "I thought you said I should tell you when I was ready. I'm ready, oh so ready," she said as she fumbled for the buttons on his shirt.

He stepped back. He smiled at her. Grace lunged at him again. He stepped away.

"You are such a tease," she cried in frustration as he turned and ran in the opposite direction. "Coward!" she shouted, following him. She was panting. Heart racing. Wanting nothing more than to tear off his clothes, to have her way with him, to feel his body against hers. To become one with him.

"When it's the right time, we'll both know," Vincente said as he opened the boot of the car and pulled out the bottles of water. He entered the Hotel lobby, and Grace followed. She had no choice but to follow him, into the elevator, along the corridor, and into the ginormous penthouse.

Once inside, Vincente drew the curtains all the way back. From their vantage point, he could think about everything that had changed since the last time he had visited Manly with his mum and his dad. So much had changed.

Before, there had been crowds of people around, walking along the promenade, laughing, and having fun. There had been boats, with their sails blowing in the breeze, like spots upon the horizon. There had been laughter, and drinking. Children swimming, playing, and building sandcastles. There had been surfers, lots of them, catching the big waves.

There had been dolphins and birds, mostly seagulls flitting around, diving in out of the water, feeding, and crying out.

Not to mention, barbequing, cafes and restaurants filled with people dining, drinking, dancing, talking, and romancing. It had been all so different then, so alive, and so remarkably busy. Vincente remembered a long wait to get into some of Manly's finest restaurants. Now, he and Grace had the entire place to themselves.

He told Grace about Manly, about how his family had rented a house on the beach. They had experienced whale watching first-hand. How the whales waved with their tails. Such magnificence. Such power.

He also shared with her that they had sometimes stayed at an Oceanside Hotel before they bought a place. It was like a small holiday. They would pack up and catch the ferry. How excited he became and how they always ate out, and swam in the pool on the roof, and then went onto the beach and had fish and chips and sat in the sand and talked a lot.

"You really miss them, your parents, don't you?" Grace said, taking his hand into hers. She loved him even more, if that were possible, when he spoke about his family, and about his memories. When he shared his memories and experiences with her, she felt like they were hers too.

"Now," he said, "We have this place all to ourselves Grace. We can stay here, live here do whatever we want here."

"Yes," Grace agreed, "I would like that."

Having cooled down a bit, they decided to go for a walk along the promenade. There were no signs of trauma from the earthquakes here. They walked along, hand in hand, talking. Growing closer every moment.

The reminiscing had created a bit of a fog. Together they felt very alone.

"Let's go for a swim." Vincente suggested as he ran towards the water, flicking the sand everywhere while pulling off his shirt, shorts, underwear, shoes, and socks.

Grace saw him, bare bummed and running into the water like someone who had never been to the beach before. She started taking off her clothes too, and when she had removed everything, she began to wade into the water.

They met and joined hands when they were waist-deep in the cool waters. The waves rushed over them, pushing them together and apart, together, and apart. They kissed and held on tight as the spray of the sea baptized them as being officially in love.

If any fish were still alive to hear them cry out, they were too polite to make themselves known.

CHAPTER 28

NOW SIDE BY SIDE in the Penthouse of the hotel having slept the kind of sleep only lovers can know, Grace had her head nestled into Vincente's chest.

He was looking down at her while she slept. Thinking about how she was even more beautiful today to him than she had been only yesterday. He pushed her hair away from her face, tucked it behind her ear. She stirred.

"Good morning, sleepyhead," he said. He kissed her on the forehead.

"Good morning." Grace echoed, as she stretched and yawned, covering her mouth with her hand while wondering if she had morning breath—worst breath of the day. She wondered how they got to the hotel.

She thought for a moment, tried to remember getting there, but couldn't recall even entering the hotel. It was like she had been on a binge, and now had totally lost her memory of the event, in addition to all the other events she had forgotten from the past. She felt annoyed because she wanted to remember every single moment with Vincente.

"If you're wondering how you got here," Vincente said. "You were sound asleep on the beach, and the tide was coming in, so I picked you up and carried you here, then tucked you in."

"Thanks," she said as she nuzzled into him. Then, she excused herself and showered. Outside of the bathroom, there was a knock on the door. She put on the hotel robe and asked, "Who is it?"

"It's me, silly!" Vincente replied, as Grace pulled the door open to find him dressed in a chef's uniform—including the hat—and pushing a feast on a trolley.

"You have been busy." Grace observed, as she took a bite of marmalade toast, and dipped a piece of crispy bacon into the softly boiled egg.

They ate and ate, until they couldn't stomach anymore, and then Vincente stood up and presented Grace with a box.

"A present? For me?"

"Who else? I hope you like it," Vincente said, and he watched Grace tear off the ribbon and push back the paper to uncover the gift.

Grace held up the most beautiful strapless sundress she had ever seen, and then she pressed it against her body. It was silk, green, and very sexy. She flew at Vincente and kissed him on the lips, then threw off the robe and put her new dress on. It fit perfectly.

"Thank you," she said.

"Now, let's see what you look like with it off!" Vincente exclaimed before he pushed her onto the bed, and they made love once again.

When they awoke, feeling a little bit hungry again, Vincente set out the chocolate fondue that he'd found earlier, and they dipped defrosted strawberries into it. They were lusciously sweet, and they fed them to each other. When they were satiated and had worked up enough energy, they made love all over again.

✳✳✳

Later that day, they walked hand in hand along the promenade, as the waves crashed up onto the shore beside them. The tide had come in, and its power was surging all around them.

"We could be very happy here, you know," Vincente said. "We have enough food to last us for months at the hotel. Combined with the other hotels, and restaurants, we probably have enough food right here to last us for years. And we could live in luxury, moving around in the hotel, never having to clean up! We can just move into another room when ours gets dirty!"

Grace was thinking about everything Manly had to offer. She too felt that the place could make a nice home. They had all the time in the world, and nothing to lose. Why not give it a try?

"I think you're right, we should stay here, make it our home. See what happens. But—" She stopped, staring up into the sky. Then she turned and looked him straight in the eyes. "What if we're not the only ones, though? What if there are others out there, across the country? Across the world? Should we be so happy, just thinking about us, when others out there could need help? When we could be out there looking for them?"

Vincente didn't answer her straight away. He looked up into the sky as well. He missed the sounds of kookaburras and seagulls. He even missed the noise of planes flying and cars honking. "I understand what you're saying, babe. But our responsibilities are to us, to ourselves. Especially when we don't know how long we have here."

"You think our time is limited?"

"Who knows? Isn't it always? I want to spend every moment with you, making you happy. Loving you. Making love to you is my priority now."

She put her arm around his waist, and they continued walking, then turned the corner, ducked under the bridge, and ran like two children. As they reached the hidden playground, Grace climbed up the slide and slid down and then jumped onto a swing. Vincente took the swing beside her, and they went up higher and higher and higher, all the while their conversation continued.

"You are my priority, too. Loving you, being with you. But maybe, if we tried to find others, we would be happier. I mean, knowing that we had at least given it a go," Grace said.

"You've just given me an idea, Grace. Maybe we should try to ring overseas, long distance. See if we can make a connection that way. We could try a cross-country call, and then we could try New Zealand, maybe Europe, England, then Canada, and the USA. We can spend time here, enjoy the days, and search that way first. Are you okay with it?"

"I think it's a good start. But for now, let's go for a swim," Grace said, as she jumped off the swing and began to run. Vincente flew off behind her, following the trail of clothes that she was leaving in her wake. He gathered up everything and watched as Grace waded into the water. She buoyed up and down then dove under. She came up again with her hair all wet, as if she were getting ready for a magazine photo shoot.

Vincente tore at his own clothes as he began walking towards her.

They went under together as the waves crashed over their bodies.

$$***$$

"Do you think we'll ever miss it?" Grace asked, as she yawned widely and sat up with her arms across her knees. She was now fully dressed again, and they had been stargazing for quite some time, resting in the afterglow.

"Miss what?" Vincente asked, as he sat up and rested cross-legged beside her.

"Learning, sports, everything that went along with being in school. Do you think we will ever miss it?"

"I, for one, don't miss failing in mathematics, and that's exactly what I was doing before Coach Anderson suggested that I get some help from you. I was lucky, I guess, but I don't miss learning. I do miss playing, the crowds cheering when I bowled the perfect bowl."

"You miss the opportunity to be a pro?"

"Kind of. The only way I was going to get into university was with a scholarship. Mum and Dad couldn't afford to send me. Not that we were poor or anything—we had money—but it would cause hardship, you know? I wanted to make it, get in on my own."

"Yeah, I can see that, you wanting to earn it. You have said before I was going to be a mathematician. Maybe I'll feel like it again when my memory returns."

"The sky was the limit for you." He stopped for a second, seeing a cloud going over her features at the word 'was,' then continued, "It still is!"

"I can't remember any of it now. When I was up there, in that tree, I often felt like—" she hesitated, afraid to admit it. "No, you'll laugh."

"So, what if I do laugh? Tell me, come on! You've got to tell me!" Then he leaned over and started tickling her and tickling her. "Are you going to tell me now?" he asked, and he tickled her again until she agreed to tell him.

"Albert Einstein," she said, "I thought I could see his face in the moon."

He didn't laugh. He looked up into the face of the moon. He could make out a moustache, now that she mentioned it, and eyes. He thought of Mark Twain, or, yes, it could be Albert Einstein. "I can see it," he confirmed. "It could be either Albert Einstein or Mark Twain up there."

"You can see it then, the moustache?"

"Definitely, but I never noticed a face so clear before. I've heard of the Man in the Moon, but how come I'm only seeing it now?"

"I don't know for sure," Grace said. Silently they stared at the moon together until Grace said, "All I know is that when I was up that tree, and when I needed hope, I found it in Albert Einstein's face. It made me stronger. It gave me hope. It made me feel certain, without a doubt, that I was going to get down from there, and that I was going to see you again. In fact, I knew that you were okay, and that I was going to rescue you."

"All because of a connection with Albert Einstein, eh? Did he… did he speak to you? From up there, I mean?"

"Not in words, so much," Grace said, "but there was definitely a connection. Like he was across the universe, reaching out to me. Lending me strength. I know it sounds silly now, but at the time, being up there so high in that tree, it seemed perfectly normal to have Albert Einstein watching out for me."

"Well, thank you, Albert Einstein!" Vincente declared, shouting up to the moon, "Thanks for bringing my girl safely back to the ground, and back to me!"

"Yes, thank you, Albert Einstein!" Grace added.

"You're probably on a first-name basis with him now, aren't you?" Vincente said, and then he started running down the beach. Grace ran after him, and they laughed and splashed in the water.

Neither noticed Professor Einstein's wink.

***

THE COUPLE RETURNED TO the hotel, determined to make some phone calls. "I'm certain if there is anyone in Australia to answer, this will reach them," Vincente said.

They sat together in the office, letting the phone ring and ring and ring. No one answered.

"Let's try something else," Vincente suggested. Vincente discovered a manual in the desk, and he flipped through it, finding the code to contact New Zealand. Same thing: no answer.

"Where should we try next?" he asked.

"Let's try…" she stood with a world map in front of her, closed her eyes, zeroed in on France, and Vincente keyed in the code. They let it ring and ring, and again, there was no answer.

"Where to now?" Vincente asked.

"South America!" Grace shouted out, and Vincente keyed in the numbers. This was the closest thing they'd had to fun in a long while, and there was renewed hope with every country they tried: China, Russia, Norway, Ireland, and England. Their hopes dwindled after they tried Canada and the United States, however.

"We're the only ones," they agreed, and returned to their room, exhausted. Neither was hungry or thirsty.

For the first time, they didn't want to make love, and they didn't want to talk. They sat alone together and drank wine. It was their world now. Age meant nothing. They could have or do whatever they wanted. It was a dream come true.

✳✳✳

V INCENTE WOKE UP AND was startled when he heard Grace talking in her sleep:

"E equals MC Squared, two times two is four, four seasons, balanced scale, three times two is six, is a female number, three is a male number, therefore six equals marriage. Six, ten, fifteen are triangular numbers, four, nine, sixteen are square numbers, the psychogenic cube is six cubed or six times six times six equalling two hundred and sixteen, Pythagoras believed that we are all reincarnated every two hundred and sixteen years, therefore, cycle. Return."

She stopped, snored a little and Vincente snuggled into her. He thought about this gift of hers, which was now working its magic within her subconscious. Her genius was permeating into her evening thoughts, rushing back to her during her resting hours. This was the first time he had been awakened by such ramblings. It was like Grace was speaking in another language. He wondered if he should mention it to her. But if he did, would the power of suggestion, rather than her own self-realization, delay the process of healing?

As the morning dawned upon them, Vincente was still awake, listening to the silence surrounding him. Grace had not spoken again, but she became restless a couple of times, and he had to move away from her. She was thrashing in her sleep, but when she had been talking about mathematics, she was very still and centered. Her voice had been filled with such passion. It was practically dripping with hope and awesome wonder although he didn't understand a thing she was saying. He formed an idea about what he was going to do when she woke up. He wasn't going to tell her about the talking in her sleep. Not today, anyway. But he had a plan, and he hoped it would be helpful to her. At the same time, he had an idea about how he could surprise her. He was optimistic today was going to be their best day ever.

CHAPTER 29

"I was thinking, Grace, it would be good to go into Sydney today. We could make a visit to the Public Library. We don't need to stop learning. We have an entire library and thousands of books all to ourselves. We can spend most of the day there!"

"Yes, I like your way of thinking. Perfect!" Grace stopped for a moment, glanced at herself in the mirror. "I'd like to also get a few things, maybe even some new clothes. Maybe I should dye my hair? Fancy me as a blond?"

"Definitely no to the blond thing, but I could use some new stuff, too. We could have a shopping spree! And the other thing I was thinking that might be handy is if we could find a CB radio. It's a more primitive form of communication, but—"

"So, you still think maybe there could be others out there too?"

"I think we may be the only two, babe. But, if we have a CB radio and we can actively use it, and if there is a chance, even a small chance that others could contact us that way, then that avenue will be open to us. To them."

"I love you, Vincente," she said as she threw her arms around him, kissing him deeply. Then she made her way towards the door. "There's no time like the present. We might as well get out there!"

"I'm all for that!" Vincente exclaimed. He put his arm around her waist, and together they made their way out of the building, and into their car. They had permanently parked out in front of the hotel, where normally only taxis and limos were allowed to load passengers. There were some perks to living in a world without rules.

"Vincente," Grace began, "I've been thinking. Although the hotel is nice and everything, it could never be home to me. Do you know what I mean?"

"Yeah, I do know what you mean. You are feeling the need to settle, to nest. And a hotel psychologically doesn't fit the bill."

"It does for now, but not, you know, in the big picture for us." Vincente stopped the car and threw the door open. She watched him run towards the window of a Salvos Store. She stepped out of the car to see what had attracted his attention, and she saw it was a CB radio!

Vincente went into the shop and looked closely at the radio. Then he found an outlet and plugged it in. He scanned the airwaves. Together, they listened intently, but there was only static and feedback. Vincente picked it up and popped it into the boot of the car, and they drove away. The radio was a long shot, they both knew it, but they didn't talk about it.

They drove through the streets of Manly, now totally used to being the only two humans in their world. They had everything they wanted or needed within their grasp: all the tourist attractions, plus Sydney's natural promise and beauty. The city was their little bit of paradise and having Manly all to themselves was a bonus of sorts.

As the Land Rover moved across the Sydney Harbour Bridge, the Opera House seemed to acknowledge their presence, and Grace took the opportunity to pick up their previous conversation. "It would be lovely to choose the home we want. To make a home of our own," she said optimistically.

"I totally agree, and we could choose any house, any mansion we wanted. But for now, I think we need to talk about something even more, well, personal. Something that we haven't really talked about before."

Vincente's expression had changed. He had become profoundly serious, more serious than Grace had ever seen him before, and she was worried. She waited for him to continue, not wanting to interrupt his thought process. She realized that he was trying to find the right words. When he didn't speak for a few minutes, Grace began to worry some more. When he pulled the car over on George Street and looked into her eyes, but was still silent, she became very worried indeed.

"Tell me, Vincente! You're scaring me!"

"We haven't been using birth control, and you could be pregnant right now. I could be looking at you as a new mum, and I could be a dad. And I was just thinking what kind of a life would it be, for a child born to us? Yes, we would love him and care for him, but what about his future? Her future?"

"What do you mean, exactly? We would adore our child!"

"Yes, but who would our child adore? Who would he or she ever love besides us?"

"Oh, you mean someone for them to marry. To spend their future with, after we are gone?" She pulled him into a strong embrace and patted the top of his head like he was a child. "Darling, you have been thinking very deep thoughts. You should have shared them with me. You shouldn't have to be worrying about anything this big by yourself. Whatever comes our way, we'll hit it head on, together."

"But a little person, with no future, other than being with us? It would be cruel. It wouldn't be right!"

"Maybe we should just give up making love, then? Yes, let's become celibate!" she exclaimed, all the while stroking his head and kissing him like he was a small boy. "If it's meant to be, it will happen. We can't worry about something now that may never happen. We love each other. I would give anything for you. I would give my life for you, Vincente, and I couldn't be celibate, not unless we separated. Unless we were apart. Then, maybe."

"That will never happen! I will never leave you! Not on purpose," Vincente vowed.

"Then there we have it. And if we have children, we will do what is best for them. Whatever we have to do. But for now, let's get to that shopping, and then let's go to the library. Then later, let's get some- thing yummy to eat! Nothing bad can ever come from our love," Grace said.

"I adore you, Grace."

They walked hand and hand into David Jones Department Store, where they shopped the morning away. Then they had lunch at an Italian restaurant, cooking up the spaghetti Bolognese together.

After lunch, they explored the library, and they took out a few novels. Grace didn't go anywhere near the mathematics section, and Vincente didn't push her to.

After that, they got into the car and drove along George Street. Unexpectedly Vincente stopped, took Grace's hand into his, and told her that there was something he wanted to show her. Something important.

Grace looked at the sign above the door, Antique Jeweller of Fine Quality Bought and Sold Here.

Intrigued, Grace followed Vincente inside.

✳✳✳

WHEN SHE ENTERED THE store, it was like she had walked into a glittering chandelier. Everything around her was alive with light. Every type of jewellery imaginable, from tiaras to bracelets to watches, to a diamond-encased briefcase was on display inside the store. She was so overwhelmed that she couldn't move for a moment. Money was no object for them now. Before this jewellery would have been way too expensive for them.

"Come on," Vincente said, "Have fun, look around! See anything you like?"

Grace moved forward, bent over, and looked inside the thick glass cases. She didn't wear any jewellery now. In fact, she wasn't certain what kind of jewellery she liked.

She walked up and down the rows of cases, zeroing in on a few things, then becoming distracted and moving along. There were too many beautiful things to be taken in all at once. When she reached the end of the store and turned around, like she was going to go out the door, Vincente stopped her.

"There must be something you like in here!"

"It's just a little overwhelming for me. I don't know much about jewellery. Maybe you can talk to me about it a bit first. Tell me about your ring. Where did you get it?" Grace asked.

"Okay, yeah, I can see that you are overwhelmed, but you must know what you like. So, we can look together. In the meantime, my ring was handed down for many years in my family. It's a family heirloom. It has always been given to the first son of the first son. I didn't realize you even noticed it."

"Sure, it changes colour in the sunlight, just like your eyes do sometimes. Hey, I like this one. It's absolutely gorgeous!" Grace picked up a ring, and as she went to place it onto her finger, Vincente reached out to stop her. He took the ring into his hand and then dropped onto one knee.

"Grace Greenway, I love you more than anything in the world. Will you marry me?"

She screamed like a little girl and ran at him, knocking him backwards onto the floor. She answered yes, and he placed the ring onto her finger. It fit perfectly, like it had been made for her. The large diamond was in the shape of a heart, with tiny diamonds all around the rim. It sparkled when it caught the light.

"Now we're official!" Vincente declared. "I mean, officially engaged."

"Thank you, I love it!"

They spun around the room, all the while embracing. Then dizziness overtook Grace, and she stumbled forward and investigated the glass case just to the left of the door. The small case had been previously obscured by the open door. Her eyes were immediately drawn to a gold band with a heart and little diamonds all around it. Diamonds that had been inset like tiny little stars. It was a magnificent ring, and Grace knew straight away that it was meant for her.

Vincente agreed, and before she could place it upon her finger; he took it from her hand and gently placed it into a box. He put the box into his shorts pocket and patted it gently. "For safe keeping," he said, "until we get married one day."

"Couldn't I just wear it?" she asked while reaching into his pocket, "I mean, who would know? Besides, there is no one here to marry us, anyway!"

"That's not the point, now, is it? It'll keep."

"Tease."

✳✳✳

"WHAT ABOUT YOU?" GRACE asked as she perused the cases, searching for a wedding ring for Vincente. She wondered if men wore engagement rings, or if that was just something for women, a female thing to indicate that she was betrothed? "I want to get you an engagement ring!" Grace said excitedly, but Vincente seemed to be somewhat reluctant. "Okay, then a wedding ring, at least," she said. She shooed him away so she could take a better look.

"Uh hum, may I help you, madam?" Vincente asked, putting on his impression of a pompous antique Jeweller.

"No thank you, kind sir," Grace said. "I have already stolen the ring I wanted!" She had just popped the ring into a box and into her pocket.

"Thank you for stealing from us. Please do come again," Vincente laughed, as they exited the boutique.

Once outside, Vincente began to walk, taking larger and larger strides. Grace could hardly keep up with him. She ran along behind him, out of breath.

Then suddenly he turned around and took her into his arms. Then he released her, breathless and excited.

"I've had the most amazing idea," he said.

"Share it!"

"You need a wedding dress and stuff, and so do I. Well, not a wedding dress for me, but you know, I need wedding attire, too. We have the best shops here at our disposal, so let's get everything we need right now!"

"But the shops aren't going to go away, are they? Why don't we just wait?"

"No, I always say, there is no time like the present, and I feel like we should get them here today," Vincente said.

In truth, Grace felt the same way, but a stronger desire was overwhelming her. Overpowering her desire for a wedding. She wanted to take Vincente's clothes off, and then she wanted to make passionate love to him.

She pulled him closer, into a tight embrace. She kissed him, giving him everything she could, but his mind was clearly elsewhere.

"You look here, and I'll go and look there, and we'll meet back here in say, one hour, okay? Right here on this spot." He paused, blew her a kiss, and said, "Have fun."

"Are you certain we can't do this whole shopping for wedding clothing thing together?" she called after him.

He stopped, shook his head, and turned back in her direction. "No way! It's bad luck for the groom to see the wedding dress before the wedding. You're on your own there, babe."

"But surely you'll need help?" Grace suggested, hoping to change his mind. He just smiled, entered a suit store, and closed the door behind him. She embraced herself. She missed him already.

CHAPTER 30

IT WAS STRANGE, BEING away from Vincente. At first, she didn't like it, being separated. Then she got into the spirit of things and started trying on wedding dress after wedding dress. Many of them were too lacy, pretentious. Some were made for size zeroes and were not complimentary of her larger figure. Others were just too complicated put on all by herself.

When she found an antique white dress with an exceptionally long train on the rack, she wasn't certain it would fit, let alone suit her. It had a high lace collar and came with a matching tiara. The buttons on the dress were pearls, with a lace frill embroidered over the top of them. The price tag read $10,000.00, and Grace was incredibly careful as she gently slid her body into it.

She held her breath and then walked out of the changing room to look at herself in the full-length mirror. Tears filled her eyes and flowed down her cheeks. She couldn't believe she could or would ever look so beautiful. She looked like a princess, just waiting for her prince to come and marry her.

She thought about Vincente and how he would feel when he saw her wearing this spectacular dress. She beamed a smile. She looked at the time, realizing she still had to find some accessories, such as shoes and some pins for her hair, a little makeup, and a pair of pearl earrings.

Mission accomplished! She had thought of everything she might need, and with still a few moments to spare. Grace took her time walking back to the spot where they were to meet.

Vincente hadn't arrived yet. Oddly enough, their vehicle had moved.

She sat down on the curb, bags flowing out onto the pavement all around her. Then she got up and took a bottle of water from a refrigerator in a nearby corner store. Finally, she sat down, dreamed about their wedding day, and waited.

***

As night began to fall, Grace was no longer waiting patiently. She was tired, and she missed Vincente terribly.

The wind had picked up, and Grace felt a chill run through her body.

She went into a nearby shop and tried on a black hoodie.

She zipped it up, put the hood over her head, and sat back down again and waited for Vincente.

And she waited. And waited.

And still waiting, wondered what happened to him.

CHAPTER 31

S HE WAS STILL WAITING for Vincente when the stars came out. As Albert Einstein's image gazed down upon her. She wished she had kept one of the novels from the library to read, but then again, the light wasn't good enough to read on this spot.

She looked down the street, so many stores but she just wasn't in the mood. Sure, she might find something to distract her, but it wouldn't alleviate her ever-growing concern about Vincente's absence.

Had one of those trees made him into a Vincente shish kebab? And why had he taken the car? The agreement had been to get our stuff and to meet in an hour. What had happened? Where on earth was Vincente Marino?

Hours passed.

Grace began to doubt Vincente's love for her.

She began to wonder if he'd changed his mind about their relationship.

This thought made her angry at first, but then it permeated deeper and deeper into her subconscious.

Somewhere, she discovered a part of her that had expected him to leave her, to change his mind. A part of her, that seemed to expect him to hurt her, to rip her apart from the inside.

She decided, since it had been inevitable for him to leave all this time, she might as well move on from the spot where they had agreed to meet. She would go wherever her heart desired, and at this moment, her heart desired to be at the Sydney Opera House.

For a moment, she considered leaving the bags right there on the side of the road. But she had found the most beautiful wedding dress in the world, and she was going to take it with her. She was going to keep it.

For a second, she thought about putting the dress back on, but the train would only slow her down.

When she reached the Opera House, its purity and whiteness greeted her with a shimmer from the light of the moon.

She discovered a ladder she had never noticed before along its side, and she climbed up, higher and higher, until she was sitting on the top of the Sydney Opera House.

Although it didn't feel soft under her, she felt like she was sitting on a giant meringue.

***

Twisting her engagement ring around and around on her finger, Grace contemplated what her life would be like without Vincente. Grace definitely did not want to live without him.

She noticed a single light atop the Sydney Harbour Bridge. It seemed to blink at her repeatedly.

It was a sign for her. One that said, if Vincente did not return for her, she no longer wanted to live.

She did not want to be the sole survivor.

She would rather climb to the top of The Sydney Harbour Bridge and fall forward into the sea. If that happened, she would put the wedding dress back on...

Then she would find Vincente in another place and time.

Just as the sun was coming up, she heard her name being sung on the wind, "Grace! Grace!"

***

When Vincente FINALLY found Grace, she refused to come down from the Opera House at first. He climbed up the ladder, wanting desperately to explain himself. She didn't want an explanation.

She didn't want to hear him. She climbed down, refusing his offer to help with the bags.

She tripped onto the pavement. Walked away from him.

All the while he tried to explain. Attempted to tell her why he was so late.

She climbed into the car. Slammed the door behind her.

He got into the driver's seat.

She told him to talk to the hand.

He pulled away from the curb. He was so mad he could have spit.

She was mad, glad, sad and relieved.

She was in quite a state.

***

"Any idea how long you are going to be mad at me?" Vincente asked.

"I'm not mad at you!" she shrieked. She loved him so much, so much she wanted nothing more than for him to take her into his arms and hold her. For him to tell her how much he loved her. That he would never let her go.

Yet a part of her wanted to be mad at him.

To hurt him. To make him pay.

The hurt she felt overwhelmed her heart at this moment, and she cried quietly to herself.

Vincente cursed himself.

All he had wanted to do was surprise her!

CHAPTER 32

WHEN THEY ARRIVED BACK at the hotel, Vincente stepped out of the car and ran to Grace's side. He needed to keep Grace in the car. They needed to talk.

"You are going to listen to me, and you are going to listen to me now."

"I-I don't—"

"You owe me. You will listen."

She looked at him with such distrust in her eyes; with such hurt and pain he couldn't bear it anymore.

"Look, if you can, just trust me. Trust me and go upstairs right now. Have a shower. Cool off. Spend a few minutes thinking about us, about how much I love you. And then when you are ready, get into the wedding stuff you bought and come back down here; but not straight away. Come back down here at exactly 6 p.m."

"So, you are going to leave me alone all day again," Grace pouted.

"I think time alone is good for both of us. It gives us some space. Time to appreciate each other. Time to think. And at precisely 6 p.m., come down and find me, and we'll talk." He gently kissed her on the cheek and took her hand into his. He looked deeply into her eyes and said, "Trust me."

She agreed somewhat reluctantly and made her way into the elevator, where she hung up her wedding dress and then laid out everything else on the bed.

She examined herself in the mirror. She looked like hell. She had been awake all night, and she had been so worried about Vincente. It was a terrible night filled with very dark thoughts. She felt ashamed of herself, and she was so very exhausted.

She lay back on the soft bed and looked at the clock. It was only noon, and she desperately needed a nap. She set the alarm for 4 o'clock, and then she began to cry all the hurt and the pain from the day before out. When there were no more tears to cry, Grace dropped off to sleep.

CHAPTER 33

T HE ALARM WENT OFF and the shrill sound of it frightened Grace. She jumped up, forgetting where she was at first. She ran around the room, looking somewhat like a goose trying to learn how to fly.

When she settled and hit the off button, her memory flew back over the past 24 hours, what had happened, how she had been forgotten, abandoned.

How she had felt more alone than ever before, and how Vincente had returned to her, begging for forgiveness.

He was so certain she would understand. So confident, and oh so sure of himself.

She looked across the room, finding her beautiful wedding dress waiting for her. She felt its fabric, and still it felt as beautiful as it looked.

A moment later, she was in and out of the shower, dried off, and was pulling her hair up and pinning it into place. She was getting ready for the time when she would pull the wedding dress on over her head. She only hoped that she had enough pins to keep her hair in place until the tiara was added—the final touch.

After she prepared her makeup, and everything about her said bride-to-be, she assessed her look, telling herself what she wanted to hear: that she was the most beautiful woman in the world. She was okay with this title, because as far as she knew, she was the only woman in the world, so there was no contest there, and it didn't seem vain to think of herself in that way.

She thought about Vincente seeing her like this and wondered if what he'd said had been true about the bad luck of a groom seeing the wedding dress prior to the wedding.

As she glanced at herself in the full-length mirror once again, she pulled her train forward and began to make her way out of the room and down the long hallway. She loved the swish-swishing sound of her dress as it followed her along the carpet. She imagined one of her best friends being there behind her, holding it. But then she diverted her thoughts. After all, this was not an actual wedding; it was just a sort of fashion show for Vincente.

When the elevator bell rang, announcing her arrival on the ground floor, Grace swished herself across the entryway, past the vacant desks and abandoned computer terminals, past the empty restaurant and the deserted bar. When she navigated the train in and out of the revolving door—which was no easy task by the way—she tripped out into the half-circle taxi lane and saw the Land Rover sitting there in its usual place. She looked around for Vincente, but he was nowhere in sight. Again. It was beginning to become a habit.

The sun was just saying goodbye for the day and setting on the horizon. The sky was coloured in that orangey-reddish hue. It was the kind that Grace thought promised a Turkish delight the following day. Or was it a Fisherman's Delight? She had no idea about the relevance of the phrase as it popped into her mind. She crossed over the road and arrived at the stone-wall still looking for Vincente.

Then her eyes were drawn to the sand. There was a single dried red rose. She picked it up and carried it with her as she made her way towards the steps. Then she spotted dried rose petals. Scattered in a trail. Showing her the way. Another dried rose met her feet, this time yellow. She picked it up and continued down the stairs, onto the sand.

There were candles left along the pathway scented with rose and lavender. Her ears detected soft music playing in the distance.

She turned her head to find its source, what she saw was overwhelming. She stood there, glued to the spot, with the wind billowing her wedding dress and train in and out, in and out. The image was like an accordion wedding dress, and from where Vincente was standing—he had never seen such a beautiful sight.

CHAPTER 34

A FTER SHE PULLED HERSELF together, Grace moved toward him. There were several steps before her, and she took each of them slowly, deliberately digging in the new heels of her antique white shoes, treading carefully. He was watching her. Waiting for her there.

She felt beautiful, in a way that she had never felt before as he beamed a smile in her direction. His face said, See! And as the sun backed out of the day entirely, it left only the man in the moon—Albert Einstein, it seemed—as witness to what was about to occur.

When she reached the bottom step and saw the sand all around her, she wondered how difficult it would be to walk across the sand with high heels on, and yet she didn't want to break the moment, so she hesitated briefly before stepping down into it.

Pausing momentarily, she appeared to be adjusting her tiara when seen from a distance, but both knew that she was taking it all in, savouring the moment. Her heart was so full she thought it was going to overflow with all the love and beauty around her.

No wonder he was so late, she thought.

She saw Vincente move for a moment. He turned the music up.

He beamed another smile her way.

She stepped down into the sand, to meet her groom.

CHAPTER 35

Vincente had created an aisle for her to walk along by stringing fairy lights and candles together, which was then entwined around dried rose bushes. It was breathtakingly beautiful. She took it all in, walking towards him, closing the gap.

Vincente was adorned in a white tuxedo jacket with no shirt underneath, and a pair of Levi's black jeans. He nervously wrung his hands and dragged his fingers through his hair, all the while beaming smiles in her direction.

He was so gorgeous she wanted to eat him up.

But she was caught in the moment, wanting to savour and relish the image as the fairy lights, candles, and the stars above twinkled in synchronicity: nature was joining in the celebration of their love.

Grace stepped carefully, trying to maintain the flowing appearance of the beauty, elegance and dignity that was expected of a bride on her special day. But in the end, she couldn't wait any longer to get to Vincente, and so she kicked off both of her shoes, grabbed hold of her train, and ran to him. From a distance she looked like she was flying, but in fact she did not actually lift off the ground.

Their eyes were locked upon each other as the gap between them became less and less, and soon they were standing side by side, holding hands, lost in one another. Lost in the moment. Lost in their love.

Vincente spoke first, "It's time for me to marry the most beautiful woman in the world."

"Thank you," Grace said, "It's more than I could ever have imagined! It's perfect!"

"Oh, but one more thing before we start. Uh, please pull up your dress," Vincente said sheepishly.

"Excuse me?"

"I mean, I have something for you," Vincente clarified. As Grace lifted the dress, Vincente said, "Higher, higher," until her thigh was fully exposed, and probably even Albert Einstein was blushing.

Then Vincente withdrew a blue garter from his jeans pocket and rode it all the way up Grace's leg until he reached her thigh. His touch sent shivers up her leg in its wake, and then when he kissed her inner thigh, he sent shivers throughout her whole body as well.

He stepped back, and a song began to play. A song Grace was remarkably familiar with.

It was that love song, and it was being played from her jewellery box.

He had returned to the house to get it. That was why...

The Bride and Groom were lost in each other.

They joined hands.

CHAPTER 36

"You remembered!" Grace exclaimed.

"Of course, I remembered."

The song repeated the words of the chorus about love going on forever and ever.

When all was silent, or with only the natural sound of the waves crashing upon the shore, Vincente gazed deeply into Grace's eyes.

"Grace, you are the most beautiful woman I have ever met. You are beautiful both inside and out, but today you are more beautiful than you have ever been to me. I have grown to love you more every day, and I want us to live the rest of our lives together. I want to make you happy. I want our love to be forever."

Tears were running down Grace's cheeks as she said, "Vincente, I have loved you from the first moment I saw you, but then it was only from afar. You were close enough to talk to, but too far to reach. The distance between us was too great. But something brought you to me, something that is more than I could ever have dreamed, and for that I am eternally grateful. I vow to love you until the last breath is gone from my body, and even then, my memory will love you still more."

Vincente moved in and placed the ring on Grace's finger. He kissed her finger gently as he slid it down, causing Grace to shiver again, but their eyes never broke their lovelock.

Grace pushed the other ring onto Vincente's finger, and following his lead, kissing his finger gently. He offered other fingers to her, and she gently kissed them too, all the while watching the hair on his hands and arms standing erect.

Locked in the moment, they moved in as close as two could be, and they kissed a most deep and passionate kiss: a married kiss, which sealed the deal.

"Say cheese!" Vincente said. He had set a camera onto a tripod, and he and Grace smiled. He moved it around, so they had a shot with the beach behind them. Then he took one of Grace alone, holding her roses, and she also took one of him.

Next, Vincente went to the stereo, and it started playing a new song. It was a very romantic song. Together they began to sway. It was their first dance as a married couple. It was their very first dance together, and her first dance ever. Joined together, they moved as one, holding each other as close as two people can get.

Vincente reached over and removed Grace's tiara, and they began undressing each other, piece by piece. When they were both entirely free of clothing, and the only thing that they were wearing was their new wedding rings, they kissed until they were down on the sand, making a marital imprint upon it.

As the waves continued to pound upon the shores, they made love for the first time as a married couple, and then exhausted, they dropped off into a deep, deep sleep.

Grace dreamed that she was tumbling out of the sky, but she wasn't falling. She was suspended in mid-air, with her arms spread open wide.

CHAPTER 37

"GRACE! GRACE! GRACE!" VINCENTE shouted.

When she woke up, half of her body was submerged in water. Everything from their wedding were gone.

"GRACE!" Vincente screamed once again, as the waves pushed and tossed him like he was as light as a buoy.

Grace began to move into the water too, once she realized that Vincente was trying to save their things. She saw him go under and she screamed out his name and waited for him to resurface.

"Forget the stuff!" Grace shouted. "Just come back; everything can be replaced!"

He didn't hear her, or he wasn't listening, so she began to make her way to him. As she fought against the waves, the undulating force of the current pulled her under and soon the burning sensation of saltwater rushed into her lungs.

Grace's mind flashed back to her wedding day, the most wonderful day in her life. Back to the vows which she and Vincente had exchanged as she fought with all her strength to survive.

"Grace, you are the most beautiful woman I have ever met. You are beautiful both inside and out, but today you are more beautiful than you have ever been to me. I have grown to love you more every day, and I want us to live the rest of our lives together. I want to make you happy. I want our love to be forever," he said.

Tears were running down Grace's cheeks as she said, "Vincente, I have loved you from the first moment I saw you, but then it was only from afar. You were close enough to talk to, but too far to reach. The distance between us was too great. But something brought you to me, something that is more than I could ever have dreamed, and for that I am eternally grateful. I vow to love you until the last breath is gone from my body, and even then, my memory will love you still more."

Vincente moved in and placed the ring on Grace's finger. He kissed her finger gently as he slid it down, causing Grace to shiver again, but their eyes never broke their lovelock.

CHAPTER 38

G RACE WALKED TOWARDS THE water. She did not look
back. When she was at the water's edge, she removed her
wedding and engagement rings, and she waded in. When she
was waist deep, she kissed the rings good-bye and made ready
to throw them into oblivion.

Vincente watched and waited, uncertain behind her. When
he realized what she intended to do he shot up like a rocket and
shouted, "Grace NO!"

She froze, cursing herself for hesitation with the rings still
clutched tightly in her fist.

"Come back," he said. "Don't do it!"

She wanted to be bare, bare of everything, just like Vincente
was. She didn't need her rings if he didn't have his.

"We'll go back to the antique store; I'll get another ring!" he
shouted. "Now please, come back!"

She still considered parting with the rings, but then the
brilliant rays of the sun reached them. It was like a sign
from Mother Nature, and she closed her hand around them
protectively.

Grace trudged out of the water, feeling a little bit angry with Vincente for taking his rings off in the first place. She had never seen him remove the family heirloom before, so why had he done so now?

When she reached Vincente, he returned the rings to her finger and then kissed it. "Well, that's a unique start to our honeymoon!"

"Yeah, a real keeper—I mean something we can tell our children and our grandchildren about!"

They smiled at each other and put their arms around the other's waist and made their way back to the hotel.

And on the way there, they decided that it was time for them to move on.

CHAPTER 39

"First, we stop in the city and get you a new ring. And then..."

"You know babe, I would rather wait, if it's okay with you, and look around some more. I don't want to buy my second ring in the same shop —it would feel strange and even unlucky. Let's look for something totally different. And as to my family ring, well it's a done deal."

Together, they packed up their sparse belongings in the hotel room.

"Come on Mrs. Marino," Vincente said, smiling at Grace, "It's time for us to get this honeymoon started!"

"Say it again," she said.

"Mrs. Marino, Mrs. Vincente Marino, Mr. and Mrs. Vincente Marino, Grace and Vincente Marino," he chanted. She swooned as if the titles were music being played and they gathered up their bags and exited. They closed the door tightly behind them and made their way down the elevator and into the lobby, then out through the revolving doors and into their waiting vehicle.

Out of the blue Grace asked, "What is the meaning of your family name?"

"Uh, if you don't like it, are you going to ask for Greenway back?" he asked all the while wearing a cheeky grin.

"No way! Greenway is boring. It means 'a green way'—big surprise. But Marino, sounds foreign, exotic – interesting."

"Why thank you Mrs. Marino," Vincente said. "It means 'seaside.' I think that's why I have always loved coming here. The ocean sounds like music to me. It's in my blood."

"After what just happened, I don't mind being away from all the water for a while," Grace confessed.

"No kidding!" Vincente said, "But we'll be back."

CHAPTER 40

A S THEY DROVE ALONG the coast, passing by new and used vehicle lots, Vincente mused, "You know what, I've always dreamed of having a two-seater candy apple red Ferrari."

As she spotted the exact same vehicle Vincente had described in one of the lots she said, "A wedding present? I think it would be great except this car has more room for storage for necessities like guns, knives and stuff."

"Yeah, you're right," Vincente said; however, he could not pass up the opportunity entirely and so he pulled into the Ferrari car lot. "It's like I died and went to Ferrari Heaven!"

"Steady, Mister Marino," Grace warned, pretending to hold him back.

"This one," he said, caressing it, "this is the baby I want!"

Grace watched as he ran his fingers along the curvaceous bumpers, touched and looked lovingly at the soft white leather interior, stroked the steering wheel affectionately, then opened the hood and nearly got in there and made love to it.

"Should I be, jealous?" she asked with a smirk.

He laughed but continued caressing the headlights.

"Seriously though," Grace said, "Hadn't we better go and look for a proper vehicle, you know with enough room to transport our worldly goods in?"

"Nah," he scoffed. "Life is too short. Come on, jump in!"

After they roared up and down the Princess Highway a few times, Grace returned to the Land Rover. She smiled as she watched Vincente say goodbye to the red Ferrari.

After a few moments he made his way back to Grace and demanded that she "Open the window."

"Why?" she asked.

"Just do it!"

"No, you get in."

"Open it Grace."

"Tell me why!"

"Come on!"

She let the window down and Vincente pushed his head into the open space and grabbed her face in both hands, and he kissed her hard, rolling his tongue over her lips and swirling it around in her mouth until she totally forgot to breathe.

"That's what you get for thinking I was going to kiss the Ferrari!" Vincente said, as he jumped into the Land Rover and made the tires screech.

Grace sat in silence, still trying to catch her breath as the red Ferrari became smaller and smaller in her side mirror, all the while remembering Vincente's mouth on hers.

"REMEMBER WHEN I TOLD you that my mum was an artist?" Grace nodded, and Vincente continued. "My mum was a painter, and a fairly good one too. My dad was with a communications company, and they sent him all over the country to work. That's why we moved around a lot when I was a kid. Mum loved us moving around, because it was good for her—artistically, I mean. She always had new landscapes, fresh scenery, new trees—"

He stopped the car abruptly, slamming on the brakes. Then made a wide U-turn.

"What's up? I love hearing about your family. Tell me more."

"I'm not going to just tell you," Vincente said somewhat breathlessly. "I am going to show you! I mean, I had totally forgotten about it, until just now. I think I may have even blocked it out."

"Tell me," Grace interrupted, but Vincente just kept on talking.

"After what happened at my grandparents' place and then at your parents' place, well it's too much of a coincidence."

"What is? What is a coincidence?"

"It's just too weird for me to explain, but I will show you and soon," he shivered and tightened his grip on the steering wheel. "Hold on, okay? Once you see it, you'll know why."

"Okay," Grace said, snuggling back into the seat. She wanted to ask more questions, but she knew that Vincente would not answer them at this time. She changed the subject. "Did you have any problems, moving around so much when you were a kid?"

"I didn't have any problems," Vincente said, "Probably because I was pretty good at sports. I tried out for things, got onto a team and 'voila'— instant friends."

"I bet you've always had girls falling all over you!"

"Ooh, look who's sounding a bit jealous? Are you jealous Mrs. Marino?"

Grace's only response was a silent smirk.

CHAPTER 41

"I T'S ONLY A FEW more minutes away," Vincente said.

"Looks like it might rain today," Grace observed, as a visible shiver went through her entire body.

"I would appreciate the sound of a real thunderstorm," Vincente said. "I miss hearing all the birds, especially the kookaburras."

Grace stared out the side window and then looked back through the windshield.

Vincente turned the wipers on as a few drops descended from the sky. They were normal droplets this time, not black like before.

"I remember they always said in school that after a nuclear war, some things would still survive like vultures and cockroaches and sharks," Vincente said.

"None of which are needed in our world."

"No, but if this thing—took them, too, what does it mean for us? Vultures and sharks are feeders from human carcasses, or other carcasses. So, as there are no bodies, they would have starved to death, too. Cockroaches eat anything—animal, vegetables, paper—you name it. Of the three, and since they fly here in good old OZ, we should have seen at least one of them by now."

Grace shivered again, "Why do cockroaches eat paper?"

"It's not exactly the paper they are after. It is the glue, which is made from animal by-products."

"I can tell you one thing I don't miss are bugs," Grace said, and her entire body shivered again. This time even Vincente noticed.

"Do you want to get a hoodie in the next mall we see, or shall I put the heat on? You seem to be shivering a lot lately. I hope you're not coming down with something."

"I'm not cold really. I just feel a little odd. I can't explain it," Grace said.

"Tell me how you're feeling," Vincente asked. "Is it like someone is watching you? Or like something bad is going to happen?"

"Maybe both; perhaps just one. I really don't know. That's why it's difficult to explain," Grace said as the goose bumps popped up on her forearms.

"We're almost there now," he said. "Hang on and perhaps a hot shower will help."

"Yeah, or a nice, long bath," Grace said. "You can give me a massage."

"I'll do you if you'll do me," Vincente said with a boyish grin.

Grace involuntarily shuddered again as the car turned around the bend. Vincente paused in front of a two-storey home, then pulled into the driveway and parked.

"Welcome to my humble abode," Vincente said, waving his arm with a flourish and bowing down like a gentleman.

Grace giggled and then examined the garden. Everything in it was dead, but some of the flowers still retained their colours. Vincente opened the door for her, and she walked toward him.

"This garden used to be my mum's pride and joy," he said, "just look it now."

"I bet it was breath-taking then," Grace said. "I mean even now, as it is, I can still tell that it was loved and cared for not so long ago."

"When I first went to school," Vincente said, "Mum started planting. She was worried about how she was going to fill her days without me. Painting is her passion, but sometimes she needed a little diversion, for inspiration. Then she discovered a talent for making things grow, and it became very therapeutic for her. Mum was an artist in many ways," he said, taking Grace's hand and leading her onto the front porch. She followed along until they stood at the foot of an overturned easel.

"When I left for school on that last day, mum was out here painting. Now..." he stopped himself, placing his hand over his mouth.

"What is it?"

"Her painting," he exclaimed. "It's still here! And look, she left the lids off her paints, and her paintbrush is bone dry." He couldn't help himself, and he fell into the chair with a thud. "Mum wouldn't have left these things out here like this. I know for certain now, and I have to face the fact that my mum is dead."

Grace took his hand into hers, and she moved beside him where she could see the painting too. "Your mum is really something."

"Was. She was really something."

Grace examined the painting, leaning over Vincente's shoulder and said, "Stunning."

"But she never had time to finish it!" Vincente bent down. He carefully placed the caps back upon the open paint jars. Then he poured some turpentine out of the bottle and dropped the paintbrush into it to clean. He lifted the unfinished painting from the ground, handed the bottles to Grace and she followed him into the house.

The first thing Grace noticed outside was the remnants of the garden. Inside, the first thing she noticed was the flowers—all kinds of flowers arranged in vases. Blue. Red. Purple, you name it. Flowers sat in coffee pots and empty jars. Flowers, everywhere. They were all dried now, just like the ones outside, but again many had retained their colours and fragrances.

Vincente's mum had filled her house with nature and love. In every space she could find, Grace knew this to be certain. Now that she thought it, she wished even more that she had met her. She regretted that she wouldn't be able to meet her now. A tear trickled down her cheek as she picked up a pair of aqua blue gardening gloves from the side table. Grace held them in her hand, almost like she was holding Vincente's mum's hand, and she carried them with her as she followed in Vincente's footsteps.

"Wait here Grace," he said. "I'll get it. The thing, the thing that I want you to see."

She sat down in the chair, all the while admiring a large painting, which was on display above the fireplace. There was something about it that was awfully familiar, almost comforting. She stood up and moved in closer to it.

***

"I CAN'T BELIEVE IT! It's gone!" Vincente exclaimed as he approached Grace who didn't acknowledge his presence. In fact, she didn't move at all – it was like she hadn't heard him.

Grace didn't acknowledge his presence or move. It was like he wasn't even there at all. He looked at his wife, standing there holding a pair of his mother's gloves in her trembling hand and then he followed her line of sight.

When he realized what she was looking at, he put his hand over his mouth. There above the fireplace was the painting that he had been searching for. The exact painting, which he had brought Grace to the house to see.

"That's it!" he shouted and touched her on the arm.

Grace jumped at the sudden touch, but she could not take her eyes off the painting. She seemed to be transfixed by it.

In her head Grace was admiring the realistic qualities. She could smell the grass and hear the cow mooing. She felt a part of it. Somehow.

Vincente tried to turn Grace toward him, but she resisted. He stood in front of her, and she pushed him away.

"Look at me!" he exclaimed.

"I can't. It's just too beautiful! I feel like, I have been there."

"Look at me!" he commanded.

Grace looked at her husband, standing there beside her, wringing his hands, with perspiration streaming down his face.

"What is it Vincente?" Grace asked, as she tried not to look at the painting.

"That painting," he said turning her around and blotting out any view of the painting, "is the one. The one I brought you here to see."

"Ok," Grace said, "and I totally see why. It's the most amazing painting I have ever seen."

"No Grace," Vincente said, "Look at the tree. Look at the tree, Grace!" and then he shuddered as he pushed his trembling fists into his pockets and then pulled them back out again. He ran his fingers through his hair, and he couldn't keep still.

She looked at the picture once again and was filled with an inexplicable inner peace. She smiled.

"Can't you see it, Grace? Can't you see it?"

"Of course, I can see it. There is beauty, peace and serenity. I see your mum's heart in this painting. It's like...I have met her before. Like I have known her."

"Ok, maybe you can't see it. Maybe I need to point it out. See there," he went to the painting, and she too drew nearer. "See there, on the tree? Right there."

"Tell me what you see Vincente," Grace asked.

"It's a face."

She moved in closer, but she could not see what he saw.

"All I see is a field filled with sunflowers and a normal tree with a cow grazing under it," Grace said.

"No!" he exclaimed, growing exasperated. "Look closer. Look at the tree!" He turned to her, pleading to her with his eyes to see what he could see, but she was unable to.

She turned to him. "There is no face, Vincente. Darling, you're seeing something which isn't there."

Vincente threw his hands up in exasperation, turned tail and ran.

At first Grace wanted to follow him, but once again she was drawn to the painting. She stepped nearer, smiled; lost herself in it.

Wait a minute, Grace thought, Vincente was petrified, and he doesn't scare easily.

She closed her eyes and then opened them again. Still, she could not see a face. In fact, this time, the rays of sunlight seemed to be reaching out to her. Drawing her in. Making it almost impossible for her to look away.

The room became warmer somehow when she gazed at the picture. She felt like a piece of the sun had been captured by the artist and was now offering itself up to her. She wanted to walk into the picture and become a part of it—to embrace the light. And when she walked forwards, she seemed to be able to breathe in the fresh hay in the fields and to hear the cow mooing. Her heart rate quickened; her breathing became shallow.

She let it overpower her for a moment, forgot to breathe. Was soon gasping for air and more than a little frightened.

Grace took a quick step back. She ran calling Vincente's name.

CHAPTER 42

Grace found Vincente in his room on his bed. Although some minutes had passed, he was still trembling with his arms folded in front of his face. She imagined how he must have looked when he was a little boy.

"Tell me about it. The painting," she asked, as she paced back and forth, all the while trying to dispel the feelings and energy that had temporarily overtaken her. She didn't want to mention what she had felt, or at least not until Vincente told her what had frightened him.

"Did you finally see it? I mean, the face?" he asked, and for that moment, with his expectations high, his trembling ceased.

Grace wasn't trying to lie when shook her head no. She was merely trying to assess the situation.

Immediately Vincente's body shuddered.

"Tell me Vincente. It doesn't matter what I see, but I can see that you are frightened darling. Tell me all about it, please. You know that you can tell me anything, right?"

His teeth chattered as he hesitated for a second and then he took in a deep breath and began to tell the story.

"When I was a kid, mum painted that landscape, and she unveiled it to me very proudly. She pulled back the curtain expecting me to love it, but instead I was absolutely terrified and as a kid, I didn't' have the words to express it. Mum didn't understand, neither did my dad. We tried again, and always it was the same for me. A small glance at it, and I'd be up screaming in the night. The nightmares spoke for me. So, my parents put it away and I never saw it again. In fact, I had forgotten all about it—until this morning. Like I said, I think I blocked it out."

"So, why did you bring me, bring us back here, then? You wanted to prove something to me, or to yourself? You wanted to face your fears?" Grace asked.

"I thought maybe it held a clue for me – for us. But you saw how I changed when you couldn't see it too. I was a kid again and had to run from the room! What do you think of your strong husband now?" he cringed at what he deemed to be an unmanly display of cowardice.

"I love him just as much—no—even more!" Grace said as she snuggled up to him.

After a few moments of not talking, Grace revealed, "I didn't see the face, but I felt something in the painting, Vincente. Something otherworldly and unexplainable."

Vincente sat up, removed his arms from his face, and said, "When I was a kid, when I looked into it deeply, it made me feel like I wanted to walk into the picture. Like I wanted to escape from this life. I could smell the hay and hear the cow. It was like a light was pulling me in, lulling me. I knew that if I allowed myself to go with it, walk into the painting, then that face on the tree would, would, would hurt me—I had to get away, I had to run away from it!"

"I felt something strange pulling me into it too Vincente, but I couldn't see the face. It was nothing like the one we saw, you know. The one that ate the raven."

They cuddled together on the bed, comforting each other, and thinking about the picture, while at the same time trying desperately not to think about it.

After a while they made love.

When Grace awoke first later, she considered how she felt about the picture. It was a magnificent landscape—there was no doubt about it. However, the light and the pull of it were something unique and maybe even, dare she say it, evil. Yes, that was it. It was the contrast of the calm and serene with a taste of something black, unknown, maybe even dangerous.

She glanced over at Vincente, still sleeping peacefully. He stirred every now and then and mumbled. She wondered if he was dreaming of the tree, the tree with the face, which he had imagined to be a part of the exact same landscape. Grace quietly got out of bed, and Vincente moved over, filling in her still warm gap.

He was still sound asleep and at peace.

She looked around his room, admiring his amazing accomplishments for which he had trophies to show: Best Athlete, Top Batsman, and Player of the Year—he had won that category several years in a row.

Then her eye zeroed in on several shelves filled with woodcarvings. Intrigued, she moved towards them in awe of the intricate details. Each one had its own separate personality. There was a ballerina pirouetting with poise and technique, there was a cricket player at bat, a cowboy wearing a gun belt around his waist and just getting ready to draw, a mountain climber, who by his expression had just reached his ultimate destination, plus numerous others.

Grace ran her eyes over the entire collection, stopping at a carving of an Aboriginal man. He was staring ahead with lost eyes. She picked him up and held him in her hand. Her skin contacting the wooden figure caused it to pulse, ever so gently. Or had she imagined it?

She stepped back and averted her eyes to her left. She was aligned with a wood framed mirror and her reflection startled her so that the wooden figure in her hand fell to the floor and bounced on the carpet. She bent down, picked it up and examined it more closely, just in time to see a tear fall out of the wooden figure's eyes. She wiped it with her fingertip and tasted it. It was salty, just like a human tear. She stood there and stared into its eyes. She felt frightened and a little more than curious. She wondered if this talk about the painting had unduly influenced her.

"What do you think of them?" Vincente asked, as he yawned, stretched, and then crossed the room to join her.

Grace was startled and jumped a bit at first. She cradled the Aboriginal man against her chest. "I had to have a closer look because their facial expressions are so life-like! Where did you find them?"

"I made them," he admitted shyly. "Each and every one was carved, from head to toe with these two hands."

"You are a real artist Vincente! Why didn't you tell me?"

"I haven't told anyone about these, other than mum, dad, and my grandparents. Do you really like them?"

"I think they're incredible!"

"I would like to carve one of you, Grace."

"That would be wonderful Vincente," she twirled pretending to be a ballerina. "I noticed each one is different, not just the characters but the type of wood. How do you choose?"

"Each carving requires a specific type of wood for everything to come together. I walk among the trees, decide what to create and wait to see what type of tree speaks to me, spiritually. Then I create the carving with the intention of making it as life-like as possible and most importantly, truthful."

"How long does each one take?"

"Once I find the wood—which takes the longest time—then I can carve the subject in two or three days. The face always takes the longest, and that's what I do last. If the face isn't right, I toss it all out and start again. Sometimes it's because the wood doesn't feel right, then I go back to the trees, searching all over again, for the right tree. Most of the time the tree is right; I just haven't captured the essence of the subject yet."

"Do you have a special set of tools to do this? Because if you do, then you should bring them with us. And I think you should bring your mum's painting with us too. Even if we do have to cover it up."

"Ah, the painting again. I want to go back down and have another look at it. I want to face my fears head-on. Will you come with me?"

"Of course, I will Vincente." She followed behind him, reaching out to put the Aboriginal man back onto the shelf, but it pulsed again. She placed it into her pocket and then said, "But I have to remind you that I did feel the painting pulling me in—and the pull was extraordinarily strong. Eerily so."

"We'll hold hands and face it together."

"Okay, let's go."

"Can we have a cup of coffee first Vincente?"

"Deal."

CHAPTER 43

Having finished their cuppas and now back in the living room, Grace and Vincente held hands and walked toward the painting.

Vincente was convincing himself that he couldn't really see a face on the trunk of the tree and Grace was convincing herself that she didn't feel the force of the painting pulling her forwards.

Their feet remained firmly planted in the same spot as they tightened their grip on the other's hand.

Grace put her other hand into her pocket, where she held Vincente's carving of the Aboriginal man. When it pulsed again, she removed it and held it up, so its eyes were facing the painting too.

The Aboriginal man began to convulse in the palm of her hand. Then he rolled from side to side. She looked down and his mouth twisted into a scream, and he was lifted out of her hand and into the painting.

Standing still in the same spot, still holding hands, Grace could now see the carving of the Aboriginal man sitting up in the tree. Above him a raven sat on a branch.

Vincente continued to stare at the painting, but he was not trembling like before. He squeezed Grace's hand for reassurance.

"Do you notice anything different?" Grace asked.

"Different? How?"

"Anything new or out of place?"

"No, everything looks the same, but the mouth doesn't scare me as much today. Maybe it's because we are holding hands."

Together they stepped away from the painting and closed the door behind them.

Instantly, the Aboriginal man pulsed. He had returned to Grace's pocket. She opened her mouth to tell Vincente what had happened, but he seemed to be less fearful, and she couldn't find the words to explain.

"I'm going to pack a few things," Vincente said.

"I think I'll stay here, if that's alright with you?" Grace asked. She watched as Vincente disappeared around the corner and then she reached up and removed the painting from the wall. She wrapped it in a blanket, and she stored it in the boot of the car. She then returned to the house and retrieved some blankets and pillows and placed them securely on top of the painting. The entire time she was loading up, the carving continued to make its presence known by pulsing in her pocket. Now she headed up to Vincente's room. The Aboriginal man stilled.

Vincente packed his carvings into a large bag. He also included his tools. Loaded up, together they went back downstairs. Vincente then wrapped up his mum's artistic kit including easel and canvas and they loaded up the car.

"Ok, let's go," he said.

"Are you sure you have everything?" Grace asked.

"I, I don't want to bring that thing with us. I'm at peace with it now and all I want to do is get out of here. Right now, I don't think that I will ever want to return here."

They moved to the entryway, and Vincente pulled the front door open, and beckoned Grace to exit first. He then closed the door tightly behind him and locked it.

Once they were back in the Land Rover and on the road again, Grace broke the silence. "We really should talk about it."

"I said," he shouted, and then toned his voice down, "I said I didn't want to talk about it. Not now, not ever. If talk I about it, I will be forced to think about how my mum, my very own mum, could have created such a painting. Mum was the sweetest, kindest woman who walked on this earth, and she would never have created anything as appalling as that thing."

Grace quietly watched the world pass by her. A storm was coming. She could feel it. Everything around her shivered, pulsed, and throbbed, including the Aboriginal man in her pocket. She wrapped her arms around herself and decided not to take the discussion any further with Vincente at this time. He would talk to her when he was ready. In the meantime, the painting was safe and secure, and it couldn't harm them.

They continued in silence.

CHAPTER 44

V INCENTE STARED AHEAD, FOCUSING his energy on the road. He tried to forget about the painting and about his mum, but no matter what he did, he couldn't separate the two things in his mind.

He looked across the car at his lovely wife. She was sitting quietly, lost in thought with her arms embracing herself. She seemed unaware that he was looking at her. He returned his focus to the road.

Grace was also thinking about the other Mrs. Marino and the painting. It seemed strange that Vincente could be so devastated by something his mum created. An idea occurred to her; they could burn it. Make a healing ritual of it.

She let her thoughts roam as she searched within her own mind for any sign of an original memory, but nothing surfaced. She believed, as Vincente did, that she still stored everything inside of her brain somewhere and that one-day, it would all float back up to the surface and she would laugh about this gap time. Burning that picture would create a gap in Vincente's memories. Was it better to have no memories at all than to have bad memories?

Meanwhile, Vincente was thinking about how lucky he and Grace were, to be able to escape the past, and to live only in the present. To leave everything behind them and to start all over again. To make new memories—together. To create some fresh imprint out of everything they saw. Every new place they visited, would become a part of them. Life would always be filled with such newness.

After some consideration about burning the painting, Grace decided that destroying Vincente's memories, was the worst thing she could ever do to him. She wanted him to have what she no longer had.

These thoughts and memories were too precious to lose—not that Vincente would lose them by destroying the object he feared, but that he would forget them in time. She wanted him to have the best chance of keeping his past with him forever. The good, the bad and the ugly.

Grace eventually broke the silence by saying, "I think we should go back to Manly." She knew that Vincente had many memories there, old, and new. In Manly, they could start anew, fresh but with ties to the past.

"So be it," Vincente said, as he turned the car around, "We can choose any house we want and then we can make it our very own."

"We don't want a house," Grace said, "We want a home."

The newlyweds smiled, happy in their decision and for their future together.

BOOK TWO:
FINALE FUSION

PROLOGUE

THE PUZZLE WAS INCOMPLETE in Grace's mind. It was like a huge gust of wind had blown right through her, turning everything upside down and inside out.

She couldn't focus on any one thing: nothing was focusable.

Colours swirled: reds, blacks, and blues ran together, turned, and tossed, assaulted with sunflower yellow, twirled, vomited into a deep grass green.

Then all the colours somersaulted her stomach up into the air and returned it back down to where it had been, as she dry-heaved herself towards the fear that left her unable to move. Everything was happening in her head but sometimes her body jerked in the flow of it.

She grabbed onto her centre and tried to regroup, to stop the swirling and twirling. But the flashes of lightning pulsed inside her head, ripping her into lilacs, violets, and bluebells.

Orange splattered onto the canvas of her mind.

Grace lost everything.

✳✳✳

"WE NEED TO GET her into surgery, now!" exclaimed a tall man adorned with a white coat. He stood among other white-coated persons scattered along the hospital corridor.

All ran like the place was on fire. A few of them cleared the path. Some pushed. Some held onto the IV. Some held onto the other machines. A few stood with gaping open mouths, empty hands, and clenched fists. Others prayed, as Grace Greenway sped by on a gurney.

She was unconscious.

Dead to the world.

But not completely dead.

At least not yet.

✳✳✳

Bᴀᴄᴋ ɪɴ Gʀᴀᴄᴇ's ʜᴏsᴘɪᴛᴀʟ room, a woman sat wailing and wringing her hands. It was Helen Greenway, Grace's mum. She couldn't believe what happened.

Her daughter had been doing so well. Recovering for some weeks now. Then Grace began to shiver, shake, and convulse until she lost consciousness.

The medical team had brought her back from death's door. When she returned, she wasn't Grace Greenway anymore. Instead, she was drooling and talking in tongues. Tearing herself apart from the outside in.

It seemed like no one knew what to do, how to stop it. Even the needles in her arm didn't calm her. Nothing worked. They tied her down.

Helen let out a sob as she remembered everything. Especially how helpless she felt then and even more so now. She threw herself onto her daughter's empty bed.

Helen's anguished sobs were heard echoing in the corridors.

***

When Nurse Burns returned to Grace's room, she found Helen curled up in a fetal position on the bed.

She looked peaceful sleeping there. The nurse thought it best not to disturb her. Besides there was no news to share, and if anyone needed rest, it was Grace Greenway's mother.

Nurse Burns tidied up Grace's night table and restacked her textbooks. As she looked them over, she felt incredibly sad. Grace Greenway hadn't even found her stride yet. She was only sixteen years old.

Nurse Burns looked at Grace's sleeping mother.

She placed a blanket over Helen and then turned off the light.

***

Several hours later, Nurse Burns was getting ready to end her shift for the day. She looked through the round window in the door and noticed Helen was no longer in bed. She pushed on the door, but nothing happened. She pushed it again more forcefully, causing Helen Greenway to fall forward.

Helen stumbled and began to wring her hands. She sobbed softly to herself.

Nurse Burns approached her and spoke in an incredibly soft and gentle voice, asking if she would like a cup of tea.

"My daughter!" Helen exclaimed. "Is there any news? I need to know how she is! No one has told me anything!"

"You were asleep," Nurse Burns said, as she patted Helen's hand. "If you promise to sit down, I'll go and see what I can find out for you."

Helen sat down and waited for the news.

CHAPTER 1

D OWN THE HALL, NURSE Burns ran into Doctor Christiansson removing his surgical mask as he rushed through the surgery doors.

"I need to get some fresh air," he said. He walked to the end of the corridor, flung the door to the roof access open wide.

Nurse Burns followed.

He lit a cigarette. Asked her if she wanted one. She declined.

After he took a drag, he said, "Grace, the Greenway girl, had been doing so well. But now that the clots have burst, it's touch and go in there."

"I'm certain she is in the best of care."

"She is now!" Christiansson said. "Now that the team of experts have arrived and taken control of the situation! I've been in there since it happened. It's been a relentless evening. We thought, I mean, we nearly lost her back there."

Nurse Burns gasped. "I will take one of those," she said. She decided to accept a cigarette after-all. She lit it up, ingested a long drag and then coughed.

"But we haven't given up yet. She lost consciousness again. It's a good thing probably. We need to stop the bleeding. We hope to keep her mind intact."

Nurse Burns and Doctor Christiansson began to pace the length of the roof. Below them sirens roared, and lights flashed.

"Her mum, Helen, is not handling things well."

"All I can tell you is," he stepped on his cigarette butt then opened the door. "Her daughter is in the best of hands."

"Nothing more?"

"Not at this time Nurse Burns. I wouldn't want you to oversell it."

"That's not much to tell her though. It's not much to tell her at all."

"Tell her to pray to whoever she believes in if she does follow that kind of belief system. And if she doesn't then tell her to send out all the positive energy she has within her heart. To send it out to the universe. To think positively and without a doubt. To believe her daughter will pull through this," Christiansson said.

They made their way back down the stairs.

"Thank you, doctor."

"Now I need to get back in there." The surgery doors swung closed behind him.

CHAPTER 2

Nurse Burns returned to Grace's room, finding Helen sitting in the exact spot she had left her. She refilled her glass of water and then kneeled down at Helen's side.

"I just saw Doctor Christiansson and he said Grace is doing fine. She's holding her own in there."

"My daughter, is holding her own?"

"Yes."

"Did he tell you what happened?"

"Yes, it was as they predicted. The clots have burst."

Helen put her hand over her mouth. She sobbed.

"Doctor Christiansson said the best thing you can do for your daughter is to pray, if you believe in prayer. Also, to take care of yourself. Get some rest. It's been an awfully long night. Now, why don't you climb back up here into Grace's bed and take a little nap? I'll awaken you if anything changes, I promise."

"I am exhausted," Helen admitted.

Helen snuggled up in her daughter's bed. She imagined she could still feel the warm imprint her daughter had so recently left there. She wrapped her arms around herself, and she sobbed. At first the tears came slowly, but then they multiplied into more tears. Sobs and tears, faster and faster and faster—almost like contractions.

Only sixteen years ago, Helen's daughter had been born right here in this very hospital. Grace was her second child, her only girl. Grace was her pride and joy.

Her first child, Daryl, had kept her in labour for forty-six hours. At times, she thought he was never going to come out. Not Grace. She had popped out and entered the world for the first time like she didn't want to miss a moment of it.

Helen remembered Grace didn't sleep a lot, even as a small child. Her daughter was afraid of missing out on life. From the first, she was in awe of everything, the light, and the colours. However, Grace didn't find her true destiny until she started to learn her numbers. When she discovered symmetry in the natural world around her that's when Grace's passion really took flight.

Helen thought about the family she once had. A loving husband, Benjamin. A brave and courageous son, Daryl. A very precious daughter, Grace. She remembered the good times they shared visiting Taronga Zoo. Going to the Powerhouse Museum. Watching movies with popcorn. Eating their evening meals together. Simple but happy days. How Helen missed them.

She hummed to herself, and tried to fall asleep again, but the memories were all too fresh, too alive, and too raw.

She sat up and remembered earlier that day when she and her daughter had been laughing and chatting.

It was like something had switched off in Grace's mind. Like she had popped a fuse. One moment she was animated, full of life, and then she was catatonic and then it was like she wasn't Grace anymore. It had all happened so fast.

Life was like that though, one moment you had a family. Then two men in blue uniforms arrived. They said a drunk driver had killed my husband and son.

On that horrible night, Helen recalled asking the two men what the punch line was. She was certain there had to be one. It must have been a joke. It was no joke. This was confirmed when the two caskets were carried up the aisle in the church. Then buried under the ground. No joke indeed.

That was then and this is now. Now, her daughter was down there fighting for her life, and she was where? In bed trying to sleep!

Helen threw back the covers and began pacing up and down the room. She thought about who was to blame: Vincente Marino.

Helen considered his selfishness, his arrogance. It was his fault and only his fault, and if her daughter died from this, then one day she would make him pay.

✷✷✷

MORNING CAME AND NURSE Burns was on staff once again. She tended to the patients who required immediate assistance first. Then she went into Grace Greenway's room to check on Grace's mum Helen.

The room remained very still, although the blinds had been pulled open. She eased her way in, noticing Helen kneeling on a chair and gazing out of the window.

When she turned to face the nurse, her black mascara ran in trails down her face. She looked like Marilyn Manson.

Helen immediately turned her attention back to what was happening outside the window. She was staring at a tree in the distance. In particular a black raven, sitting on a branch opening and closing its beak as if talking to an imaginary friend.

Helen felt jealous of the bird. A bird free to fly away. To take off at will, but remained by choice. She also envied its lack of emotional attachment. Attachment meant pain, in the end. You always lost the ones you loved the most.

She turned around to face Nurse Burns again. She asked in a soft far away voice, "Any news?"

✳✳✳

"Hasn't Doctor Ackerman been in to see you this morning?" Nurse Burns asked. Doctor Ackerman, the new specialist on Grace's case, had promised to visit Helen Greenway first thing to update her.

Helen's blank expression said it all.

"I'm certain the Specialist Doctor Ackerman will be quickly visiting soon. Why don't I go and check with him?"

"That would be very kind," Helen said as she folded her arms around herself. She turned her attention back to the raven. It jumped a few branches higher up in the tree.

Nurse Burns turned to walk away. She stopped and asked Helen if there was someone she would like her to call—someone who could sit with her. Perhaps a friend or a Chaplain or Minister. Helen shook her head, and then continued staring out of the window at the movements of the raven.

As the door closed behind her, Nurse Burns could hear Helen Greenway softly weeping.

Helen was thinking about the husband and the son she had lost. And also, about the daughter who she feared she may lose. She sobbed and covered her hands over her face like a child would in a now you see me now you don't kind of game.

Only the raven noticed she was playing.

✳✳✳

WHEN NURSE BURNS ARRIVED at the surgery door and tried to enter, her way was blocked. Specific orders from Head Surgeons Drs. Ash and Ackerman indicated that Grace's case may have a turn for the worst.

She returned to Helen Greenway without any specific message. She tried to reassure her everything was going to be all right. Then she changed the subject.

"Would you like something to eat?" Nurse Burns asked, as she poured Helen a cup of hot tea from the recently arrived tray. The tea had been sent for Grace's breakfast. Clearly the doctors hadn't still updated her charts. Nurse Burns would have to check on who had made that error, for budgeting purposes, but for now it served as a small amount of encouragement towards getting some sustenance into Helen Greenway.

"I'm not hungry, or thirsty," she insisted. "I want to see my daughter. I want to see Grace." She let loose a shrieking sob.

Nurse Burns was tidying up the room when Doctor Smith, the hospital's newest surgeon entered with a confused look on his face. He was tall, dark, and handsome, so much so that even a look of confusion made him seem to be ever more attractive to most women; however, Helen Greenway did not notice.

Helen was remembering Grace. How she once sat under a big umbrella tree and read about Einstein's Theory of Relativity or Fibonacci's Liber Abaci. She imagined her daughter on a soft bed of plush grass, shaded and protected in the arms of a tree.

Doctor Smith approached her cautiously, looking first at nurse Burns and then back at Helen Greenway. Helen did not stir or even acknowledge his presence.

"May I see you, outside for a moment?" Doctor Smith asked.

"Yes Doctor," she replied.

They backed out of the room. Helen Greenway didn't even notice.

✳✳✳

"WHAT'S THE MATTER WITH her?" Doctor Smith asked. Nurse Burns put him into the picture.

"She needs to tone it down," he said, "because she is disrupting the other patients. I just came on duty, and there have been several complaints made. This needs to stop. Either we get one of the doctors to approve sedation, or we encourage her to move away from the ward for a little while."

"I'm doing my best," Nurse Burns said a little too defensively.

Doctor Smith took her hand and looked into her eyes. He had learned this move from watching re-aired episodes of E.R. Staff members and patients' hearts alike always melted on the show, ensuring George Clooney's popularity.

"I know you are," he chided, "and I appreciate all you have done. All you are going to do in order to assist both myself and the other patients on the ward."

She smiled back at him but inside thought he was as phony as a two-dollar note.

She turned and made her way back to Helen Greenway's room. Unfortunately, Helen was no longer in it.

CHAPTER 3

"I NEED TO GET out of this room, out into the fresh air," Helen whispered to herself as she snuck past the doctors and nurses. She made her way onto the elevator; certain no one would miss her.

As the doors squished shut, Helen watched the stretchers being pushed, pulled, or escorted along the corridors. She covered her ears when she heard their squeaky or scraping wheels gathering traction. She jumped when one was misdirected and scraped the wall. The hospital staff didn't seem to notice the hullabaloo.

She felt relaxed when the doors were firmly closed behind her. All she had to distract her was the elevator music. A familiar tune from a musical brought back memories of she and Grace bonding as mother and daughter. Early days, before the mathematical gap and teenage years separated them.

Once she arrived on the ground floor, Helen stepped out with a keen sense of purpose and destiny. She wanted to feel the breeze on her face. She wanted to be outside in the calm, fresh eucalyptus scented air.

No one stopped her or questioned her, or even seemed to notice her. She entered the revolving doors and flowed with the current outside.

At the exact same moment, a screeching screaming ambulance pulled into a stop alongside of her with sirens blaring and lights flashing.

The noise was deafening, not at all the kind of peace and solitude Helen had envisaged. She wanted to get away, to escape from it. But the sound seemed to wrench at her, taking away her energy. Her feet seemed to be firmly planted in the concrete.

Unable to move or run, she backed herself up against the wall, and covered her ears. All around her was chaos, pushing, pulling, and scraping instead of the peace and serenity, which she so craved.

Overwhelmed Helen passed-out cold and dropped to the ground.

CHAPTER 4

"Vincente?" Grace sobbed. "Vincente, are you there?"

Grace's eyes were wide open, and she searched around the cold metallic room for him, but he was nowhere.

The men and women in masks leered down at her.

The bright light above her pulsed with heat and energy, forcing her eyes closed once again.

"Vincente?" she whispered repeatedly.

A lone star burned brightly. It danced in front of her eyes. Soft and gently warm at first, it soon burned into her skin.

Then everything went back to black.

CHAPTER 5

"WE ARRIVED AT THE hospital with one patient and found another one on the pavement!" the ambulance driver shouted as the team assessed the situation.

"Two for one emergency," his co-worker said with a smirk.

"First dibs go to our man in the ambulance," the first man said. He and his co-worker jerked the stretcher along the pavement. "Incoming," they said as they pushed their way through the doors.

"There's another one out there," the second man said to the receptionist.

By this time, Helen had already come to and was attempting to stand up. Little white stars flickered and twinkled all around in her head. It was like she was in one of those Wile E. Coyote cartoons. After the Roadrunner had pounded a sledgehammer into the furry beast's head. She tried to steady herself, but her legs went all weak, and she once again dropped to the ground.

"Does anyone know who she is?" a woman inquired. Visitors and hospital staff, recently coming on duty, had gathered around Helen. One staffer spoke into a radio and requested a stretcher and trauma surgeon to immediately report to Emergency.

Helen opened her eyes and looked up. A group of strangers was staring at her. She tried to stand up again, but the strangers encouraged her to remain down.

"Can you tell us who you are? Do you remember your name?" the woman who had spoken into the radio asked.

"Yes, my name is Helen, Helen Greenway."

The woman spoke into the radio again. "On the ground out here in the entryway we have a Caucasian woman. Approximately sixty years of age, name: Helen, Helen Greenway. Anyone know her? Is she a patient? Escaped from the Psych Ward? She is in street clothing, I repeat, she is in street clothing."

A young doctor arrived with his medical bag in tow. He knelt down beside Helen and asked her if she was injured. When she shook her head, he proceeded to check her vital signs.

"I'm fine," Helen said. "It's my daughter who is ill!" Once again she tried to stand up.

"Helen," the doctor said, "you need to stay down, until I am certain your vital signs are normal."

Helen nodded meekly, like a scolded child.

After Helen's vital statistics were deemed acceptable, she was encouraged to stand up. A wheelchair was brought out.

"Now," the doctor said, "you sit down and let's go and find your daughter."

"I can walk," she chided.

"I'll push," he insisted.

✳ ✳ ✳

WHEN THEY ARRIVED ON Grace's floor, Nurse Burns ran towards them. "Thank goodness you're okay Helen!"

"You know her?" the doctor asked.

"Yes, we're kind of old friends," Nurse Burns smiled.

"Well, she fainted outside the building, that's why she is in a wheelchair. I have checked her vitals. She seems e fine, although possibly a little sleep deprived. Also, starving and dehydrated."

"Yes, she's been so focused on her daughter's health, it has been difficult to get anything into her."

"Speak to her doctor then. Perhaps put her onto a drip, if necessary, but we can't have her wandering around in this state. She needs food and water, and she needs it immediately. Who is her daughter's doctor?"

"Her daughter has a team of doctors—Christiansson, Ash, and Ackerman."

The doctor hesitated. He had heard about the operation going on, about the surgeons being called in on an emergency basis. One was flown in overnight. It was a dire situation indeed. He empathized even more now with the woman in the wheelchair.

"In that case, see what you can do," he said to Nurse Burns. Then to Helen, "You need to eat, drink, and then rest, for when your daughter wakes up. You need to be extraordinarily strong for her."

His words did not reach Helen, because she was already fast asleep in the wheelchair.

CHAPTER 6

Helen awoke fifteen minutes later, back in Grace's bed. She had no memory of how she had gotten there. She pressed the button on the bed. Moments later Nurse Burns arrived with a tray full of hot food and fresh coffee.

"I'm afraid I can't eat a thing," Helen said.

"It's either this way or intravenously. You decide Helen. I am going off duty shortly, and I promised the trauma doctor that I would make sure you ate before I left for the night. If you don't comply, then he is going to organize it with your Doctor for you to be on a drip and fed and watered that way."

"I refuse both ways. In fact, I have a phobia about hospital food. I want to get out of here and get something else to eat. Away from here."

"Yes, understandable. I think we can do that," Nurse Burns said as she turned and exited.

In a moment, she returned with her coat on and together she and Helen left the hospital. They were going to a little café just down the street.

It would be a welcome break for both.

CHAPTER 7

"HER BLOOD PRESSURE IS dropping. It's off the charts! If we don't do something now, if we can't stop the bleeding, then we are going to lose her," Doctor Ash said.

All present in the surgery scrambled and moved in closer.

"Blot it, damn-it!" Doctor Ackerman ordered.

There was so much blood pumping out. Even with all hands-on deck they couldn't do enough fast enough. The cardiac machine flat lined.

It screamed.

"We've got to get her back! We've just got to!" Doctor Christiansson exclaimed.

CHAPTER 8

A T THE CAFÉ, HELEN Greenway was digging her fork into a pile of mashed potatoes. She sliced a piece of steak and pushed it between her teeth. She chewed and chewed and tried to swallow but it did not want to go down.

"That's right," Nurse Burns said, "you'll feel better in no time."

Helen felt a chill go through her body, like someone had opened the door on a cold winter's day. The door remained closed, but goose bumps formed on her arms. She folded into herself, trying to keep warm. From somewhere unknown, she heard Grace calling out her name. Seconds later, the Nurse's phone rang.

"This is Doctor Christiansson. I'm calling because I understand you are there with Grace Greenway's mum Helen. Is that correct?"

Nurse Burns nodded but said nothing as she maintained a poker face.

"Grace has just flat-lined, again. I'm uncertain..." He broke off, leaving the dire statement incomplete. He was exhausted.

"I understand," she said. "We'll come right back."

Helen Greenway dropped her fork and tears streamed out of her eyes. Helen ran toward the hospital with the sound of her daughter's voice ringing in her ears.

CHAPTER 9

"Grace, you have got to hold on!" a voice said.

It was a voice Grace recognized as Vincente's. He had gone away. He had left her side and now he was back. He had returned.

"Where have you been?" she asked, all the while searching the room for him. Searching for his cobalt blue eyes.

"I'm here," he said, as he took hold of her hand. "I've always been right here."

"But why can't I see you? I was so frightened." She paused, feeling his hand closing around hers. "And then the lights went out." She paused. "I don't think I can hold on Vincente. I don't think I'm going to make it."

"Yes you will," he said, as tears fell down his cheeks and onto their entwined hands. "I've only just found you! We're newlyweds and you promised you would love me forever."

"I will always love you Vincente. Forever."

"Then you must find a way to stay," he said. "I'm nothing, nothing, without you!" He fell onto his knees, like he had been hit in the heart with a bolt of lightning.

"I'm trying, Love," she said. "But it's so dark, so dark in here. I need to see you!"

"I'm right here," Vincente said, and he squeezed her hand tightly.

"I can hear you. I can feel you. But where are you?"

He stepped into the light.

"I can't see you! Why can't I see you?"

"It's night-time, Love," he said. "And the lights might hurt your eyes. But trust me, I am here. I've been here all along. I promised I would never leave you and I always keep my promises."

"Sing something to me."

He sang the song from her jewelry box, the song, which had become their song.

The operating room was aflutter with all kinds of medical equipment and medical staff who were running around and bumping into one another. When the sound of the flat line ended and the normal tone for her heartbeat resumed, a small cheer rang out in the surgery.

"We did it!" Doctor Ash exclaimed.

"We still have a lot of work to do," Doctor Ackerman reminded him. "Grace has lost a lot of blood. She may need several transfusions and we're still racing against the clock with the clotting."

"I'll speak with her mother," Doctor Christiansson said. "She may be able to donate some more blood. It's always better when a family member donates."

He slapped both of the lead surgeons gently on the back and looked at Grace. He watched the heart monitor for a few seconds, taking it all in. Everything seemed to be normal, or as normal as it could be for a young girl who had just flat-lined twice in less than 24 hours.

✳✳✳

"You're doing brilliantly," Vincente said, as he caressed her forehead.

"I want to stay, but I'm just sooooo tired."

"Remember our wedding day? Remember our house in Manly? How we decorated it together? Remember how you promised me forever, Mrs. Marino?"

"I do remember," she said. Then she looked up, and the light that had once been far above her, seemed to have moved, closer to her now. It was like a star pulling her while at the same time fighting for its own life. Grace was very tired, and she longed to rest, to be at peace. She longed to go into the star shine.

It was a ball of starlight. It twisted and turned, pushing inwards and outwards all the while beckoning for Grace to come and join it. It was a Fibonacci star; a part of the Milky Way and the only thing holding her back from joining with it, as her very own Golden Mean, Vincente.

"Grace," Vincente said.

His voice seemed to be so extremely far away, and she felt very cold and very much alone. The searing heat at the core of the star breathed upon her and warmed her from a distance. To join with it would only be a breath away. It would be so easy.

"Oh no!" Doctor Ash shouted. "Not again! Not so soon! We're losing her!"

"She's lost too much blood!" Doctor Ackerman exclaimed. "Where's Doctor Christiansson with the news about the blood transfusion? We need to give her more blood immediately! We can't wait for her mum. Begin the transfusion now."

Seconds later, foreign blood was being pumped into Grace's limp body.

At first, her body seemed to accept it. To drink it greedily. However, it wasn't long before the new blood rejected the old blood.

Then the battle really began.

"Vincente?"

"Yes, love."

"I'm afraid of dying."

"It's not your time," he said. "It can't be your time."

"How do you know?" she asked as heat raged within her body. She was burning up and then icy cold. All the while the starlight beckoned.

"Because I only live for you."

"But this feels bad, very bad, Vincente."

"What does it feel like, love? Tell me."

"It feels like I am up above the ground and I'm looking down at myself on the stretcher in the surgery. I can see them poking, prodding, and scuttling around."

"They are helping you, love."

"Yes, but it hurts me so."

"Can you stay? You must stay. Please. Do it for me. For your husband."

"I can't bear the pain. I want—I want—"

"I know what you want Grace," he said. "I bet you would love to see your mum."

"But Vincente, my mum is dead."

"No, she's alive and she's on her way now. Hold on."

"How can she be though? One moment we were at Manly, and no one existed in the world, no one but you and I—and now—this. Lots of people everywhere. And extreme pain, relentless pain."

"Remember the clots Grace?"

"The clots, yes."

"There was more than one. They burst. We're all fighting for you. Don't let go Grace. You have got to fight, too. I love you. I can't let you go. Please don't let go!"

"Vincente, I am sooooo tired! Perhaps it is time—for you to let me go."

"Never!" he shouted. He watched as her eyelids fluttered and closed. Finally, he whispered into her ear, "Rest then, my love. Yes, close your eyes and rest. I will sing you a lullaby, but please don't leave me."

She continued to breathe in and out. Vincente sang more of their special song with tears streaming down his cheeks.

CHAPTER 10

Helen and Nurse Burns returned to the hospital where Doctor Christiansson was waiting. "How are you feeling, Helen?" he asked, all the while guiding her towards the surgery.

"I'm fine, it's my daughter I'm worried about!"

"I understand you were feeling unwell earlier, and passed out? Is that correct?" He looked at Nurse Burns and she nodded.

"I did faint, but what does that have to do with anything? What is happening with my daughter?"

"I'm concerned we may need to take some blood from you, for a transfusion. It's always best when it comes from someone in direct relation to the patient."

Helen nodded, then put her hands over her face. She felt exhausted beyond belief, but she wanted to be able to help. She needed to be able to help.

"Let's get you upstairs to the blood room for observation." Then to Nurse Burns, "Has Helen eaten anything lately?"

Nurse Burns nodded and showed him how much. It wasn't even enough to keep a bird alive.

"There, there," Nurse Burns said to Helen as they made their way along the corridor.

Doctor Christiansson's pager sounded. "One moment please," he said. He moved away from them. "Change of plans. I need to take you to see your daughter—now. Come along and get scrubbed up."

Nurse Burns made a move to return to her station, but Doctor Christiansson asked her to remain.

"Before we go in," he warned, "I must tell you Mrs. Greenway—Helen—that we already lost your daughter a couple of times back there."

"Lost her?"

"Yes. Meaning that she flat lined. Her heart stopped, but only for a few moments."

Helen fought back a sob.

They entered the surgery.

Grace was unconscious on the operating table.

"Mum!" Grace exclaimed.

Helen went to her side and took her hand into hers. She looked into her daughter's eyes.

"This is Grace's mother, Helen," Doctor Ackerman explained to the others on the medical team.

"Thank you for coming, and so quickly," Doctor Ash said. "It's good to meet you. Grace is a very brave girl indeed."

"How is she doing, I mean really?" Helen asked.

"It was touch and go there, but her vitals have stabilized. We're keeping an eye on her and she's holding her own."

"Thank you," Helen said. "Thank you all!" and she felt a big lump in her throat.

"Uh, excuse me Doctor Ash," one of the nurses who had been keeping an eye on Grace's vital signs spoke up. "Could we have you over here for a moment, please?"

He went to her and immediately his eyes zeroed in on the screen.

"Mum! It's me, Grace, mum!"

"She can't hear you," Vincente said.

"What? What do you mean she can't hear me? She's standing right there! Of course, she can hear me! Mum, it's me, Grace...Vincente and me. We're married now and we love each other, mum. Mum!"

"Love, she can't hear you," Vincente repeated, all the while caressing her hand. He reached over and kissed her on the forehead.

"She can't hear me, but she can see me. There—she's holding my hand. Wait a minute—she can't see you, can she? Why can't she see you or hear you, Vincente?"

"I don't know."

"Vincente, are you dead?"

Vincente laughed, ran his fingers through his hair, "Of course I'm not dead. I'm right here beside you, holding your hand."

"But the others can't see you, not the doctors or my mum. They move around you, through you. Why can't they see you or hear you? Why am I the only one who knows that you are here? Am I dead? Are we both dead?"

"We are together always because we love each other. Our love is stronger than everyone and everything."

Grace's spirit had been drifting around the room before, but now she re-entered her body.

Once inside, she tried to fight the pain, at first. Then she tried to live the pain, to go with it, but it was too much for her to handle. She couldn't hold on. She fragmented.

"Her vital signs are falling! We're losing her all over again!" Doctor Ash shouted. Everyone moved closer to Grace's side, pushing Helen out of the way.

"The bleeding had totally stopped," Doctor Ackerman confirmed. "She was doing so well. I can't find any reason for this sudden relapse other than..." He hesitated and looked over at Helen Greenway standing away from the table, wringing her lands like Lady Macbeth.

"Get her out of here!" Doctor Ash shouted.

"What are they saying now, Vincente?" Grace asked.

"They are blaming your mum for your relapse. When you returned to your body and came back out again, something happened. They think you are dying."

"But I'm not dying! I want to live!"

"We're losing her!" Doctor Ackerman shouted. "Clear the decks!" he exclaimed as he moved in and began cardiac resuscitation.

"No, I won't leave her!" Helen shouted as she was pushed through the swinging doors and into the corridor.

"Mum!" Grace shouted, "Mum!"

"She's bleeding again," Doctor Ash confirmed. "We've got more clots here. I can't count how many. I don't know how long she can hold on!"

"We're doing everything that we can for her."

Grace's spirit slipped back into her body. She tried to make herself stand up. In her head a kaleidoscope of colours began to swirl and twirl until she could no longer see or hear Vincente.

"Vincente don't leave me!" she screamed.

 ✳✳✳

"Vincente?" Doctor Ash asked. "Who is Vincente?"

"He's the boy who put her in the hospital," Doctor Christiansson replied.

"Perhaps we should contact him and ask him to come to the hospital?"

"It's the middle of the night? It might not be possible to get him here."

"Just do it!" Doctor Ash shouted. "We need all the help we can get!"

"Grace, listen to me," Doctor Ash said as he leaned in closer to her. "We are doing everything we can for you. I hope that you can hear me. We heard you. We are calling Vincente. He will be here and at your side soon. So please hold on. Be strong."

Grace could not hear him. She was somewhere in the dark all alone.

CHAPTER 11

O UTSIDE IN THE LOBBY, Helen Greenway whispered into the phone, "Hello, Vincente, I'm sorry to disturb you so late."

"Who is this?"

"Sorry," she hesitated and then continued after identifying herself. "It's Grace. Grace is the reason I am calling you so late. It's her mum, Helen Greenway, speaking."

"Is she okay? She's not...?" he stopped himself, and his voice trailed away. He was afraid to hear what was coming next. Had he killed her? He couldn't stand it, if that were the case, although he knew that it wasn't his fault. He couldn't have known. His mind snapped back to the present. He was fairly certain that Helen Greenway had already answered. On the other end of the phone there was complete silence.

"Are you there, Vincente?" she asked, as she awaited his reply. She had explained it all, stated her case. He was silent. Reluctant to come to the hospital? Surely not. No, he probably just hadn't fully woken up yet. When there was still no reply she prodded, "Grace, my Grace, needs you, Vincente."

His head snapped back with a sense of relief to know she was still alive and breathing, "I'll be there first thing in the morning."

"No, please come straightaway. Grace needs you now. She is calling for you. The doctors say you need to come to the hospital now, before it's too late."

Vincente's head was reeling from being woken up in the middle of the night and with thoughts of how he was going to get to the hospital. He would need to wake up his mum and ask her to drive him there and then she would be filled with all kinds of questions. Not to mention, how would he get home?

"Please say yes, and I'll send a taxi over for you. Just a moment," Helen held her hand over the phone. A nurse confirmed a car would be sent to Vincente's house to pick him up and return him home. "A car will be sent to pick you up Vincente. Please confirm that you will come to the hospital to see my daughter. She is asking for you. Please."

"Okay, but give me a few minutes to get dressed and to leave a note for my mum."

"I need to confirm your address," the receptionist on Helen's end of the phone asked after checking the hospital's records.

"Yes, that's correct," Vincente said.

"The car is on the way, please be waiting."

"I will be," Vincente said, as he signed off and began to pull on his black jeans and white t-shirt. He combed his hair, and then threw a red hoodie over his head, which mussed it all up again.

Next he took two steps at a time down the stairs. He wrote a short note to his mum and stuck it to the fridge. Seconds later, the vehicle arrived.

He was in the car, buckled up and en-route to the hospital. He rested his head on his arm and watched the darkness fly by.

Every now and again the face in the moon seemed to beckon. The man the moon looked oddly familiar, some kind of a cross between Mark Twain and Albert Einstein.

He focused his mind on the moon and the stars, trying to keep himself from falling asleep.

He wanted to be wide-awake. He wanted to...

✳ ✳ ✳

H ELEN WAS PROUD OF herself for she had convinced Vincente to come to the hospital.

Although Helen was kind of baffled as to why her daughter had been calling out his name. What kind of a hold did he have on her heart, for her to call out to him like this? Perhaps she had underestimated him. Or maybe he meant more to her daughter than Helen realized? He was just a high school boy, a classmate, a crush. Then again, hadn't she herself married her own high school sweetheart?

Helen paced up and down the corridor. When Nurse Burns came out she said, "I can't stand it! Not knowing what's happening in there with my daughter! It's all too much!'"

Nurse Burns understood the strain that Helen Greenway was under, but her over-reacting and general impulse to panic had a ripple effect on the other patients, and to family members who were waiting to hear news about their own loved ones.

Nurse Burns guided Helen by the firm place in her back away to a quiet corner, where she spoke to her in a whisper, "Your daughter is in the best of hands. I know it is difficult, but you must try to remain calm."

"If only I would have been able to remain with her, to offer my support," Helen said.

"Grace is holding her own in there, and the doctors are only thinking about her—and what she wants and what she needs. Your daughter's survival is the hospital's number one priority."

"Yes, but I'm her mum! Aren't I owed any explanations? Don't I have any rights around here?"

"Indeed, you do have rights, but you have been given an important task, to bring Vincente here. I understand he's on the way?"

"Yes he is. But I might have been able to help my daughter, if you hadn't pushed me out of the room."

"Helen," Nurse Burns said somewhat crossly, "your daughter's state altered when you were with her. You seemed to cause her nothing but distress in those moments." She hesitated. "The doctors noticed this change in your daughter's stability. That's why they removed you from the operating room. It was for Grace's sake."

"But there is no reason for Grace, to decline—because of me. I love her. She's my life."

"Well, the evidence spoke for itself."

"If I'm not needed here," she said pouting. "I might as well go downstairs and wait for the Marino boy. I need to do something."

"It sounds like a very good idea," Nurse Burns said. She patted Helen on the back of her hand, but this time Helen pulled her hand away. She stuffed both of her hands into her pockets and sauntered off along the hallway. The sound of her boot heels echoed as she went.

"Please ask Reception to buzz us up here when he arrives," Nurse Burns shouted, as the elevator doors closed.

"Will do," Helen answered.

✳ ✳ ✳

AS THE ELEVATOR DOORS swung open on the ground floor, Helen stepped out into the reception area. Immediately she spotted Vincente. He was moving within the revolving doors; his hands jammed into his jeans pockets and shoulders hunched.

Helen stood still for a moment, examining the boy who had put her daughter in the hospital. He looked disheveled and out of his comfort zone. Still, he was very handsome in his red hoodie, which made his blue eyes seem even bluer. He looked like a cross between James Dean and Robert Redford.

She walked towards him. He had not yet noticed her.

When he flashed his eyes in her direction she was caught off guard. For a moment, she couldn't breathe. He was not your average boy. There was something, something quite different about him.

"Hi Vincente," Helen said, proffering her hand to shake his. She was a little bit overwhelmed and so she introduced herself to him as if they had not met before.

Vincente thought the introduction was kind of strange, since they had met very recently. He gave her a pass since she had big bags under her eyes and looked like she had been sleeping in her clothes.

He accepted her offered hand and shook it firmly. He allowed her to tuck her arm under his and to lead him to the front desk. Helen asked the receptionist to confirm his arrival and to relay it to the eighth floor.

Helen then led him towards the elevator. They stood side by side in front of the doors, entwined but still virtual strangers as they made their way upstairs.

After a couple of floors, Vincente felt the need to ask about Grace, about how she was doing and so he did. Helen explained how she had not been informed about her daughter's condition. However, she could confirm that Grace had been asking for Vincente.

"I'm happy to help her in any way I can," Vincente said. It was true —he was happy to help her—but he still couldn't figure out why she was calling him back to the hospital in the middle of the night. He kind of felt sorry for her, if she had such a sad and lonely life that there was no one else she could call for help.

Vincente looked straight ahead at his reflection in the elevator doors. He ran his fingers through his disheveled hair hoping to tame it, but his attempt was unsuccessful.

"Have you any idea Vincente, why my daughter would be asking for you like this?"

"To be honest, it's a mystery to me. Perhaps, she is deluded into..."

"Deluded into what?"

"I don't know. We hardly know each other. Besides, she's just not my type."

"By that you mean that my daughter isn't popular enough or pretty enough for you?" Helen asked with a nasty edge to her voice, which didn't get by Vincente.

He was trapped in an elevator with a woman, who had her arm wrapped around his. Her fingernails were now grappling his sleeves like talons.

"Ouch. Uh, no, I didn't mean that," Vincente said, as the bell indicating that they had arrived on the eighth floor rang. The doors flung open. Vincente pulled himself away from Helen and stepped out, and moved towards the reception area. There were other people over there, and most importantly witnesses—in case Helen Greenway totally wigged out.

Helen remained frozen outside the elevator, but she still had Vincente pinned to the spot with a stare.

Vincente looked over at Helen and realized he hadn't exactly made a good impression. But then again, it was the middle of the night, and he was still half asleep, and he had no idea why he was here. Sure, he knew that Grace Greenway had a crush on him, but so did half of the girls at school. When you were hailed an all-around sports star, it was par for the course.

Moments later, Vincente was being led along the corridor by one of the Doctors. Helen followed behind, with her eyes firmly planted on the back of Vincente's head.

Ackerman introduced himself. He filled Vincente in on the details, then they scrubbed up and donned the necessary medical garb.

"I understand you are a very good friend of Grace's?"

"Uh, kind of, sort of."

Doctor Ackerman ignored the noncommittal reply. "Grace has been asking for you for quite some time now. She will be incredibly happy, to know that you are here for her."

"Uh, glad I can be of service."

"Son," Doctor Ackerman continued, "Grace's condition is stable now. She had a tough time of it there, a very tough time. And, well…"

"How tough?"

"That's uh, confidential, but let's just say, it was touch and go."

"You mean to tell me that she nearly died?"

"I mean things haven't been good. And please don't say or do anything to upset or distress her. Happy thoughts only today, okay?"

"Happy thoughts?"

"Yes," Doctor Ackerman, said. "Now, follow me."

✳✳✳

THEY ENTERED THE SURGERY theatre side by side through the swinging doors. The medical team parted the way for Vincente like he was a rock star.

He immediately zeroed in on Grace. She was in the middle of a table with several machines tethered to her like tentacles.

He took a deep breath and moved closer to the table. He was afraid, although he didn't know exactly why. Perhaps it was because there were pairs of piercing eyes watching him. What were they expecting him to do —a miracle?

He looked at Grace's prostrate body. He saw her chest moving up and down.

Grace was breathing. She was alive. He saw her chestnut hair falling over her shoulders. He saw her eyelids fluttering, like a nervous tick. She was alive in there somewhere behind the shutters.

He stepped closer, and his body bumped into her hand. It was there by her side, and it was open.

Vincente took Grace's hand into his.

He said her name.

Her hand was cool and did not respond to his touch. He closed his hand around hers and said, "Grace." He waited, but nothing happened. She was unconscious. She couldn't feel him or hear him, so what was he doing here? What was he supposed to do now? He looked around the room, at the vacant faces. They were no help. No help at all.

Yet, all eyes were still on him. What should he say? What should he do? He wanted to run from the room.

Vincente wanted nothing more than to return to the warmth of his own bed.

CHAPTER 12

GRACE HAD RE-ENTERED HER body, but her senses were stifled. She could not feel Vincente holding her hand although she could see that he was doing so.

"Grace, it's me, Vincente," he said, hoping that she would acknowledge his presence in some way.

Grace heard him, but his voice sounded different. Distant.

"Talk to her," Doctor Ash prompted. "Talk to her about anything!"

The medical team moved closer. The only sounds heard were the machines.

Beads of sweat began to form on Vincente's forehead. He said, "We miss you, Grace. We miss you at school. You've been away for too long." Vincente realized this dialogue was lame, but he was just going with the flow. He was trying to establish normal conversation; unfortunately, it was all one-sided.

Grace questioned his identity. Who was this strange boy with the short blond hair and dark eyes and red sweatshirt? If he were her Vincente, he wouldn't be talking to her about school. School!? That's where they faced the raven-eating tree!

"We won the cricket match the other day!" Vincente said, overly enthusiastic. He ran his fingers through his hair again. He tried to jam his fists into his pockets, but with the surgical stuff on, it wasn't possible. However, the mere attempt at his normal coping mechanism made him feel more relaxed.

Grace wondered if someone was playing a trick on her. She looked at all the unfamiliar faces, the staring eyes. She didn't know most of them, but they were able to see this Vincente. They were watching him.

Grace removed herself from her body and began to float around the room.

From above, she watched this Vincente. He didn't seem like himself at all. He was cold. She couldn't feel his touch, but she so wanted to. When she noticed he was holding onto her hand, her heart began to thump and pound. Too quickly she jumped back into her body.

The heart machine responded with another flat line.

***

Grace looked towards the light as tears poured down her face. Below her, the hospital attendants were running around the surgery like the world was ending. She knew the only thing ending was her own life.

She had been fighting the starlight, which had been beckoning to her. Calling for her.

Now it was blinking and nodding, and she realized that it was her time to go. Time to move towards it. It was finally time to burn with the Fibonacci star.

"Tell her that you love her!" someone shouted.

"But I don't!" Vincente replied meekly.

Soon, the starlight grew hotter and hotter and hotter. It was no longer waiting for her to come to it. It was coming for her.

"I love you, Grace!" he shouted.

Too late.

***

As they led Vincente out of the room, he was still shouting out the words. True, to him they were meaningless, untrue sentiments. Words he was only saying to be kind, to save her from the brink.

He shouted it out again. This time his voice echoed along the corridors and out into the universe, "I love you, Grace Greenway!"

"I love you too, Vincente!" she shouted back to him. With the mayhem and the hoopla as they attempted to save her life—he did not hear her.

Suddenly the hot star began to spin and rotate. Soon it was no longer coming toward her or burning her with its heat. Instead, it threw out pulsing waves and became a neutron star.

Grasp on her gone, "I want to live," Grace Greenway declared to herself. "I want to live."

CHAPTER 13

TWO DAYS LATER, GRACE Greenway awoke clot-free and no longer in danger. She would need to be monitored closely for the next little while, but soon she would be able to go home.

"Vincente; Mum," she said groggily, as tears streamed down her cheeks. They were tears of pure happiness for being alive. Tears of gratitude for having this moment to share with the two people she loved the most in the world.

She outstretched her arms, to embrace both of them together. They folded into her, against her. She felt the warmth and strength of their bodies, almost like she was gaining strength with their combined energies.

Vincente and Helen were looking at each other, waiting for Grace to let them go.

"Are you in any kind of pain?" Helen asked.

"I feel tired, that's all, Mum."

"I'm glad you're feeling better," Vincente said. "I'll go and get the doctors—let them know you're awake."

He turned and backed out of the room. He stood there for a moment, feeling grateful that she had recovered fully. Thinking that now perhaps he had done his duty, and he could go home. He hoped that she had forgotten or had not heard what he had been forced to say to her in the operating studio. He was glad Helen Greenway hadn't been there to hear his forced and false declaration.

He accepted the fact that he had done the right thing in order to help her. His only hope now was that this would be the end of it. He wanted his old life back again. And that life did not include Grace Greenway.

***

"So, mum, do you like him?" Grace asked.

"He's a nice boy," Helen said. "I can see why you are attracted to him."

"Attracted to him?" Grace exclaimed. "I'm more than attracted to him, Mum. We're married! See!" she said as she pushed her ring finger towards her mother. There were no rings.

"It's okay Grace," Helen cooed, noticing her daughter's distress. "It's okay if you are a little out of it. You've been through a great deal over these past few days."

"Mum, it's true! You don't believe me, do you?"

"Uh, now don't upset yourself, dear" Helen said, as she patted her daughter on the hand.

"We're married, Mum. Married!" Grace said again. The doors swung open, and Helen escaped into the hallway, leaving her daughter in a distressed condition and all alone.

Strange, Grace thought. Very strange. Where are my rings?

***

In the corridor, Helen Greenway barreled headlong into Doctor Ackerman. He was on the way, after hearing the good news from Vincente that she was awake and lucid.

"Oh. Doctor Ackerman!" Helen exclaimed.

"Oh my, what's happened? Should I go straight in? Has she relapsed? Vincente said she was doing well. Awake and talking. Completely alert."

"That she is, Doctor Ackerman. She is up and talking but she seems to be under the delusion that she is married to Vincente Marino!"

"Oh my, how can that be?"

"She told me they were married. She and Vincente. Plus, she tried to show me her rings. She was very distressed to find them missing."

Vincente stepped out of the open elevator then, carrying a tray of cappuccinos. He made his way toward them.

Doctor Ackerman looked at Vincente and stopped him with the wave of his hand. He then led Vincente towards the seating area where he asked him to remain. Ackerman returned to Helen.

Vincente sat down and began sipping from one of the cups.

"I would like to speak with Grace—alone—for a few moments," Doctor Ackerman said. "Please wait here with Vincente, Helen, I'll have a chat with you both afterwards."

Helen seated herself beside Vincente. He offered her a cuppa. She politely refused it and then folded her arms around herself.

Vincente knew something was up, but he had no idea what. He had another sip of coffee and hoped they would let him go home soon. He was exhausted, and fairly certain Helen wanted her daughter all to herself.

After all, in his opinion, this was a family matter.

***

When Doctor Ackerman exited Grace's room, the concerned expression on his face said it all.

Helen immediately stood up and went to his side.

Vincente also immediately noticed the doctor's somber expression. Whatever was happening in Grace's room, it definitely wasn't good news. He wondered if he would ever return home.

"Helen," Doctor Ackerman said, "we need to talk—in private. Please come to my office."

"What about?" Helen averted her eyes away from where Vincente was sitting.

"He'll be fine where he is until we return," Doctor Ackerman said. Then to Vincente, "If you could please wait, we'll put you into the picture shortly."

Vincente nodded, and then began to sip on the second cappuccino— Helen's drink. After all she didn't want it, and he had paid for it. Why let it get cold? Besides, he needed the caffeine to keep him awake. He took out his phone and played a game of Bejeweled Blitz, and then scanned through Facebook. He had one message from Missy Malone. She wanted to get together later. He hoped that he wasn't going to be too tired from all this Grace Greenway business.

Curious, he went to Grace's door and looked in through the glass. Grace was fast asleep. Strange, he thought, since she had just woken up. Vincente returned to his seat. As he thought about Grace, he took another sip of Helen's coffee. He drank Grace's cup too, before they came back to get him.

CHAPTER 14

"HELEN, WE WERE HOPING Grace's memory loss would have been rectified. However, it seems like we now have additional concerns."

"So, she told you, too? That she is married to Vincente?"

"Yes, and she not only told me that they were married, but she described everything in great detail. It was almost like she was living through it again. It was so real, such a complete picture. I could almost hear that romantic song playing in the background."

"What romantic song?" Helen asked.

"She said it was a song from an old jewelry box."

"Yes, I remember that one. Grace's father and I gave it to her for Christmas when she was a little girl."

"Ah, a childhood gift, which she has now imagined to be her wedding song. Your daughter definitely has a very vivid imagination," Doctor Ackerman said.

"So, what do we do Doctor? Tell her the truth? We have to tell her the truth."

"The mind is a very fragile thing. Perhaps when Grace was fighting for her life, she created this situation as a survival mechanism. To give herself something to live for, to fight for. It's a primal technique. When we are at death's door, we sometimes create or fabricate an alternative reality."

"But my daughter already had so much to live for!" Helen said.

"Yes, you think so and I think so, but would Grace agree?"

"So, what are you saying doctor? What do we do?"

There was a knock on the door. Doctor Christiansson poked his head inside. "Pardon me for interrupting. Doctor Ackerman, you wanted to have a word?"

"Yes, if you could give us one moment please Helen," Ackerman said. He motioned for her to sit down and then he and Doctor Christiansson left.

Helen mindlessly flipped through a magazine or two. The doctors privately discussed Grace's precarious situation.

"I'm afraid we have no choice in this matter," Doctor Christiansson said. "We must go along with Grace's fantasy. She is not strong enough to be able to face the truth at this time. If pushed too hard, the consequences could be quite detrimental."

"I agree," Doctor Ackerman concurred. "The best thing we can do for Grace, until she is ready to hear the truth, is to enforce her own delusions. The thing is, we need to ensure Vincente is on board with this. We need to tell him everything Grace has told us. We need to get him to agree to go along with the ruse, until Grace is ready, I mean strong enough both mentally and physically to be able to handle the truth."

"Yes, the Marino boy was able to help Grace before, and I'm hoping he will be able to help her again," Christiansson said.

"And when she is well enough, strong enough, then we will tell her the truth," Doctor Ackerman confirmed.

"I don't like it," Helen said, once the doctors filled her in on their plan. "We will be feeding her imagination, and fostering lies and more lies."

"But they aren't lies to Grace. She believes every single word of it, and she is the one who we have to put first here," Doctor Ackerman said.

"Well, what if the boy doesn't agree to go along with it?" Helen asked.

"He has to," Ackerman said. "There is no alternative. Grace has come so far, and she's on her way back to recovering her health, physically. Her body may not survive another relapse. Grace's mental stability is critical at this time."

"Grace has created this dream, and Vincente is a big part of it. He must agree to help her. We have to convince him of his importance to her," Doctor Christiansson said.

"How long will we all have to play this game?" Helen asked.

"We will play until she is ready," Dr. Christiansson said, "and not a moment longer."

"What do I tell the boy then?" Helen asked. "How can I make him understand when I can't even understand this completely myself? I don't like the idea of deceiving my own daughter."

"He will have to trust us, to trust Grace. When she is ready to face reality–to hear the truth—then and only then will things return to the way they were before," Ackerman said.

"I'll do my best to convince him."

"Good luck," Doctor Ackerman said.

"If you need me to help..." Dr. Christiansson interjected, "...if you want me to speak with him, to clarify anything, then send the boy to me."

"Thank you," Helen said.

CHAPTER 15

Helen went into the ladies' room and washed her hands. Being in the hospital 24/7 seemed to necessitate a paranoia of germs.

She held her right hand out, and noticed it was shaking. She had no idea how she was going to convince the boy to go along which such a strange pack of lies. Anyone with experience in life surely realized truth was always best. Yet here she was being forced to convince Vincente to be an accomplice in support of Grace's delusion.

She reached into her handbag and felt around, producing two sticks of lippy. She applied one and somehow it made her feel a little bit better. Another venture into her handbag, produced perfume and sprayed a small amount behind her ears. Now she was ready to go out and speak with Vincente.

Helen closed the door behind her and entered the busy corridor. She was pushed up against the wall for a few seconds, as hospital staff bulldozed a gurney through. She took a deep breath, composed herself, and then began walking towards the waiting room.

She spotted Vincente and he spotted her. She waved, and then wondered if she was being a little over familiar. She reined it in by placing her hand on the leather strap of her bag. Now she looked like someone who was afraid of being mugged.

Vincente saw Helen Greenway making rapid movement towards him. He looked at her for a second, and then looked at his feet. He immediately noticed she had dolled herself up and wondered why. Perhaps she had her eye on one of the doctors? Wasn't it a little soon after her husband died? He wasn't sure, but he was not one to judge neither what people said, nor what people or did.

Helen took a seat opposite to Vincente and said his name. He looked up and waited for her to say something else, but she didn't. He looked back down at his feet again. He was so tired, dead tired, but the three large coffees had wired his mind.

She said his name again and leaned forward, her elbows resting on her knees.

Vincente sat back in his chair and pretended he needed to stretch and yawn. The silence was becoming increasingly uncomfortable.

Helen waited for him to finish moving about, and then went straight into it. "Vincente, I need your help with something, something rather personal."

He hesitated and leaned in, now curious.

"May I speak freely and openly with you?" she whispered.

Vincente was genuinely curious now. He'd been hit on before by older women—but not usually women who were this old—and not by women who were mothers of his schoolmates.

He suddenly felt uncomfortable. His initial reaction was to cut her off right there and be completely blunt with her. Then again, although he wasn't interested in the least, he was curious as to what she was going to say. How she was going to go about it. And he wondered, maybe if the shock of what Grace had been through had taken its toll on her, too. So instead of saying anything, he sat still and waited.

Helen leaned in closer, "What I have to ask you is rather embarrassing," she hesitated and giggled nervously. "I mean, it's ludicrous! But I hope you will say yes and agree to help me nevertheless."

Helen batted her eyelashes and hesitated. She straightened up and then leaned back in again. This time even closer to Vincente, so much so that their knees were almost touching. Then she seemed to wave her hand, creating a gap between them, and letting her hand brush ever so lightly against his knee.

She was so close he could feel her breath on his face.

Vincente moved back in his chair awkwardly. Pulled his feet under the seat. Crossed his arms against his chest. He focused his attention on the floor. He fought the urge to take out his phone to distract himself from the crazy scenario.

"It's Grace, Vincente. She seems to have. Well, this is difficult for me to say. Especially to someone as young as you are, someone who I imagine has a girlfriend already. Or, maybe even more than one girlfriend?" Helen hesitated before dropping the bomb and looked him straight in the eye. She was trying to relate to him, to connect on his terms. If she could bridge the age gap between them, then maybe he would understand. Maybe he would agree.

Vincente thought this was getting embarrassing. He wanted to put her out of her misery, "I do have a girlfriend, uh Mrs. Greenway. We're not exclusive, although we do have an understanding, if you know what I mean?"

Did he just wink? Helen was sure she had seen him wink! And she didn't like it, not one bit.

Vincente wished she'd go away. He was really tired, and all he wanted to do was go home. Impatient and disgusted, he stood.

"Yes, I do uh—understand what you mean Vincente," Helen said awkwardly, "Please sit down."

Vincente did. He crossed his arms again creating a physical barrier between them.

"Vincente, my daughter has a crush on you. You know that don't you?"

"Yes, I know that she likes me. Grace is great! She has saved my life by helping me with math. Without her I would have been thrown off the team by now."

"Did she now? I didn't know that. So, you did kind of know her, one on one then?"

"Not one on one like boyfriend and girlfriend, no. But we were mates. Friends."

"But you're a star cricketer, and you are handsome. I can see why she was, uh, infatuated with you. But what I have to ask you is," she stopped and stammered finding it difficult to get to the point.

"Sorry Mrs. Greenway, but I must cut to the chase. It's been an exceedingly long night and I'm tired. I must tell you that I am flattered by your—errr—by the attention you are showing me, but as I said before, my girlfriend, Missy and I have kind of an understanding."

"I'm sure she won't mind, under the circumstances because you will be helping someone out—someone in need. After all, this is a life-or-death matter," Helen said.

"You are being a little melodramatic now aren't you, Mrs. Greenway?" Vincente uncrossed his arms and moved closer to her. "I'm flattered and everything, but, I mean, can't you find someone more, you know, closer to your age? Like maybe one of the doctors?"

"What!" Helen exclaimed, moving her entire body as far away from Vincente Marino's as it could get while still sitting opposite to him. Then she stood up and moved even further away with her back to him. She took a deep breath, regained her composure just as Vincente gently patted her on the bottom. She jumped, fighting the urge to slap him silly.

"For your information," she corrected now furious, "I don't find you one bit attractive, you silly, silly boy!"

"Sure, sure, I reject you, then you get all nasty—I see what your game is now. But don't play me too much, I might just like it," he moved even closer to her.

"Now you quit that!" Helen said with a trembling voice as Vincente Marino moved in closer and closer to her. She was backed firmly against the front of the chair now – and forced to sit down. Her face was flushed, and her entire body was shaking.

"I've had enough of this nonsense," Vincente said. "I came in here in the middle of the night to help your daughter out...fine. But she's back in the ward now, and I'm hanging around for what? I don't know. Not to be hit on by her mum!"

Helen's face resembled the colour of beetroot. "Vincente, I need a favour from you, so I am going to ignore this miscommunication and come straight out with it. Beating around the bush wasn't a clever idea!"

Vincente nodded impatiently but continued to listen.

"Grace is under the delusion that you and she are married."

"What?"

"It's true. She woke up and is stuck on this idea about the two of you. She has created a fantasy in her mind."

"Married? Grace Greenway and I, married?"

"Yes, that's what she believes."

"So, tell her the truth. Why are you telling me this?"

"Because the doctors believe that we must go along with it, for the time being."

"By 'we' you mean me, right? You expect me to play husband and wife with Grace?"

"I know it is a lot to ask of you Vincente. But if you could find it somewhere in your heart, to help her, it could be a matter of life and death for her."

"This is too much to ask," Vincente said, and he stood up and started to leave the waiting room, "way too much."

Helen caught him, grabbed his arm.

"It's the least you can do! You put her in here, with that hit to the head. You did that! Surely you must have a moral compass somewhere inside, a conscience. Grace wouldn't be in here if it weren't for you! And, as you said, Grace helped you to ensure your spot on the cricket team."

Vincente knew this was all true, although the hit had been an accident. "What is it exactly that you want me to do?"

"Act like a husband would. Be there for her. Speak with her. Hold her hand. My daughter is a bright girl; she will tell you what she needs."

"But what if she wants us to do the things that married people do." He smirked. "Then what?"

"I'm sure before we get to that point, she'll either start to remember the truth or I will tell her."

"Why not save this drama and tell her the truth now?"

"That is of course what I want to do, but the doctors have advised against it," Helen said. "They feel Grace is in too delicate condition to shock her with that much reality at this time."

Vincente felt like he had no choice in the matter, he had to go along with this. While he totally disagreed with the doctors, he would play along. "What about school?" he asked. "I have a game tomorrow—I mean today."

"Grace will remember that you are in school. In the meantime, perhaps you can invite some of the other students from school to visit her. Familiar faces may jog her memory."

"I can't think of anyone she's friends with offhand, but I will try. Now, can I go home?"

"Not until you've spoken with her. And remember, she just told me the news—the two of you were recently married—and I didn't believe her. I ran out of the room and found her doctor. So, I expect that my daughter will be very happy to see you and quite cross to see me. She may also want to introduce you to me as her husband."

"I'll do my best, but I'm not a very good actor, and I've never been a good liar."

"Well then, let's make this an award-winning performance!" Helen coached as they walked towards her Grace's room.

"Here we go!" Vincente said, as he pushed the door open, and held it for his new fictional mother-in-law

CHAPTER 16

G RACE LOOKED UP, AND saw her mum enter her room followed by– Vincente! She sat up, smiling from ear to ear, and opened her arms to him. He moved toward her so slowly that she intuitively knew that something was wrong.

"Darling," Helen said, in a chirpy tone of voice, which startled Vincente. "I had a word with Vincente, and he told me all about it. All about your wedding. Didn't you now, Vincente?"

Vincente first looked at Grace and then at Helen. She was throwing him to the wolves, making him lie. He had no other choice. "Yes, I told your mum all about us," he said. He moved a little closer to Grace, who enclosed him in a heartfelt embrace.

While she was holding him, Grace sensed a distance there, which she had never felt before. She felt like she was holding onto a wooden plank.

They separated and Grace looked deeply into Vincente's eyes. He was hiding something. Or maybe just embarrassed? Perhaps it was just this, that she was being over-affectionate in front of another person. They had been alone before, so this was something that they would have to get used to having other people around to witness their love.

Grace reached out and took his hand into hers and said, "I totally understand how you are feeling, given the circumstances. We're not used to being affectionate like this—around others."

Vincente felt like crud. He was being forced into this, and he felt sorry for Grace, who had no idea he was only acting. But from the sound of it, his performance left a lot to be desired. "Yes, that's it," Vincente said. "You always were very perceptive to my, uh feelings."

Grace continued to observe his discomfort. Vincente, sensing she was watching him very closely and worried that she might become distressed, lifted her hand up to his lips and kissed it. When he looked up, he was staring deep into the eyes of his alleged wife. Alleged on her part, but on his, all he saw was Grace Greenway—a plain Jane, with an above average, nearly genius mathematical ability. They were total opposites. He would never marry her, not even if he and she were the final two persons left on the planet.

Grace turned her attention to her mum, who was standing in the background, watching the two of them. Yes, that was it. Her mum had everything confirmed now, but she didn't agree with their choice. After all, they were only sixteen years old, and without the permission of a parent perhaps in her mind their marriage was not legitimate. Not to mention, neither a minister, nor a priest or even a justice of the peace had made it official. They had exchanged vows and rings. It wasn't a real wedding, and all her mum would have to do is annul it. Maybe that was why Vincente looked so freaked out?

Grace looked at Helen, who was standing there with tears in her eyes.

"Aren't you happy for us, Mum?" Grace asked.

"Of course, I'm very happy for you both, darling," Helen said, as she caught both of them in a group hug.

So close now, Grace looked into Vincente's eyes, and he looked away. She said, "I know that I probably look hideous," as a tear fell down her cheek. "It's been such a long ordeal, what with the operation and everything." She took a deep breath, pulled herself together. Vincente tried to encourage her with a smile, and then she continued, "I can't wait until we are able to get back to normal. Until we can go back to our house and swim on the beach like we used to."

Vincente looked away again. Like a caged rat, his eyes darted nervously from side to side.

"I'm certain Vincente can't wait for that moment, darling," Helen nudged.

Vincente let out an "Humph," which he had only meant to be an echo inside of his own head. Unfortunately, the sound was heard and noted by all present. Helen glared at Vincente, like he had just committed murder. Grace looked so hurt that more tears spilled from her eyes.

"You don't want to go back there? To Manly? To be happy again?" Grace was certain that Vincente had changed. Something in him had altered his love for her, and the realization was breaking her heart in two.

Helen dug her elbow into Vincente's side. He guffawed and gulped in some air before saying, "Not until you are well again Gracie."

"You know how I hate that!"

"What? What do you hate?" Vincente asked. He was totally confused, and definitely not doing a decent job of this acting gig. He had warned Helen that he was not a good liar, and now, he was making a mess out of this. Making a mess out of Grace. The poor girl.

"You know what I mean!" Grace shouted. "You know what I hate. How it makes my skin crawl."

"Oh," Vincente said, finally remembering. Yes, he had called her "Gracie" once before, and she had gone crazy on him. Now he repeated it. What an idiot he was! "I'm so sorry Grace, it totally slipped my mind. I'm so tired; I haven't had any sleep. My bad—it was just a brain fart."

The trio laughed and the laughter continued until Grace broke it with, "If you're tired, love, go home. We can catch up tomorrow."

Vincente considered it. His escape was so near that he could taste it. He was desperate to get out of there, to end this pathetic charade. "I have a game this afternoon, so I won't be able to come back for a visit until this evening."

"That's okay. You need to rest up for the big game," Grace said.

"Vincente," Helen said, "Grace and I appreciate you doing everything you have done to help. We understand if you need to go home now. I'll organize a taxi for you."

"No need," Vincente said, "Mum called a little while ago and said she would wait outside for me. She saw the note I left, and she was concerned."

"I'd like to meet her one day," Helen said.

"Yes, me too!" Grace agreed. "I feel like I know her already, since you showed me her paintings. That landscape with the tree and the cows especially became a conversation piece for both of us."

"The one with...what?" Vincente stuttered out. He was totally confused about what Grace had just said. He hadn't shown that painting to Grace—or anyone else outside of his parents and grandparents. In fact, it had been in storage since he was a child. "When did I show you mum's painting?" he asked.

"It was over the mantelpiece, at your parents' house."

Vincente stumbled backwards. Helen caught him. She had no idea what this exchange was all about, but Vincente seemed to be more distressed by it than Grace was.

"Are you okay?" Helen asked, legitimately concerned.

"I'm fine," he said, but he certainly wasn't fine. He wanted to escape, but at the same time, he had to be sure that they were talking about the same painting. Maybe Grace was simply confused, "And was there anything special, about the painting? Anything special that I told you about it?"

"Yes," Grace said matter-of-factly. "You told me that you were frightened of the painting when you were a child, because you thought the tree had a face. That's why your parents put it into storage. But when we visited your parents' house, it was right there hanging up over the mantelpiece."

Vincente was more than gob smacked. It was the truth, about the painting but not about it hanging over the mantelpiece. That would never have happened. He wondered how she could have possibly known about that painting.

She continued, "But now the painting is in our house, our house in Manly. It's still in storage. We both thought it would be best to put it away. You must check with your mum if she would like to have it back."

Vincente stumbled across the room to Grace, and mumbled something about yes, he would do that. Distracted he whispered something to himself, and then to Helen. He had no idea how Grace could possibly know the things that she seemed to know.

"Mum," Grace said, "I think you would really get on with Vincente's mum, because you both love some of the same things, like sunflowers. Vincente's mum has sunflowers in most of her paintings, and you have sunflowers all over the house."

"That's lovely dear," Helen said.

"And you should see the amazing figures that Vincente carves!"

Vincente sat down hard into the chair. His face was now ghostly white.

Grace continued, "He's much more talented than he lets on about other things besides sports. He's an amazing artist in his own right. It must be in his blood."

"How, how could you know about those?" Vincente asked, "They are in my bedroom."

"Your bedroom!" Helen shrieked.

"And no one has seen them—no one—except for my mum and dad and grandparents."

"You showed them to me, silly and we brought them with us to our house in Manly. Wow! You must be really, really tired, to have forgotten so much. You really should go home and get some sleep, Vincente."

Vincente felt like his blood had been drained out of his body, and he looked it too.

"Do you want me to escort you out to your mother's car?" Helen asked. She was genuinely concerned because he looked like he might faint. "Do you need to see a doctor?"

Vincente had the urge to turn and run, but a part of him also wanted to reach out and kiss Grace Greenway.

Kiss Grace Greenway!?

It was a need, a desire, which he had been fighting for the last few moments. He was holding back, emotionally. He thought perhaps he was feeling a pull from her, a need from her. Perhaps, because she wanted him to kiss her?

Vincente stood up and walked towards the bed. Grace was looking at him, but her eyes were calm, full of love. Love for him.

He leaned over and calmly kissed her forehead.

But Grace had other plans.

She moved her head, sensing his embarrassment in front of her mum, so that he kissed her fully on the lips. Then she pulled him in to her, clung to him, and he relaxed into the embrace. She was holding him so tightly that he couldn't let go, and pretty soon he didn't want to.

Somehow, she reached deep inside of him. He was lost, lost in her. When he caught his breath and backed away, he stood staring, like a window had just been opened up in his heart.

He didn't know how she knew the things that she knew. He hadn't told her any of it, and still she knew it, somehow. He was aroused and creeped out at the same time. He wanted and needed to get out of there.

And yet a part of him wanted to kiss her repeatedly and again. Still another part wanted to run, and to keep running and running and running.

"Darling," Helen said, "I think Vincente really should go now." She noticed his robotic behaviour. It was like he was under a spell.

"Night Mr. Marino," Grace chimed.

"Uh, goodnight Mrs. Marino," Vincente said on impulse. She smiled the biggest smile, like the sky had opened up and was pouring out golden sunshine onto him. He ran his fingers through his hair and then he backed himself out of there.

Once he was through the doors, he began to run.

He ran down eight flights of stairs.

And out into the street.

He would have continued running, all the way home if his mum hadn't flagged him down first.

CHAPTER 17

S EVERYTHING ALL RIGHT Vincente?" Ellen Marino asked her son. Vincente's cheeks were flushed, and he was mumbling under his breath as she made her way towards him. She opened her arms to him, and he fell into them with an audible sigh. She patted his head like she used to do when he was a small boy. This emotional connection caused him to sob uncontrollably.

"There, there," she said.

Although Vincente felt warm and safe, he could not stop thinking about Grace. He tried to be in the moment, but even his mother's soothing words could not ease his mind.

While he snuggled into his mum's embrace, his brain was playing a child's song over and over in his mind, "Vincente and Gracie, sitting in a tree k-i-s-s-i-n-g."

He couldn't explain how he was feeling to his mum. He couldn't even understand it himself.

Still, he could not get that kiss out of his mind. And it was a beautiful kiss. A deeper, more memorable kiss than any kiss he had ever experienced, and yet—why was he crying like a baby?

Vincente stepped back from his mum. He tried to pull himself together.

Ellen looked into her son's eyes and cradled his chin between her fingers. She kissed him on the forehead. He lost control and started sobbing all over again!

"Tell me, Vincente, what's wrong? Did the girl, your friend...Did she die?"

"Vincente shouted "No!" louder than he had expected to. He stepped away, landing firmly with his back against the wall. His fists were clenched, and he felt angry, sad and happy, like every emotion possible had rushed in upon him like a Tsunami.

"Talk to me!" Ellen coaxed.

"I want to go home, mum. I just want to go home." Vincente said as he choked back his tears. He felt like such a fool.

Ellen folded her son's hand into hers, like she had always done when he was a little boy. Until that one-day when he was nine and he wouldn't let her hold his hand anymore. But tonight, he didn't argue as her fingers clasped around his and then tightened their grip. Whatever was upsetting her son, it was bad. So bad that he couldn't get control of his emotions.

Vincente Marino wasn't the kind of boy who cried, even when he would get hurt as a little boy. He always tried to put on a brave face. Especially when others were looking on. Usually when they were alone together, it was different. Or it had been, until today.

When they were buckled up, Vincente let his mind wander back to Grace again. Not to the kiss this time. Instead, he was thinking about how she knew the things that she knew. Like the painting—how could she have known about that particular painting? It was impossible for her to make it up or to guess at the things she seemed to have knowledge of.

"Guess what happened yesterday?" Ellen asked.

"I don't know, Mum."

"Well, I sold another painting!""

"Great news Mum! Which one was it this time?"

"I'm not even certain you'd remember it. I painted it a long, long time ago."

"I'm sure I would remember Mum. I bet I can guess which one it was. I bet it was the one with the field full of wildflowers, so realistic, that you could almost smell them!"

"Oh, you are a lovely son, thank you. But no, it was one that I painted a few years ago, when you were a little boy. I put it into storage because something about it frightened you."

Vincente sat up straight. He was listening intently now. It couldn't be.

She went on, oblivious of Vincente's increased tension, "It's in a field, with a big tree and a cow."

It was the same painting. The exact same painting he had discussed with Grace Greenway earlier. Perhaps the sale had been publicized? That would explain Grace's knowledge about it. He hit himself on the forehead. Yes, that would explain everything!

"It only happened last evening. A private dealer heard about it and came to see it, then bought it on the spot for his client. He's off to Europe now and going to pick it up when he returns."

"So, the sale, it hasn't been publicized in any way?"

"No, I haven't even told your father yet!"

Grace couldn't have heard about it unless, she knew the man. No, what with her condition and all, it couldn't be.

As they drove along the city streets, Vincente was determined not to think about anything. Not the painting. Not Grace. Not the kiss. Especially not the kiss.

CHAPTER 18

WHEN THEY RETURNED HOME, Ellen asked Vincente if he was feeling better. His response was a vague grunt, which meant that he was feeling more like his old self again. She offered him food, but he said he wasn't hungry.

"I'm exhausted, Mum," he confessed. "I want to get some sleep."

"I have to ask you, before you go—is the girl you went to see…"

"Grace?"

"Yes, is Grace, is she getting better?"

"Yes, she's uh, improving," Vincente said as he rounded the corner and put his foot onto the step. He turned around and looked at Ellen, "But I could really use a favour."

"Would you like me to pop in and see Grace?"

"No, but thanks. What I'd really like is for you to call coach. Tell him I'm not feeling well, so that I can rest for a few more hours before the game."

"Vincente, you know what we—your father and I—think about sports. You must go to school, do a regular day at school or you can't play."

"But this hasn't been a normal day, Mum!" he protested, "I've been at the hospital all night and I'm beyond tired."

"Okay, love," she said, "I will let it go this one time. Now off to bed with you!"

Upstairs in his room, Vincente searched for his pajamas to no avail. Too tired, he climbed into the bed with just his black underwear on.

Vincente tossed and turned, quickly coming to the realization he was almost too tired to sleep. He was also pretty wired from the coffee, and the not Academy Award winning performance earlier.

Problem was–Grace hadn't been acting. She believed every word she said, and he felt it in her kiss. She was pouring her heart and soul into him.

He flung the curtains back and watched the tree outside of his window as it swayed back and forth on the whim of the wind. The drops fell against the window and flowed downward on the glass like pearly tears.

As the droplets fell, one by one, the tree swaying, and the sounds and the motions seemed to administer to Vincente like a lullaby. In a few moments he was fast asleep.

CHAPTER 19

"GRACE? GRACE, WHERE ARE you?" Vincente yelled as he ran up the steps leading to the Sydney Opera House. Almost there, he continued calling out to her like he expected to find her sitting on top of the giant white meringue-like sails.

After searching around the Rocks area, he began running down George Street, towards Parramatta Road. He called out Grace's name over and over again, until he was so exhausted by the hot Sydney sun that the seagulls, cockatoos, and ravens seemed to be screaming, too.

He had to find Grace. He just had to.

On Parramatta Road, in a new car lot—a red Ferrari caught his eye. It was a convertible, with the top down, and he climbed in. The tires squealed as he pulled out of the lot. Where on earth was Grace? He honked his horn. Where are you, Grace?

Vincente turned the stereo on, and a song he didn't know, a sappy love song, played. At first, he wanted to change the track, but something about the song made him leave it on.

When the song ended, the display on the stereo revealed it to be a duet by two pop singers. The song began to play again. Vincente immediately changed the track, only to find the same song playing again but this time sung by two rhythm and blues singers. He flicked the switch again, only to find the same song again, this time sung by two country singers. What kind of a CD was this? Every track played the same song! He tried to eject the disk, but the icon showed that the slot was empty. What the...?

Vincente slammed on the brakes, which caused the vehicle to do a 180-degree turn, and then came to a full stop. "Grace," he cried out, "Grace Marino, where the hell are you?" He leaned his head on the steering wheel in exasperation, just as the two pop singers' voices filled the night air again. Still Grace was nowhere to be found.

Vincente was all-alone in a sports car, the car of his dreams—his dream car—but it meant nothing to him without Grace beside him. "She's not even my type!" he exclaimed, as he peeled out. This time he turned the stereo off, but still that damned song kept playing repeatedly in his head.

As the wheels flew into a roundabout Vincente lost control of the car, and wham—crashed it straight into a tree. The bonnet of the car was crushed inward, but he was alive. He was breathing heavily. Smoke billowed from under the hood, as he whispered into the air, "Grace."

His whisper was returned, "Vincente?"

"Grace!" he repeated. Vincente sat up, now alert, and said into the air, "Grace, where the hell are you?"

In his fist, he held something. It was a balled-up piece of his shirt. It was red now, red with his thick warm blood. And when he opened his fist, it formed into a shape: the shape of a heart.

And when he closed his fist and sang out loud the chorus of that romantic song and then opened it again, it was once more in the shape of a heart.

Then the pain began pricking him, and he noticed the spots. Large droplets of blood were dripping onto the floor, and they also slowly covered the seat and the floor. Droplets hung on the rear-view mirror and along the inside of the windshield.

Blood was everywhere, on the floor, the walls, the ceiling. "Grace!" he called out one last time before he closed his eyes and disappeared into the darkness.

CHAPTER 20

WHEN VINCENTE AWOKE, THE sun was peeking into his room through a gap in the curtains. At first, he did not remember where he was. True, he was on his own bed but outside of the covers. He was safe. It had all been a crazy dream! He laughed at the thought that it could have been anything else.

He glanced at his athletic awards for a moment, before looking at the carved figures. He noticed that one of them was missing. The first one he had ever created: The Aboriginal. He looked everywhere for it, but it was gone.

A kookaburra called out and his laughter filled the air as Vincente pondered on the missing figure. A fly buzzed around him, which he waved away.

Vincente looked at the time and realized he was late. He had slept the school day away and now he was going to be late for the game too if he didn't get his butt into gear. He could not let the team down.

Vincente rushed into the bathroom, splashed water onto his face, brushed his teeth. and stuck out his tongue. He looked like he hadn't slept in weeks.

He felt the stubble on his chin and looked at his watch again. He didn't have enough time to shave, so he slapped on some aftershave and sprayed on some deodorant. Next, he threw on a pair of black jeans and a t-shirt and jumped down most of the stairs in one go.

It didn't make Vincente feel any better, to know how much the team needed him. He didn't take any pride in it being the absolute truth. But the other players—his teammates—never seemed to hold it against him. They knew he had a gift, but sometimes he wished the pressure would ride on someone else's shoulders, not only his.

Once downstairs, he grabbed a bottle of water from the fridge and called out to his mum. When, she didn't answer he didn't worry. He knew where he would most likely find her–outside on the porch painting.

Sure, enough she was there, working away, lost in her world of creativity. He stood there, watching her for a moment, taking in her creative spirit, before she sensed that he was there. When she did, it was like a string of creative thought had been broken, but she turned incredibly happy to see him.

"Ah, you're awake, how are you feeling love?" she asked, as Vincente leaned in to kiss her on the forehead. Then Vincente jumped over the railing and landed like a cat in the garden. "Watch the flowers!" she exclaimed. Then looking up at the brooding sky she said, "Wait, I'll get an umbrella for you."

"Not necessary," Vincente replied. "I'll run, and none of the raindrops will be able to catch me!" Vincente began to run, fast, only turning around once for a brief few seconds to wave goodbye.

CHAPTER 21

Back at the hospital, Grace was missing Vincente. She wanted to be alone—with her husband. She wanted things to be like they used to be, with the two of them on their own in the world.

She closed her eyes and remembered their most shared kiss. He had held back—no—he had hesitated.

Helen moaned in her sleep, then stirred, yawning a noticeably big yawn. She stretched and sat upright, looking directly across the room, only to discover her daughter had been watching her. "Sorry I overslept," she said. "How are you today?"

"I'm fine. I've been awake for hours. Thinking."

"Thinking about what? Vincente, I expect," Helen said.

"Yes, he has been on my mind since I woke up."

Helen stretched again, yawned.

"You were snoring mum."

"I do not snore!" she said.

"You most definitely do, and I will have to record you doing it next time, so you can know how loud it is!"

"I was dreaming about your dad; I miss him."

"I miss him too mum," Grace said, realizing this was the perfect time to ask for her help.

Grace took a deep breath and crossed her fingers.

CHAPTER 22

"M um, I miss spending time with my husband."

"I know you do love, but Vincente still has responsibilities to his family, and he has schoolwork and sports. You two are young. You have lots of time."

"But we are newlyweds, and we ought to be spending more time together."

"You need to get well first," Helen said, after standing up and going to her daughter's bed and taking her hands into hers. "You need to focus your energy on healing, so we can go home."

"I do want to go home mum, but I want to go to our home."

"Yes that's what I mean love."

"No, not your home, but to our home—I mean mine and Vincente's."

Helen took in a deep breath. She knew Grace was fantasizing, and she had to go along with it, but this lying was getting increasingly difficult. Helen said, "It's been less than seventy-two hours since your surgery. You might not realize how close you were to catastrophe, but I know how close it was, and I don't want to take any chances with you. You are still under strict observations here. Doctor's orders."

"Will they ever let me go home then?" Grace asked.

"Yes, when you are fully recovered."

"But how long? How long will it take?"

"Doctor Ackerman said they need to take some new blood samples today. They might need to change your medication. You are under the best of care here."

"I know, but I want to be with my husband."

Helen tried to change the subject. "Tell me a little bit about your house. Where was it?"

"Our house is in Manly, right on the beach."

"On the beach you say?" Helen knew that real estate in that area was worth millions. She asked if they had won the lottery.

"Of course not, Mum. Money was no object. Before that house, we moved around and stayed in hotels."

"And how did you earn a crust? Did you work? How did you make a living? Buy food and clothing for yourselves?"

"Because money meant nothing, we simply went out into the world and took everything we needed. It was only the two of us then, there was no need for money. We survived on an abundance of everything, including our love for each other."

This was going nowhere fast. Helen said, "I'm going home to change and wondered if you would like me to bring you anything more—like your laptop? Or any other books?"

"I'm fine, Mum. I don't want anything but my husband. Plus, I have this pile of books here, which I've been reading. I do still have problems concentrating for prolonged periods of time. I can't seem to focus. What I really need Mum, is your help in convincing the doctors to let Vincente spend the night here with me. That is what I need more than anything else."

"Honestly Grace, you'd think that life before Vincente Marino never existed!"

"It feels like we were together for a lifetime and now we are apart, through no fault of our own," Grace said. "I miss him so much. It's different when you are here, or the doctors are around. He is not himself. We need to be alone—like regular newlyweds should be."

"Grace, he will be here soon, after the game is over. But it's not good for you to get so distraught and upset. Try to focus your energy on getting well. Leave it with me and I will see what I can do for you, if you'll be a good girl now and close your eyes."

Grace leaned back onto the pillow and Helen kissed both of her eyes shut as she had done when Grace was a little girl. Her eyelids fluttered under her touch, like two butterflies. She said, "Vincente will be back here before you know it."

"Please ask the doctors if he can spend the night here with me in this room, Mum. Please! One night. All I ask is for one night."

"I will ask," Helen said, as she backed her way out of the room. In her heart of hearts, she knew that it would never happen.

There was no way Vincente Marino was going to spend the entire night in the same room with her daughter alone. Especially not when Grace believed they were man and wife.

"Over my dead body!" Helen said to herself as she closed the door to Grace's room.

CHAPTER 23

T HE TWO LOVERS PROMENADED along the beach, hand in hand, totally immersed in each other. Every now and then they would stop for a kiss. Then they would continue to walk a bit further, stopping into listen to the sound of the waves crashing upon the shores.

"I lost my rings!" Grace exclaimed.

Vincente told her not to worry. He said they would find them, and if they couldn't find them, then he would buy her more rings. He said that although the rings had sentimental value, they could be replaced. The rings were empty circles, while their love was full and round and centered deep inside of their hearts.

"I had them before, but now they're gone! Maybe one of the nurses stole them from me? Maybe they removed them when I went into surgery?"

"Grace, why are you fretting so? Don't worry. We will find them," Vincente soothed.

"The rings are missing—and I am being held in this hospital as a prisoner. It feels like I have been here forever."

"You can come and go as you please my love," Vincente said.

He walked in front of her, with his back turned away, and his front facing Grace. He reached out his open palms to her and she took his hands into hers. Connected once again, they walked further along the beach. They maintained eye contact this way, sharing wordless thoughts.

"Even if you tell me that I can leave, I cannot. They will not let me go."

"Are you having a bad dream my love?" Vincente asked. "Wake up now and all will be well. I promise."

"No," Grace said. "It's the other way around. It's all backwards. When I wake up, you are different. We're not the same. "

"What are we then, love?" Vincente asked.

But no answer came.

CHAPTER 24

ELEN WAS ABLE TO track down Doctor Ackerman—or
to corner him— depending on who told the story. She
explained the situation about Grace wanting to spend the night
in her room alone with her alleged husband.

Doctor Ackerman didn't react like this suggestion was a
surprise. In fact, he had anticipated such a request.

"Why didn't you warn me then?" Helen asked.

"It might never have happened," Doctor Ackerman
explained. "And you would have been worried and your
response to Grace might have seemed unnatural."

"So, what are we going to do? We can't leave her alone all
night in that room with that boy! He is so full of himself; he
might take advantage of her and the situation."

"Helen, your daughter is still in the early recovery process. I
have to say that it would be best to continue to play along with
this delusion. To in fact push it to the limit even, because it may
be the only way for Grace to break free from the fantasy—and
to choose reality."

"So, you mean, he stays in there with her, and she realizes that he's not who she thinks he is?"

"Yes, you've got the picture. If he is not who she believes him to be, if his image cracks in the mirror of her mind, then and only then can she accept reality, refute what is fictitious, and return to being Grace again."

"And the boy? Who will convince him? Especially when he doesn't see Grace in the same way that she sees him. He has nothing to risk, and pretending to play house, like they are a real married couple may be too much to ask."

"Vincente doesn't have anything to risk, but he has everything to gain. When this episode ends, he can get back to his old life. He will no longer need to act, to come to the hospital, to pretend he is something he is not. Surely, it will be enough incentive for him to help us?" Ackerman suggested.

"True, I hadn't thought of it in quite that way," Helen said. "In fact, now that you put it that way, I am anxious to make it happen—and the sooner the better. There is only one problem. What if Grace becomes amorous with Vincente and desires him to share a marital bed?"

"Yes, that could be a problem," Doctor Ackerman confirmed.

"Well, the boy needs to be warned that Grace may, in her current mental condition, have certain expectations for the evening, which he should not under any circumstances reciprocate," Helen said.

"I am certain we can convince him to 'play the game' without going too far."

"But, he is a man," Helen said. "No offense. He is accustomed to girls falling all over him—giving him everything he wants."

"Send the boy to me, for a chat, after you have spoken with him. I will explain things to him man to man."

"What reason should I give him," Helen asked. "What reason for you to speak with him?"

"Just send him to me after your conversation, Helen. I will do the rest."

Helen looked at her watch. "Vincente is expected to visit Grace any time now. I will broach the subject with him, then send him in to see you."

"And how will you explain your tête-à-tête to your daughter, not to mention his sudden disappearance?"

"I will stall Grace. She has asked me to arrange a stay-over for him, and I will tell her I am working on it."

"Sounds like a good plan," Doctor Ackerman said.

"Then we'll send Vincente home tonight, to get his clothing, etcetera, and the big night will be tomorrow night."

"Yes."

"I'm depending on you to protect my daughter."

"Don't worry, I'll see to it," Doctor Ackerman said.

Helen stood outside of her daughter's room for a moment while she pulled her thoughts together. When she was finally ready, she took a deep breath and peered in through the window before she opened the door.

CHAPTER 25

G RACE WAS OPENING DRAWERS and closing them again. When Helen entered the room Grace said, "Thank goodness you're here, Mum! Thank goodness!"

"I'm never far away," Helen said, as she placed her arm around her daughter's waist and guided her back towards the bed. Helen gazed into her daughter's face. One thing resonated with her—something she had failed to notice before—Grace was no longer a little girl.

"Mum, I can't find my wedding rings!"

"Darling, you mentioned these before, remember?" Helen parroted back. "They couldn't have gone too far; now could they have?" She felt incredibly sad then. Her daughter was still searching for things that did not exist. She sniffled a bit but then composed herself again before Grace could sense the shift in her mood.

"I swore never to remove them, and now, they're gone!" Grace exclaimed.

For a moment, Helen visualized shaking her daughter, forcing her to snap out of it, to face the truth. But it was a battle Helen couldn't afford to fight on her own. She needed the backing of the medical staff before she could blow her daughter's fantasies wide open.

On the other side of the room, Grace was ranting, "Don't you see, you've simply got to help me, Mum! Maybe they fell, under here?" she asked as she bent down to the floor and searched under and in each nook and cranny.

When she was alone, Grace had gone over every single reason why Vincente's attitude could have changed toward her. She decided it was because she had lost the rings. In defeat, she sat down on the floor and started to cry.

Helen knelt beside her and took her hands into her own. She was going to speak, but Grace opened her mouth first and cried, "I have absolutely got to find them before Vincente returns. When I find them, then he will be the way he was before. Then he will be my Vincente again."

"Darling," Helen said, lifting her daughter's chin up so that their eyes were level. "Your rings can't be far away. Perhaps, they were removed when you went into surgery? Yes, that would explain everything," Helen chided as she lifted her daughter up. When she saw a spark of possibility in her eyes, she continued. "Yes, I bet they are waiting for you to be released."

"But can't they be returned to me now?" Grace asked. "It's not like I'm in prison!"

"True, you're not in prison, but sometimes hospitals have rules in order to keep their patients' things safe," Helen said. "Would you like me to inquire about them? Ask if they might make an exception to the rule for you?"

"Yes Mum! Yes, please!"

Helen thought about how she was going to ask about rings that did not exist. Clearly her daughter wasn't going to forget about the rings. She had to return with either an answer – or with the rings.

"Grace, I was thinking. Remember when you first came to the hospital? Did you have the rings on then?"

"Of course not!" Grace exclaimed. "We weren't married then."

"So, it was later, after you were married, that Vincente brought you back to the hospital?"

"Yes," Grace said.

"Perhaps you could describe them for me, in case I need to identify them."

"Yes, clever idea. Or maybe they put them in the vault under the wrong patient's name, and someone else has my rings! Oh, I hope not!"

"Don't fret about that now, tell me what they look like. I bet they were beautiful!" Helen soothed.

"Yes, Vincente has wonderful taste. My engagement ring is in the shape of a heart with diamonds all around the outside. My wedding ring has gold stars all around it, and within each star is a diamond. I simply have got to find them Mum."

Helen stepped back. She paused before she asked, "And where did you buy these rings? They sound expensive. We should probably insure them."

"From a little jeweler on George Street, specializing in unique, one-of-a-kind items."

"What end of George Street? It is a very long street," Helen asked.

"Close to the Circular Quay end, near The Rocks."

"Okay Grace," Helen said. "I will see about your rings. Fingers crossed you will have them back on your fingers very soon."

Helen had no choice, she had to make her way to that jewelry store, and she had to describe the rings to the jeweler. She had to find out, if he knew of any such rings or if he had something similar in the store.

Helen closed the door behind her. She stood still with her back against the wall, thinking. A few things were now clear to Helen Greenway. One was that her daughter believed she had been in the hospital for quite a long time, much longer than her actual stay.

The second was that Grace believed she and Vincente had fallen in love and left the hospital together. They had married and returned sometime later. Sometime after they lived life together for a while and had enough time to set up a home.

And lastly, she had discovered the alleged rings had been purchased locally. At a jeweler Helen was familiar with. A jeweler where paying thousands of dollars for a single item was considered modest. If it was indeed the same jeweler, how had Grace and Vincente paid for such expensive rings?

Helen took a deep breath, fought off a breakdown. She wanted to run away. She felt guilty for wanting to run and she felt guilty for not knowing what to do. She gave herself permission to bolt.

"Taxi!" Helen signaled outside, and one pulled up to her at the curb. "Take me to The Rocks, and drop me somewhere near

George Street," Helen said. "I'm looking for a jeweler, a very exclusive and expensive jeweler. I don't know the address, but it's on George Street."

"Yes, I know the one," the driver confirmed as he pulled away.

Helen sat in the back, wondering why she was letting herself get so drawn into something she knew to be untrue.

While she sat in bumper-to-bumper traffic, listening to horns honking and sirens blaring, she could not for the life of her answer her own question.

CHAPTER 26

A CHEER RANG OUT as Vincente Marino was carried off the field, upon the shoulders of his teammates. Once again, Vincente had led his team to victory. To show their appreciation, they were chanting his name repeatedly.

Vincente was elated. His performance had even surpassed his own expectations.

As he was thrown into the air, he turned his head for a moment and caught the eye of Missy Malone. She was jumping up and down. He admired how cute she looked when everything bounced in synchronicity. She blew him a kiss, and he nodded in receipt.

When he had first arrived on the field, Missy ran to his side. He had seen her making her way towards him, lips pursed. He let her grab him. He let her kiss him with everything she had—but he felt nothing for her.

The kiss from Grace Greenway surpassed all the kisses of Missy Malone combined. She would never believe that truth in a million years. He could hardly believe it himself.

Still, no matter how he felt about her, Vincente knew that Missy would hang on to him, even if he didn't respond. Why? Because

Missy Malone considered herself an accessory to Vincente. She thought they went together like Lamingtons and coconut, like vegemite and toast, like a pie and chips.

If he wanted to let her go, he would have to be brutal. He would have to tell her, directly, that he no longer wanted her. He would have to tell her to go away.

Vincente looked at her now, at how pretty she was. How sweet and full of expectations. Then he looked down at his teammates, still cheering his name and tossing him into the air and any thoughts of Missy flew out of his mind. She meant nothing to him.

For a moment, Vincente's mind drifted back to the hospital, and he looked at his watch. Visiting hours were ending. He needed to see Grace. He had promised to visit her.

Worst thing was, now he was even dreaming about her! He wondered if he should break the promise. Leave her in the lurch. Then he could maybe try to forget about her. Maybe then she would try to forget about him, too.

That wouldn't solve anything though since Grace Greenway was caught in a romantic fantasy. She was stuck in a dream, which she believed at this moment was real. The power of her dream had swelled inside of him with that kiss. For a moment, he even believed it was real. That he loved her, and she loved him. It felt real. Just for a moment.

Vincente shivered, almost causing his mates to drop him onto the tarmac. They lifted him higher and continued their recitation.

Bored with it all, Vincente returned to thoughts of Grace, knowing full well that nothing could come from that line of thinking. No matter what happened between them, Grace Greenway just wasn't for him. She was simply not his type.

The crowd joined in with the chant and surged forward. Vincente detached himself now and asked to be set down. He told the guys that he had to leave for a couple of hours to keep a promise to a friend.

Disappointed to hear this news, they chanted his name even more loudly. Vincente waved, promised he would return later.

They asked him to stay. They crowded around him. Closing him in. Trapping him.

Missy Malone moved in closer too. She and the others blocked his way.

Vincente felt like he owed Missy an explanation, but he couldn't even explain things to himself right now. He knew that if Missy found out about Grace, it would cause problems. Not that she would be jealous, exactly. She would never believe he would prefer Grace to her. Not to mention the guys – they would think he had totally lost his mind!

Vincente once again remembered the kiss that he and Grace had shared.

He shivered. "It's all a fantasy. And even I'm getting caught up in it."

He imagined what would happen if he told the gang that Grace Greenway believed he and she were married.

She would become a laughingstock and him right alongside of her. They would never let him forget this mathematical state of Grace.

"Catch you later!" Vincente shouted, as he pushed his way past the reluctant crowd and got himself out of the school grounds.

Once through the gates, he ran and ran and ran, refusing to slow his stride.

Missy watched him go. She crossed her arms, fully assured that Vincente Marino would be back. Back to her—because she knew that Vincente Marino could never get enough of her.

CHAPTER 27

H ELEN RETURNED TO THE hospital ring-less.

Grace was sitting up in bed with her hands clasped together, eyes focused on the door waiting for Helen's return.

As Helen glimpsed through the porthole at her daughter, it looked like she was holding her breath. However, as her skin wasn't blue, she must've been breathing. They were just very shallow breaths.

Helen went over what she intended to say to Grace which was nothing. She intended to divert her daughter's attention to other things.

The jeweler had been extremely helpful. When Helen described the rings, he knew exactly which ones she was referring to. He said they had disappeared, some weeks ago. He and the owner had reviewed the surveillance video recordings repeatedly. The rings were simply there one moment and gone the next. POOF. No explanation. Very strange.

"Look at your hair, Grace!" Helen exclaimed. "Vincente will be visiting soon, and you need to look beautiful for your husband."

Grace examined herself in the mirror. Deciding her mother was correct she sat down, and Helen began to comb and style her daughter's hair like she had done many times before.

Grace relaxed. Helen gathered her makeup bag, and applied a light foundation of powder, followed by a little blush. Grace smiled, happy to share in these mother and daughter moments.

Soon, Vincente made his presence known by the scuffing his shoes.

He spotted Grace, seated with Helen touching her hair, and the scene before him made him smile. He decided without delay that he would carve this moment into wood. He beamed a smile in Grace's direction.

Grace jumped up, and immediately hid her hands. She didn't want him to touch her. She didn't want him to notice the lost rings.

He caught her with his smile, pulling her towards him like a magnet. Resistance was futile.

When their lips met for a hello kiss, sparks flew—on both sides. Grace moved in, to take the kiss to another level, but Vincente pulled back, leery of Helen Greenway's presence.

Vincente acknowledged Helen's presence next, planting a small kiss on her cheek. He'd never kissed Helen on the cheek before in greeting. He had no idea what he was doing. It was like he was under a spell.

Still remembering the jolt he'd received from Grace, Vincente moved into the background and shoved both hands deep into his jean pockets. He leaned with his back against the wall, his left foot on the floor and his right foot resting against the wall almost as if he were posing for GQ.

"Mum, would you mind leaving Vincente and I alone for a moment?"

You're throwing me out?" Helen asked, pretending she was offended on the outside, when she really was offended on the inside. In fact, she was offended to the core, but she also wanted to speak with Doctor Ackerman, and this would be the perfect opportunity to seek him out.

She was worried about the way they kissed—the way the sparks seemed to fly. Even Helen was metaphorically dodging them, and feeling the temperature rise in the room. Or was she just imagining it?

No, it seemed real. This was making the decision to let the two of them stay in the room together overnight. Somehow, this fantasy didn't feel like it was one-sided.

However, Vincente had said repeatedly that her daughter was not his type.

Helen decided that she must have imagined the connection—had let her imagination get carried away right along with her daughter's. Maybe this condition was contagious.

"I'll take a walk," Helen said, and then turned and whispered so only Vincente could hear, "Can I trust you?" He nodded, and his face oozed sincerity. Helen didn't trust him as far as she could toss him. "I'll be back real soon," she said.

After she left the room, Helen stood outside the door. Vincente could see her peering in through the round window, keeping an eye on them. He tried to be cool, to act naturally.

Grace had not noticed her mother was eavesdropping. She moved in on an unsuspecting Vincente and planted a hot kiss onto his lips.

Vincente's last glimpse was of Helen's face turning a shade of red he had never seen before. Then he lost himself in the kiss for a moment, let himself go.

Grace abruptly ended the kiss, stepped back and said, "You don't love me anymore. Do you Vincente?"

In his head, Vincente could hear his own voice echoing and bouncing around saying, *WOW-WOW-WOW-WOW-WOW-WOW-WOW.*

His hands were still jammed deep within his jean pockets, and they were now balled into fists. He couldn't hear what she said, what she had asked. All he could focus on was the WOW factor of that kiss.

"What? What did you say?" he asked, his senses slowly returning.

"You need me to repeat it?" she asked as a tear rolled down her cheek.

The *WOW! WOW! WOWS!* in Vincente's head smashed into the far wall of his mind and shattered, then somersaulted into the words she had said. He had heard them, but the message hadn't reached his brain yet. Now her words echoed, "You don't love me anymore." His stomach lunged.

Vincente looked into her hazel eyes and travelled deep within them. It was like he was jumping into a swimming pool, so inviting, so alive.

Yet somehow, she looked lost, and the worst thing was—he had made her feel this way, albeit unintentionally.

Seeing her that way made him long to comfort her, to bring her back to him. In pursuit of this, he moved closer, so their bodies were touching, and he initiated a kiss.

This time it was even more powerful. So much so that he wanted time to stand still. He wanted everything to stop and yet, he wanted it to continue. He wanted everything with this girl, to share everything with her—and yet she wasn't even his type. He wanted to give her the world and to make her happy. To share himself with her. To become her world.

And he wanted it all now.

Vincente remained silent. Afraid to speak. Afraid of what he was feeling. Afraid of what he might say and do. Instead, he continued to swim in the pool of Grace's eyes, losing himself in her depths.

His silence and confusion were heart breaking for Grace. She was crumbling, breaking into pieces, and crying pools of water from those hazel eyes. Big, fat, salty tears were coming down, falling.

He reached up and caught one on his fingertip. He gently transported it to his mouth, placed it upon the end of his tongue where the saltiness of it exploded. He caught another and another, each one bursting upon his tongue. All the while, Grace continued to cry and cry and cry, in disbelief at Vincente's strange actions and silence.

He loved her, and yet he knew that he couldn't love her. She didn't even love him, not really. She only loved him in her fantasy. But he loved her, in the here and in the now. His love was real.

He turned and ran.

CHAPTER 28

I N THE CORRIDOR, WITH his back to Grace's door, Vincente understood that he had left her in a desperate state. He knew that he should investigate the room, to check how she was. He recognized that he had acted like a barbarian. He was ashamed of himself.

"Ah, just the lad I've been looking for," Doctor Ackerman said, noticing Vincente was breathless, almost panting. He slapped him on the back in a fatherly way, and asked, "Is everything all right?"

"I, I don't know. I don't know anything anymore!" Vincente declared in a shaky voice.

"Come with me, young man," Doctor Ackerman said. "We can talk privately in my office, and you can catch your breath."

"Yes," Vincente relented. "But I don't want to talk about it."

"Well, I want to talk to you about Grace."

"Grace?" Vincente said and he started to shake.

"Yes, come along. My office is around the corner."

Moments later, they arrived. Doctor Ackerman invited Vincente to take a seat, and then poured out a glass of icy water. Vincente's hands trembled when he lifted the glass up to his lips.

Vincente was remembering the salty tears. The exploding salty tears.

"Calmer now?" Ackerman asked.

Vincente nodded.

"All right then, let's talk about Grace. You understand the present situation, correct? How Grace Greenway has deluded herself into believing you two are in a relationship, in fact a married couple—newlyweds?"

"Yes, I understand that is how she feels, but what I don't understand is why. Why me?"

"Only she can answer that question, Vincente. Perhaps it is something we will never know. She will never know. However, in documented cases such as this, the reason for creating a fantasy is based upon denial of some reality. Possibly something that has nothing to do with you at all. For whatever reason, she has created a world in which you and she mean everything to each other. It's like you and she are like the main characters in a novel, and you're battling the world together."

"Characters in a novel? Oh, I never thought of it like that," Vincente mused. "Still, sometimes when she weaves this fantasy, includes me in her fantasy, sometimes—it even feels real. To me." Vincente looked at the floor. He couldn't bear to look Doctor Ackerman in the eye. Not when he'd admitted that he was being drawn into the net.

Ackerman looked at the boy sitting across the room from him. It suddenly occurred to him that this was a totally different boy than the one he had first met. "Do you love her?" he asked.

"I don't think so. I don't know. She's not my type. I don't even know her, not really, and yet she knows things about me. Knows things that no one could possibly know unless I told her myself—which I haven't." Vincente wrapped his hands around his head. Talking about it made him feel physically ill. The room was spinning around.

"Put your head between your knees lad," Ackerman said. "You're turning a few new shades of green, which even I haven't seen before."

Vincente followed the instructions immediately and without question. The room soon stopped spinning, but now there were stars sparkling all over the ceiling. Stars which only Vincente could see.

Ackerman continued, "I'm not sure how she could know such personal things about you. Maybe when she was between earth and wherever spirits go when they are travelling between worlds, maybe her spirit in some way connected with your spirit. I know it sounds impossible. But I've heard stories about near death experiences which are difficult even for me—a man of science—to dismiss."

"Just now, she asked me if I loved her, and I couldn't answer her. She thinks she loves me, but she doesn't. Not in reality. I wanted to say yes, some crazy part of me wanted to say yes, but how could I? I don't understand her. I don't understand anything anymore! I sometimes think she must be a witch, to know the things that she knows."

"You believe in witches?"

"Not really.'"

"I think you've been watching too much television. Grace Greenway is not a witch. She's an impressionable, young girl. A girl who is sixteen years old and has recently lost both her father and her brother in a tragic accident. A girl who, for whatever reason has chosen you to be a part of her fantasy. She has chosen you as her husband. She needs you, in the role of her husband now, while she is still unwilling to face the truth."

"So, you're saying that she is unwell mentally, and that I'm to go along with this—this farce, no matter what the cost is to me?"

"Grace is in no way out of danger. We are monitoring her vitals. Keeping an eye on her. That's why she has not been released yet. She is under our care. Vincente, you are at the heart of this situation. You are the catalyst. If you abandon her now..."

"If I walk away, then I'm responsible for what happens next. Is that what you are telling me?"

"She is very vulnerable now. She needs something from you and perhaps if you give it to her, fulfill that wish for her, then she will be able to face reality and give you up. She needs someone to believe in, something to look forward to, and she has chosen you. All roads lead to you. I don't know why, perhaps it is because you brought her here to the hospital."

"I hurt her, but it was an accident, Doc, I swear."

"Yes, you hurt her in some ways, but you also saved her life because she was brought here, with the best of care around her when the clots finally ruptured. Had she been at home or at school when that happened, she might not have survived."

Vincente sat silently for a moment, realizing how much of an impact he had already made on Grace's life. He longed to get back to her, to make everything all right once again. He stood up, "I need to get back to her. She asked me if I loved her, and I turned and ran like a coward."

"Yes, go back to her now, and don't tell her that you love her unless you really mean it. Unless you are willing to give her your heart, and to be by her side once she knows the truth about you and once the spell has been broken."

"No pressure!" Vincente scoffed, as he made his way towards the door.

"Come back here, to talk to me anytime Vincente," Ackerman said. "And don't forget how important you are to her. Don't forget what you mean to her."

Vincente nodded, and then turned and ran back toward Grace's room.

✳✳✳

IN HER ROOM, GRACE was sound asleep. He bent over the bed and kissed her on the forehead. She still had tears on her cheeks, and he gently wiped them away.

He sat beside her on the bed, and she did not stir or move. He watched her sleep. He watched as her chest rose and fell with every breath. When she whimpered in her sleep, he took her hands into his and reassured her that everything was going to be all right. In the dark there, alone with her, he told her that he loved her. And then he kissed her on the forehead again.

Grace stirred briefly in her sleep, almost like the words he had spoken had touched her dream in some way, and then she settled back into a deep sleep.

Vincente left Grace there, sleeping safely and soundly. He returned to thank Doctor Ackerman for all his help and advice before he made his way home for the evening. He was exhausted...so tired, and yet invigorated in a way that he had never been before.

Never before had Vincente Marino felt so alive.

***

Standing outside of Doctor Ackerman's office, Vincente overheard raised voices. He hesitated before knocking. When the voices quieted slightly, he knocked and was invited to enter.

"You should be ashamed of yourself!" Helen shouted as she flung herself at him and began to hammer her fists into his chest.

"Calm down," Doctor Ackerman commanded.

Helen continued to thump upon Vincente's chest.

Vincente took a deep breath, hoping she would pound out whatever was bothering her. It wasn't hurting him. When he realized, her anger was not going to burn itself out, he grabbed a hold of both of her wrists and held them tightly until she was forced to calm down. She continued by hissing into his face.

Vincente held on even tighter and asked, "What the?" while looking in the direction of Doctor Ackerman who was trying not to lose his temper.

"Vincente, when you came here earlier, after leaving Grace, Helen found her in quite a state. She was distraught. Devastated. She was unable to communicate. All she could do was sob and cry."

"I can see where she got that from!" Vincente said, looking into Helen's eyes.

She growled at him.

"Don't make it worse lad," Doctor Ackerman pleaded. "In order to calm Grace down, they had to sedate her."

"I was just in there and Grace was asleep. She looked very peaceful to me."

"What did you say to her, to put her into such a state?" Helen demanded.

"I made a mistake. I ran away, but I went back. I went back."

"Too little, too late!" Helen exclaimed.

"Look, I didn't ask for any of this!" Vincente pointed out; hands held up in surrender.

"Now both of you sit down and calm down," Doctor Ackerman directed, "and let's stop the drama. We need to focus on Grace. Grace and only Grace."

"Agreed," Vincente said.

"Agreed," Helen huffed.

CHAPTER 29

A S THEY LED VINCENTE out of the room, he was still shouting out the words. True, to him they were meaningless, untrue sentiments. Words he was only saying to be kind, to save her from the brink.

He shouted it out again. This time his voice echoed along the corridors and out into the universe, "I love you, Grace Greenway!"

"I love you too, Vincente!" she shouted back to him. With the mayhem and the hoopla as they attempted to save her life—he did not hear her.

Suddenly the hot star began to spin and rotate. Soon it was no longer coming toward her or burning her with its heat. Instead, it threw out pulsing waves and became a neutron star.

Grasp on her gone, "I want to live," Grace Greenway declared to herself - "I want to live!"

CHAPTER 30

DOCTOR ACKERMAN ASKED, "WHEN you returned to see Grace, how did you feel, I mean when you saw her again?"

"I felt the strong need to take care of her, to, to love her, to protect her, to make her my own. God, I'm so confused. Why am I feeling this way?"

"Yes, let's examine this Vincente," Doctor Ackerman said. "Grace makes you feel something different, something new. Correct? Different than the other girls in your life have made you feel?"

"Yes, she's not my girlfriend. I do have a girlfriend at school—she would do anything for me," Vincente said.

"But would you do anything for her?"

"I, she's low maintenance—if you know what I mean."

"Right then, let me put it another way," Doctor Ackerman said. "Does your girlfriend need you?"

"She's popular, and I'm popular. We're meant to be together. Destiny. Everyone says so. Everyone expects it."

"Expectations? What do other people's expectations have to do with true love? Love, true love, is between two people. Only two people. Now think about it Vincente, think about it before you answer. How do you really feel about Grace Greenway?"

Vincente shuffled his feet, fidgeted. "Enough of this—this psychoanalyzing B.S. This isn't about me. It's about Grace getting well. What do you want me to do now? Marry her?"

"No, I don't want you to do anything which will make you feel uncomfortable. However, Grace has requested your presence. She has asked us to ask you, if you would spend the night in her room with her."

"What? Are you serious?"

"She is serious, so we have to take her request very seriously."

"And her mum, the dragon-lady, agrees?"

"Reluctantly, as you've probably already surmised. You heard me say that I would speak with you. That I would make you understand Grace is not to be hurt or played with or taken advantage of."

"You think I might jump her bones? More likely she would jump mine!"

"If you care about her, really care about her, and she as you say, 'jumps your bones,' then you will have to find a way to let her down gently, without rejecting her outright."

"I still don't get how spending the night in the room with her is going to help."

"It is what she wishes, Vincente."

"But there are no guarantees, right?"

"There are no guarantees, Vincente, but Grace will get well. It's our ultimate goal."

"I'm for that," Vincente said.

"So, Helen will tell Grace that you needed to go home to get some things. You will return tomorrow evening, with the intention of spending the night in her room. As you know, there are two beds. The beds will not be pushed together in any way, understand?"

"Yes Doc," Vincente said. "I'm going to head out now, get myself some sleep—since I won't be getting much tomorrow night!"

"I sincerely hope you don't mean that the way it sounded!" Ackerman exclaimed.

"I meant; oh, you know what I meant."

"Goodo then, come see me tomorrow or anytime you want to talk. I'll remain on staff all evening, at your disposal so to speak."

"Thank you, Doctor Ackerman."

"Goodnight Vincente."

"Night Doc."

CHAPTER 31

I N THE EARLY HOURS of the morning, Grace awoke and for a moment she forgot where she was. She vaguely remembered Vincente being in her room. One minute he was there and then the next, he was gone. Why had he departed so abruptly? Had she done something to upset him? Said something?

She hoped to find him there in the room somewhere, waiting for her to wake up. Only Helen was still there, and she was asleep.

Grace got down from the bed and made her way into the loo. She removed her hospital gown and stepped into the shower. As the water heated to a near boiling temperature, she closed her eyes. She longed for Vincente's touch.

She turned off the water, acquired a new gown from the shelf. She folded herself into it deciding that no one could look attractive in a gown such as this.

When she returned to her bed, Helen was fussing around the room.

"I have good news for you!"

"Really? I'm not still dreaming Mum?"

"Yes, Vincente will be spending the night with you."

"Tonight? This very night?"

"Yes."

"I need my things, I need my nice nightgown, and my perfume."

"You will find the things that you need in the bag in the bathroom cabinet."

"I can't wait!"

"Vincente will, of course, sleep in—that bed."

Grace was already envisioning moving the two beds together, making one bed. Sharing a bed with her husband. Two beds for show, yes, but they would only need one. Grace hugged herself as goose bumps appeared on the flesh of her arms.

"I will be leaving around teatime, but should you require assistance, Doctor Ackerman will be at your disposal."

"We're married, Mum!" Grace exclaimed.

Grace ran towards her and threw her arms around her mother. Helen was pleased to see her daughter happy—any mother would be, but it was the lies that were troubling her. The lies and the charade she was not happy about. She felt like a fraud. Duplicitous.

Grace went into the cabinet in the bathroom and pulled out the overnight bag. In it was the prettiest, most virginally white linen nightgown she had ever seen, with a red tie up on the front.

"Mum, it's beautiful," she exclaimed.

Nurse Burns arrived and noticed that Grace was looking a little flushed.

"Are you feeling well, Grace?"

Grace was filled to bursting with excitement in anticipation of her night with Vincente. She wanted time to fly by so he could be there beside her—now.

"Try to eat something," Nurse Burns suggested. "I understand you'll be having a visitor spend the night, so you need all your strength."

"Yes, you should eat something dear," Helen agreed.

Grace had a bite of toast and sip of coffee and then her stomach lurched. "Maybe later," she said. The smell of coffee made her feel ill. "No, take it away," Grace said.

"Was Vincente happy when you told him that he could stay, Grace?" Nurse Burns asked.

"I didn't tell him, but I'm sure he was happy," Grace said. She then changed into her nightgown and made herself ready for Vincente's arrival.

CHAPTER 32

A T 6:15 P.M. VINCENTE Marino arrived at the hospital, clutching a box containing a dozen long stemmed red roses. They were tied up with a crimson ribbon.

When he entered Grace's room, Helen somewhat reluctantly made herself scarce.

Vincente immediately went to Grace's side and kissed her on both cheeks. He presented her with the box, then watched as her eyes grew bigger and bigger when she undid the blood red ribbon.

He felt nervous, but so did she. There was a powerful sense of purpose in the air.

After thanking Vincente with a peck on the cheek for the beautiful roses, Grace asked the on-duty nurse for a vase. She returned with one, and Vincente set to arranging the flowers in it. He had seen his mother arrange vases filled with flowers hundreds of times before.

He began by pulling one rose out of the box, and then caressing it nonchalantly before he placed it into the water. Grace watched him intently, noticing the contrast between his strong athletic fingers and the thin thorny stems of the roses. When he caressed the rose, his actions made her shiver.

She watched as he picked up one rose, two roses, three roses. Without even being aware he was doing it, he lightly caressed the stem, felt the pain of the thorn in his finger for a second, and then gently placed the flower into the vase.

Each movement took Grace's breath away. Moved her heart up into her throat. It was almost like he was holding her heart between his fingertips.

Vincente was trying hard not to make a splash as he deposited one rose after another into the translucent glass vase.

Every now and then, he glanced at Grace. Her stare was transfixed on him. He was glad he chose roses—she obviously adored them.

He suddenly began to feel quite self-conscious. He reached into the box again and pulled out the next rose, observing Grace's breathlessness. He put the rose into the water and then reached into the box for another. She seemed winded again, only this time, she also looked faint.

"Are you all right?" Vincente asked.

Grace's cheeks were scarlet, and she seemed to be having increased difficulty catching her breath. He wondered if he should call for someone to help. He didn't want her to have a relapse now, especially when it looked like things were coming to a head.

"I'm—I'm perfect," Grace said, as she played with the red tie up on her nightgown. "Let's talk about something while you finish with the flowers."

"What did you have in mind?" he asked, as he caressed the stem of another rose.

"Oh," Grace said, as she watched him put the stem into the water, then she was able to speak. "How about we tell each other something the other person doesn't know? Maybe a misconception you had about me, and I'll tell you a misconception I had about you."

"Okay," Vincente agreed, as another rose was placed into the water. "You go first," he said, as water droplets splashed out of the vase, landing on the back of his hand.

Grace watched the droplets, as he went into the box for another rose. He raised the flower upwards, and the water ran down his forearm.

He picked up the next rose and looked at her. Her breath caught in her throat. Time seemed to stop.

CHAPTER 33

"I ONCE HAD A special name for you, before I really knew you," Grace revealed.

Vincente rolled the current rose between his fingers. He placed it into the water. He noticed that Grace was now breathing more normally, and her cheeks weren't as flushed. He nodded, encouraging her to continue.

"I used to call you my Golden Mean."

"Why?" Vincente asked.

"Remember in math class when we learned about Fibonacci's Golden Mean? Well, you were my Golden Mean."

"You mean, all the way back then, you felt that way about—me?" Now he was really confused. She was saying she loved him then before any of this happened. He knew that she had a crush on him, but it wasn't love, it was an infatuation. Lots of girls were infatuated with him. "Refresh my memory on Fibonacci," he said.

"It's the concept where the first number and the second number add up together to achieve the sum of the third number like one, two, three, five, eight, thirteen, and so on."

"Oh, yes, I do remember something about that and something about nature, like waves and flowers?"

"That's right! See, you do remember!" Grace said, as he popped another rose into the water. "There is symmetry in nature, with waves, snowflakes and flowers, all reinforcing Fibonacci's theory of the Golden Mean. So, you were my Golden Mean."

"Thank you," Vincente said, not knowing what else to say. "It's amazing you can still remember a name you had for me, considering what you've been through. How you lost your memory."

"It came back to me recently. I had forgotten, but when I dreamed about you, about us, it all came back."

Vincente continued with the roses, and Grace continued speaking. "When I thought you didn't love me anymore, I dreamed about you, and in my dream, you promised that you'd never leave me."

"I'm sorry Grace, forgive me," Vincente said as he placed the final rose into the vase.

"I believe you, this time."

Vincente lifted up the vase and placed it on the nightstand beside Grace's bed and said, "I did come back, you know."

"When?"

"Last night."

"You couldn't have. I would have known."

"You were sound asleep when I came in. I kissed your forehead like this," he bent over her.

"Don't," Grace said. "Don't...unless you really mean it."

He took a deep breath and stepped back. He walked over to his bed and kicked off his shoes and dangled his legs over the side of the bed. He kicked them back and forth, like a small boy would.

"Now it's your turn," Grace said.

"Hmm, let's see," Vincente, pondered for a moment. "Well, I thought you were shy, especially around guys, but you don't seem to be very shy around me."

"Is that it? Is that the best you can do?"

"Hey, I'm new at this—remember it was your idea. I bet you can't produce another one for me?"

"Can too!" she said. "This one is going to make you laugh, but once, a long time ago, I thought you were a vampire."

"Me? A vampire?"

"Yeah, I know it's crazy, but I even went so far as to lean over you and expose my neck to you, to see if you would, you know, bite me. It was the very first time we kissed—remember? I leaned over like this, and I waited for you to sink your teeth in."

"That's weird!" he said, as he looked at her white exposed neck having a powerful desire to kiss it.

Grace shivered and her nipples tingled at the mere thought of it.

"So, I must have been a real disappointment to you when you realized that you married a mere mortal?"

"That's funny. You could never disappoint me," she smiled. "Now it's your turn."

"Well, before, I thought you were weak, a weak person. But now…"

Grace interrupted, asking "Weak, in what way?"

"Weak, as in lame," he said, searching her face for a reaction that he had said the wrong thing, but she seemed to be okay with it. "It was probably because when you saw me, or when I saw you, you were always looking at me in a weird way. Now that I think about it, if you thought I was a vampire, then perhaps that's why you were looking at me like that. Anyway, you're not weak or lame—you're a strong woman. And you seem to be getting stronger."

"Well, that's better than the first one," Grace said as she leaned back into her pillow and closed her eyes.

Neither spoke for a moment, each lost in their thoughts.

"Can we talk about it?" Grace asked. "Can we talk about whatever has changed for you about me?"

"Grace nothing has changed, it's just that..."

"You feel trapped?"

"Kind of. Maybe, but it's not your fault. It's totally not your fault." He took in a deep breath then continued, "Could I ask you something, something which has been bothering me?"

"Sure Vincente. You can ask me anything, anything at all."

"Who really told you about my mum's painting?"

"You did."

"Really Grace, you can tell me the truth. Who told you? Did you read about it on the net?"

"I don't tell lies Vincente. Like I said before, you told me about it, and you showed the actual painting to me when we went to your parents' house."

"But why would I want to show that painting to you?"

"Because of the trees!"

"The trees?"

"Honestly, which one of us experienced the memory loss around here?" Grace rolled her eyes. "The trees—like the one that skewered and ate that raven, the one that I was held captive in?" Grace waited for Vincente to show some sign of recognition, but none came. She huffed her impatience at him.

Vincente was fairly sure that Grace was cracking up. He didn't know whether to agree with her, or to disagree with her, so he remained silent.

Moments passed. Grace crossed and uncrossed her arms refusing to give up. "And because of those trees, you wanted me to see your mum's painting."

"But I still don't get it—why would I want to show you my mum's painting?"

"Because you were always afraid of that painting. Because you said that as a child, you saw a face in the trunk of the tree, and it terrified you."

"My mum sold that painting the other day. It had been in storage in the attic for years. True, something spooked me about it, but I never told a single soul."

"You told me, and you showed me."

Vincente moved across the room. He sat by Grace's side. "What else did I tell you?"

"Lots of things! I mean we spent every day together, 24/7."

"Tell me," he said.

"You really want me to?"

"Yes."

"Let's see. You always dreamed of owning a Ferrari, a red Ferrari, and we drove one off the lot on the Princess Highway. You were in heaven driving that thing and I was a little jealous."

Vincente thought back to the dream when he was driving a red Ferrari searching for Grace. Weird. He decided to change the subject. "Did I tell you anything else about my mum?"

"You showed me her studio, and she was in the middle of painting a new work. It was a picture of her garden, but it wasn't finished."

Vincente took in a deep breath. It was the same painting his mum had been working on this morning. He went back to the idea that Grace must be a witch. He waited for her to twitch her nose like Samantha Stevens on Bewitched, but nothing happened.

Grace pulled him into herself and kissed him passionately on the mouth.

Vincente was on top of her now, kissing her. Trying to move away but wanting to lean in while every stored-up emotion exploded inside his head. She kept kissing him, until he was breathless.

"You're out of practice, aren't you?" Grace asked, as she allowed Vincente time to catch his breath.

He stumbled off the side of the bed.

"I've finally done it!" she exclaimed. "I've finally given you spaghetti legs! About time too—you always gave them to me!"

"Where did you learn to kiss like that?"

"Very funny, Vincente, you taught me everything that I know."

"Are you telling me, I'm the only man that you have ever kissed?"

"Yes, you're my one. My one and only."

He changed the subject again. "What else did you see at my house?"

"You showed me your beautiful wooden carvings, and I still have this one." Grace reached into a drawer and pulled out the Aboriginal man.

Vincente's mind was racing a mile a second. He needed to escape. To get out of that room – now.

"Where did you get that?" he asked.

"I took it from your room."

"You took it, but when?"

"When we visited your house. I had it in my pocket, and somehow one moment it was there and then the next it was sitting inside of your mum's painting."

"In the painting? In your pocket?" he exclaimed.

"Yes, sorry I didn't tell you it was here. It kind of shocked me too – one moment in the painting, the next moment in my pocket again."

"Uh, I'm feeling kind of thirsty, I'm going to get a soft drink. Can I get you anything?" Vincente asked. He was shaking. His entire body was shaking. He needed to get out of there now. To leave. To run.

"You are going to get a drink? Now?"

"Yes, I need a drink."

"Okay, but hurry back," Grace said. She blew him a kiss and then placed the Aboriginal man back into the drawer.

Outside Vincente wanted to bolt. Instead, he made his way along the corridor to speak with Doctor Ackerman.

CHAPTER 34

"Doc!" Vincente shouted, as he hammered on Ackerman's door repeatedly. "Doc, I need to speak with you!"

Doctor Ackerman put down the phone receiver as Vincente entered his office.

"Doc, you've got to get me out of this! I can't stay overnight. I'm drowning in there, and she's so crazy that she's starting to make sense to me!"

"Whatever do you mean? Take a deep breath, Vincente. Calm down!"

"She told me about a conversation. Well, not a conversation as such, but she told me about something that happened only yesterday. She knows things that no one else can possibly know and then..."

"Then what? She didn't want you two to—? To—?"

"No Doc, but she's keen and—she's getting to me."

"Are you telling me that you are falling in love with her? For real?"

"I've never been in love before, but I have made out with a few girls. No girl has ever kissed me like she kisses me and yet she tells me that I'm the only man she has ever kissed!"

"So, you are going into emotional overload, and you want to go home? To run away. Are you afraid of losing control?"

"I'm saying that she has put a spell on me. She's not even my type! It must be a spell!"

"Yeah, you said that before, mate, and it didn't make any more sense then, than it does now. So, what do you want me to do, tell her that you've gone home? That there's an emergency, so you can't stay?"

"Maybe you can go in and give her a sleeping pill, then I'll go back in and sleep. It'll be morning before we know it."

"I can't give her a sleeping pill because you request it."

"But Doc, she's telling me stories about us. About things we have seen and done together. Things which never happened. She speaks with her heart in hand about us, like we are one person, and she is convincing. It's almost like I know what she is talking about."

"Now," Ackerman said, "this is serious. You are telling me that you, without a doubt, are being pulled into this fantasy? That her descriptions even seem to be real to you sometimes?"

"God help me, yes."

"Okay Vincente, I hear you. You're not my patient, but you are helping out Grace who is my patient. Under this circumstance, you need to go home. I will give you a prescription, so that you can sleep and perhaps, in future, it would be best if you stayed away."

"But I can't!"

"You must, Vincente. You are no good to anyone in this state."

"I can't go without telling her myself, without saying goodnight to her. I promised her that I would never leave her alone again."

"You do love her, Vincente."

Vincente nodded as he closed the door behind him.

He walked slowly along the corridor, past Grace's room, into the elevator. When he arrived on the ground floor he exited the hospital into the dark night. He strolled across the tarmac and found a tree standing in a solitary state. He leaned his back against it and wept.

CHAPTER 35

G RACE ANXIOUSLY AWAITED HER husband's return. When the door swung open, in walked Doctor Ackerman.

"Where's Vincente?"

"How are you doing, Grace?"

"Where is Vincente? What have you done with him?"

He smiled. "I'm glad you were able to spend this extra time with him, but some of your tests have returned, and the results are questionable. I need to get another sample of blood. Just to double check that all is well. I've asked Vincente to postpone his overnight stay, while these tests are being completed."

Grace put on her saddest face and held out her arm for him to find a vein. He popped the needle in effortlessly. She didn't flinch or feel any pain because the pain in her heart was already unbearable.

Doctor Ackerman finished putting the blood work away. "Vincente was disappointed, as you are, but we will arrange it for another night. It can't be helped Grace. Your health is most important."

"I want Vincente!" Grace called and she began to thrash and twist and turn in the bed. She threw the covers off and pulled the plaster off that he had placed onto her arm. The vein reopened and blood spurted out.

Doctor Ackerman restrained her. He pushed the emergency button for a nurse's assistance. "I'm sorry," he said as he sedated her.

CHAPTER 36

Doctor Ackerman needed some fresh air and walked across the tarmac. He spotted Vincente there, leaning against a tree.

"Did you see her?" he asked.

"Indeed, I did, and I explained everything."

"And how did she, take it?"

"She didn't take it well. I had to sedate her."

Vincente clenched his fists and stood up. His face was only inches away from Ackerman's face. "I said I would come back. You didn't have to do that. I needed time. Time was all I needed."

"You need more than time, Vincente. You need distance. I'm not certain what will happen to that girl, if you fall in love with her, and if the fantasy she created collides—to become reality. I'm not sure what will happen then."

"If she has dreamed it and then it comes true, then she would get well straightaway, wouldn't she?"

"Vincente it could happen, and then again, things could go the other way."

"Meaning?"

"Grace is standing on the edge of a cliff. The truth could push her over. She may realize that everything around her is a lie. That we've all been playing along with her fantasies and then, where will she be?"

"So even though I do love her now, I should back off, leave her alone, go back to school—to the girl everyone else expects me to be with, and just hope that Grace Greenway eventually gets over me? I don't want her to get over me! And she'll think I left her again; she'll think I broke my promise—again."

"We need to take your feelings into consideration in how we proceed with this, this, whatever it is. We need to rethink, to regroup. Go home now. Come back in the morning. Grace will sleep for at least eight hours. See me when you return, and I will update you. Do not go straight in and visit Grace. Come to me first."

"Deal."

Vincente and Doctor Ackerman crossed the parking lot, where a line of taxis awaited passengers. Vincente climbed into the backseat of one and was soon on the way home.

Home—where he hoped to sleep without dreaming.

CHAPTER 37

I N THE MORNING, GRACE awoke to an empty room.

She felt alone and betrayed, as one of the nurses fluffed up her pillow and placed a breakfast tray in front of her.

She pushed it away. The mere smell of it made her feel ill.

"I'm not hungry," Grace said.

When her room was clear of people once again, Grace leaned back on her pillow and closed her eyes.

She played her wedding day repeatedly in her mind, until once again she drifted off to sleep.

CHAPTER 38

T HE NEXT DAY, DOCTOR Ackerman summoned Helen to his office. He urged her to sit down, with a very perplexing look on his face.

Helen knew that he had bad news to share. She also knew that she shouldn't have left her daughter alone with that boy.

Doctor Ackerman sat down opposite Helen so that their knees were nearly touching.

He looked directly into her eyes and said, "Grace is pregnant."

Helen laughed.

"Grace is pregnant," he repeated.

"What?"

"We did some blood work the other day, and the test came back positive. I took some more blood last night, and it is confirmed—your daughter is pregnant."

"She can't be! I'll kill that little bastard!"

"Now how will that help anything?" he asked. "You need to calm down and listen to me. Listen to me carefully."

She took a deep breath. Unclenched her fists.

"It's early on and your over-reacting will not help you or Grace."

"Does she know?"

"No, you are the first to be told. I thought it appropriate. We need to discuss how to proceed."

"How to proceed? There is no point in discussing this. We need to get rid of it."

"Grace is sixteen, she has rights."

"It has to be Marino's!"

"Not necessarily. She has been here, with staff and visitors around her, every day. He hadn't been alone with her until last night and by the way, he only stayed a couple of hours before I sent him home."

"My daughter goes to school and comes home. She works on math and experiments in the evenings. She doesn't know other boys. It must have been Marino!"

"But we have to be certain before we go accusing anyone. And most importantly, we must tell Grace."

"First, we need to confirm that he's the father and then we can tell her," Helen said.

"Vincente cares for your daughter deeply. He is confused, and he has told me that the two of them haven't done anything more than kiss. However, Grace does believe that the two of them are a married couple. Therefore, if we tell her, she will be 100% certain that she is carrying Vincente's child."

"If it's not his, then what? An immaculate conception?"

"All I know for certain is that we need to tell Grace. She will need your help in deciding what to do," Ackerman stated.

"If it's not his, then the proof will be self-evident, that we have been cruelly playing with her by going along with her fantasies," Helen said. "It might be too much for her to handle."

"We'll need confirmation as soon as possible. I will ask Vincente if he agrees to some tests when he comes to see me later, today."

"And if it's not his, then she will more than likely agree to do away with it."

"Do you wish to tell her now that she is pregnant? Once Vincente's tests are in, we can broach the subject of who the father might be with her, assuming he is not the father," Ackerman said.

"Yes, I think we should tell her. The sooner the better."

"Let's go to her room now and see how she is. We can assess the situation and decide then what to do."

"She needs to know. My daughter needs to know."

***

Vincente arrived on Grace's floor at the exact moment when Helen and Doctor Ackerman came out of his office.

"Doctor Ackerman, I wanted to speak with you," Vincente said. And then, "Hello Helen."

She looked at him with daggers in her eyes.

"We need to go in and talk to Grace, but please wait for me in my office. I will be back shortly and then we can talk."

Vincente ran his fingers through his hair. He watched Helen and Doctor Ackerman amble away. When they arrived at Grace's door, they hesitated briefly and then entered. He wondered what the hesitation was all about.

He felt guilty for leaving Grace alone. He wanted to see her—to make things right between them.

Once inside Doctor Ackerman's office he closed the door behind him and poured himself a cup of water. Vincente sat down and picked up a sporting magazine. He flipped through while he waited, but his mind was too distracted. He couldn't stay seated, so he got up again and paced. He jammed his fists into his pockets. And he waited.

***

"I'm so happy!" Grace exclaimed. "This is the best possible news for Vincente and me. We're having a baby!"

Helen hugged her daughter, who was trembling with excitement.

"Grace, you need to keep up your strength and you need to eat. What's this I hear about you skipping breakfast?" Dr. Ackerman said.

"I didn't feel up to it then, but I'll eat something now. Bring it on! I'm so excited!" Grace exclaimed.

After taking few deep breaths Grace said, "Please ask Vincente to see me. I can't wait to tell him the news!"

CHAPTER 39

"Thank you for waiting, Vincente," Doctor Ackerman said.

"How is Grace this morning?"

"She's radiant! Sleep has done her a world of good, and you look rested too. Did you sleep well?"

"Yes, I slept straight through."

"I realize you're not one of my regular patients, but I'd like to request permission to run a blood test?"

"A blood test. Why?"

"You seemed overwrought last night, and I thought it might be good to check you out to make sure that you are in ship shape."

"I have been feeling really tired."

"Just as well, we'll check you out then," Ackerman said. "Please roll up your sleeve and I'll get the sample from you straightaway."

After the sample was taken and the vial stored away, Doctor Ackerman presented a release form to Vincente to sign. It authorized him to use the blood samples to perform all necessary tests.

"May I see her?" Vincente asked.

"Not today but see me tomorrow. Perhaps you can see her then."

"But you said she was radiant and well-rested."

"Yes, and we want her to remain that way! You go home, come back tomorrow. Give her some space, some time. She is with her mother now."

"Okay Doc. See you tomorrow then."

"Thank you, Vincente," Doctor Ackerman said as he rushed out carrying the blood samples. He couldn't wait to get them to the lab.

***

Twenty-four hours later, they were all gathered in Grace's room.

When Doctor Ackerman finally arrived, he did not smile. He didn't speak or make eye contact with any of the three people present. He held the results close to his chest on a clipboard.

Grace was all a-twitter with excitement.

Helen had clenched fists and a clenched jaw. She resembled someone who needed to go to the loo rather badly.

Vincente was clueless.

"Good morning, everyone," Doctor Ackerman began. "It appears, based upon blood tests, that Grace and Vincente are expecting a baby."

Grace exploded into a cheer and opened her arms up to Vincente.

Vincente stood looking at Grace. He was whiter than the sheets on the bed. "How can this be?" he asked himself and then he said out loud, "how can this be when all we have done is kissed?"

Helen fainted and fell to the ground with a thud.

CHAPTER 40

"**G**RACE? WAKE UP GRACE. It's time for us to go," a child's voice whispered.

Grace shivered. The room was very cold and dark. She watched, as across the room the blinds seemed to wave back and forth with the breeze. It appeared that the window was wide open.

Hospital windows don't open, she thought.

A tiny hand took hold of Grace's and pulled her out of bed.

Grace, still half asleep and half-awake walked alongside of the child. Together they walked toward the open window, as if in a trance.

The little girl was also dressed in a white linen nightgown with a red tie-up, "Hold on tightly," she said as she placed a soft blanket into Grace's arms.

Grace cradled the blanket instinctively and closed her arms around it.

Their nightgowns blew and whispered as they made their way toward the window.

In the light of the moon, Grace recognized the little girl who had shown herself twice before. Once when in the middle of the road, and the second time when Grace was stranded in a giant tree. She shivered as the little girl's nightgown shimmered in the moonlight.

The little one climbed onto the window ledge, all the while still holding Grace's hand in hers. She pulled, but Grace's feet would not move.

"Where are we going?" Grace inquired.

"To the heart of the world," the little one explained.

Grace held the blanket firmly against her chest and looked at her feet. She tried to block it out of her mind, the thing that had happened last time when she had been pulled out of the window into the night.

The little one continued to watch Grace impatiently, "I am the chord," she said. "You must come with me now. They are waiting."

"Who, who is waiting?" Grace inquired.

"You will see," the little one said. "Come."

With one hand, Grace held the blanket and with the other, she twisted the red tie-up around and around and around. She was stalling for time – she did not want to sit on the window ledge. She did not want to go out into the night. This time she didn't have to go. She didn't want to go.

"Hurry Grace. They have been waiting for you for forever," the little girl explained.

Grace backed away.

When Grace would not join her, the little girl climbed down from the windowsill. She took Grace's hand into hers once again. She held her hand tightly and led her to the window. For a few seconds, their feet rose from the floor and soon they were seated side by side on the windowsill.

Together, they sat and looked into the face of the moon.

"Take a deep breath," the little girl said and then she softly counted down, "5, 4, 3, 2, 1!"

And together they fell forwards into the Cimmerian night.

CHAPTER 41

After they fell for many minutes, which seemed like hours, they landed on the back of a waiting beast.

This beast was not the same one, which had carried Grace some time ago and deposited her high up in a tree.

This beast was not furry or feathery. Instead, it had wings made of metal, which reflected the moonlight and the light of the stars as it swooped across the blackened sky.

Grace had so many questions to ask, but the wind was howling, and the beast let out a thunderous roar every now and again. Grace clutched the blanket; all the while wishing it were Vincente she was holding onto.

The little girl tossed her dark hair back and lifted her face up toward the moon. She closed her eyes and began to hum a soothing lullaby. Grace recognized the tune; it was their song, hers, and Vincente's. Grace closed her eyes and drifted off into a deep dream.

CHAPTER 42

T HEY FLEW FOR AN exceptionally long time, until Mother Sun began to give birth to a new day.

That was their cue, to begin their descent. Grace and the little girl held on tightly to the metallic beast as the sunlight reflected off of its body causing bolts of lightning to fire forth in all directions. The sky was lit up, with daytime fireworks as they fell through the clouds.

Then the clouds began to part, as they descended toward the heart of the Earth.

In the distance, Grace could see a giant red stone, which was a-fire in the sunlight. It was surrounded by sand.

Yet, when she blinked her eyes open and closed a few times the ocean started and ended around the edges of the rock. Waves crashed and rolled, but they never broke beyond the edge of the monolith. It was like the ocean began and ended here at the rock.

Now moving closer, Grace could distinguish a pattern of concentric circles. From the air, what she saw below looked like a giant dartboard.

Now, recognizing the pattern, Grace was able to divide the distance between the subsequent rings and to distinguish one region for another.

On the outside, the red sand, which rose up sporadically as the earth, inhaled and exhaled. The next circle as we have explained was the ocean, starting and ending as the waves kissed the red rock without overflowing. The red rock formed a ring, and from it grew a circle of trees.

The trees held out their branches, one to the other, but one tree towered above all the others: an olive tree. It reached up into the clouds far above the metal bird, which Grace was riding on. Beside the olive tree, were normal sized maple trees, palm trees and eucalyptus trees—to name but a few. This section began and ended with trees and then a dividing circle of red sand again was visible.

Inside the trees, there was another section of flowers. It was made up of sunflowers and golden wattles and tulips and roses and many, many more.

Then more red sand, followed by very tall animals like dinosaurs, giraffes, elephants, and bears.

Where that section ended, another one began. Red sand, then other circles of water creatures like whales, sharks and jellyfish. Water rushed over and around them without touching any of the other sections since they were protected and contained.

In a circle, were all the flying and gliding animals. There were ravens, foxes, butterflies, and cockatoos. They rose and fell almost like an imaginary puppeteer was holding them down. The beast, upon whose back Grace and the little girl had journeyed, would take his place within this circle.

Next after another circle of sand came a section of reptiles, marsupials, and numerous other animal sections followed so that each phylum and species was represented in kind.

There were far too many sections for Grace to count them all. The sounds coming from them rose from the Earth, almost like they spoke in one voice.

Now as they drew nearer and nearer, Grace could see circles of people, too.

Men and women, both young and old, were divided into sections. They came from all over the world representing every Aboriginal and Indigenous culture. Some were dressed in traditional garb. Some carried spears. Some carried boomerangs. Others were adorned in furs and feathers, and a few had painted faces. While others made music from rain sticks and drums.

As they drew closer, all the circle dwellers intrinsically felt Grace's presence. In synchronicity, each segment began to sway. The red sand rose and fell within its circle boundary.

Closer and closer now they flew and for a moment she thought she saw Vincente. It was true. He was standing in a circle with other boys who were the same age as he was. Each boy had blond hair and was wearing a long floor length robe like a monk might wear.

Vincente's eyes connected with Grace's. He waved his Aboriginal carved man in the air to acknowledge her presence.

In the sunlight, Grace noticed his family heirloom ring was back upon his finger. Together the boys raised their arms in her direction. Grace was blinded momentarily as the sunlight hit each of their rings at once. They were all wearing the exact same ring as Vincente.

Blinking back to reality, Grace saw each of the boys remove his ring and place it in front of himself on a small square of fabric.

Inside the section of boys was a circle of girls. Again, there were thousands, one girl for each of the boys. The girls were all dressed in white linen nightgowns with red tie-ups around the collars. Each girl was holding a blanket in their arms.

As they nearly landed, Grace watched as the red tie-ups drifted up and down in the breeze, then stilled, and then rose and fell once again.

Vincente's eyes locked onto Grace's. She nearly jumped off of the beast's back, but Vincente looked away almost like she was dead to him. Her feet touched the sand. She would have run to him, if the little girl hadn't prevented it by taking hold of her hand.

Grace joined into the circle where the girls waited in silence. Grace had many, many questions which she wanted to ask, which she needed answers to. The little girl put her finger to her lips and said, "Shhhh."

Grace's red tie-up now rose and fell in time with the other girls as the warm breeze caressed them. Although she was warm, Grace shivered.

"Put the blanket on the ground in front of you," the little girl demanded.

The other girls in the circle followed Grace's example.

Again, Grace attempted to ask a question but as before the little girl only said, "Shhh."

CHAPTER 43

Now four new sections had been added. A circle of red sand, followed by a circle of fabric with a ring upon it in front of the boys. This was followed by another circle of sand and a circle of blankets in front of the girls.

It was then that the chanting began. It began on the outside and moved from section to section. Each segment had a sound to make, which together formed into a song. Together they rode on the wings of melody as the sun pushed its way higher and higher into the newly born day.

As quickly as it had started, the chanting stopped.

For a moment there was absolute silence. Then together they roared in one voice, one song.

It was a beautiful sound, calming and soothing, not at all what one might imagine, but it was so loud that Grace covered her ears.

The little girl saw Grace's fear and she whispered into her ear: "The pain has been borne by the Earth, for such a long, long time. The Earth is now releasing the pain. Its survival depends upon it. Do not be afraid. You are witnessing the healing."

Grace lowered her hands and closed her eyes and when she was no longer afraid, she could feel and appreciate it all.

Mother Sun poured her rays into the hearts of all those who were present. She seemed to be drawing out heartbeats, synchronizing them. Making them reverberate into the single heartbeat of the universe.

"Say it now," the little girl said. "Grace, speak the words."

Grace shrugged her shoulders in confusion. She had no idea what the little girl wanted from her.

"Say it now. Say the words, the words. The words, which you have been taught. You are the last one. You must say them now. We are all waiting."

Grace's mind flew back to the song that the little girl had spoken to her some time ago. She wasn't certain that she could remember the words. Yet somehow, she knew instinctively she did remember them.

All were quiet. All were waiting.

Grace took a deep breath, but she could not bring forth a single sound.

"Speak from your heart," the little girl said. "And the words will flow."

Grace quieted her breathing and closed her eyes. The words poured from her mouth into the open air like a gift:

"I am the woman-drawer,

I am the cry;

I am the secret voice,

I am the sigh;

I am that which is heard
Low in the dusk;
Birds by a note reply,
The flowers in musk;
I am that dolorous plant,
Uttered where calls
A lone bird wand'ring by
Dim waterfalls;
I am the woman drawer,
Pass me not by;
I am the secret voice,
Hear ye my cry;
I am the power which night
Loses abroad;
I am the root of life;
*I am the chord." ***

The girls in the section began to chant. One song for one, one song for all. Then they joined hands and swayed in the warmth of Mother Sun.

The little girl smiled at Grace and then transformed back into a raven. She flew toward the section where she was greeted by the sound of their wings flapping.

While they were singing, men and women began to gather outside of the circle. They were dressed in traditional garb, and they had come to the red rock from many, many distant lands. They stood together in couples, and they held hands. Soon, the hands were parted, and the men stood in the line leading into the circle of men and the girls stood in line leading in the circle of girls.

An Aboriginal boy stood in front of the first blond boy, and they embraced. Then the blond boy picked up his ring and the square of fabric and placed it into the open hand of the Aboriginal boy. The Aboriginal boy placed the ring upon his finger. They embraced again and the Aboriginal boy waited.

The boy's partner stood in front of the first girl wearing a white linen gown. The two girls embraced as the boys had done. The girl gave the Aboriginal girl the red ribbon tie-up from her gown. They embraced again and then she bent down, picked up the blanket and she and her partner walked in the direction of the sun. As the couple walked into the light, they vanished.

This same incident occurred repeatedly for many, many hours. Together, the men and women bridged the gap of time. There was much weeping and embracing. Soon, the only two people left were Vincente and Grace and a couple outside of the circle.

The last Aboriginal man entered the section, and he and Vincente made the exchange.

And then the bundle at Grace's feet began to cry.

It wasn't just a blanket. It wasn't an empty bundle. It was a child. Grace and Vincente's child.

Grace bent forward to pat the blanket, but the Aboriginal woman was already there, and the ceremony had already begun.

The baby continued to bawl at Grace's feet.

She looked at the woman's hand and saw that it was shaking.

The woman embraced Grace.

Grace glanced over her shoulder to confirm that the woman's partner was now wearing Vincente's ring. He was, which meant that Vincente had given his permission.

A defiant tear rolled down Grace's cheek.

Next in the ceremony was the gift of the red tie-up. If Grace refused to hand it over, then the deal would not be done. She wanted to see her baby, to comfort her baby.

The woman embraced Grace once again.

And then it happened.

CHAPTER 44

T HE WAVES SURROUNDING THE red monolith rose up, higher and higher and higher, until they had curled their way around the red rock and formed into a new section of circular ginormous-max movie screens.

Once the new circle of screens was complete, then the ground under Grace's feet began to shake and shudder, as it broke apart. The platform raised Grace and her child up higher and higher and higher.

There in front of her the history of the world's Aboriginal and Indigenous peoples began to flash across the screens. She witnessed babies being taken, stolen, and handed over to strangers and parents weeping repeatedly through days, years, and centuries.

And with every child who was taken, the olive tree twisted and slashed a wound onto Grace's body. At first, she cried out with the sting, but as she gazed into the wounded eyes of those babies being torn away from their families, she opened her arms, and she welcomed the pain, and she embraced it as a part of her being. She recognized now that the olive tree was the constant.

The connection between here and there, between them and us, between worlds.

When she had accepted the pain into her body, she glanced in the direction of Vincente. He had tried to run to her, but his feet would not allow it. It was like they had been concreted into the ground.

She swirled, blood dripping from her gaping wounds and called out to Mother Earth who brought down the screens and returned Grace back to level ground where the Aboriginal girl waited.

As soon as she was back upon terra firma, Grace had no hesitation whatsoever in embracing the Aboriginal woman, whispering an apology into her ear, and in presenting her with the red tie-up ribbon.

The Aboriginal woman picked up what was now her own baby. She waved and did not look back as she comforted her child, and they moved in the direction of the warm sun's rays.

At first the baby's cries resumed, but soon she was comforted, and the air was calm, very still and noticeably quiet.

And then came a pandemonium of noise, as all the trees and animals bellowed out in synchronicity.

A raven flew down to where the last two, Grace and Vincente stood. She turned back into the little girl and reached out for Vincente's hand and then for Grace's hand.

Balance now restored for Mother Earth; the trio walked into the sunlight.

"One more thing," the little girl whispered and then she let go of their hands.

CHAPTER 45

T HE EARTH BEGAN TO shake and convulse under their feet.

Grace and Vincente held to each other as the forces pushed them together and apart, together, and apart.

They held hands as they lifted off the ground.

They twirled and twirled in a black tunnel, almost like they were inside of a whirling black umbrella.

They held together. They kissed.

A unified call rang out.

In a blink of an eye Mother Earth returned everything and everyone to where they were meant to be.

And once again the red monolith stood alone.

EPILOGUE

A YOUNG MAN STRADDLED his surfboard at Manly Quay. He was waiting for the big wave.

In the distance, he spotted something flickering and bobbing.

He paddled toward it. It was a camera.

He put the strap around his neck, and when the big wave finally arrived, he rode the surf into the shore.

Later, he walked up and down the beach for quite some time, asking if anyone had lost a camera. No one claimed it.

Curious, he took it to the local photo shop. The film inside was not damaged or wet. He asked to have it developed.

A few hours later, when the film was ready, the surfer dude returned to the camera store. The young woman behind the counter apologized because there was only one photograph on the film.

He opened the envelope.

A young man with blond hair, wearing a black tuxedo jacket, shirtless and a pair of black jeans stood arm in arm with a woman with auburn hair, wearing a tiara and a lace wedding dress. They looked very happy. Behind them fairy lights, the moon and the ocean had provided the perfect backdrop for their wedding.

Recognizing neither of them, he tossed the photo and the camera into the bin.

Three ravens cried out in the distance.

AFTER WORD

As it was

And as it always shall be...

Children pay the price,

For history.

ACKNOWLEDGMENTS

***DAME MARY GILMORE (1865-1962)**

Dame Mary Gilmore's Poem entitled "The Song of The Woman-Drawer."
is included in this book courtesy of the Publisher ETT Imprint, Sydney, Australia.

I hope you'll want to read Mary Gilmore's other works too!
Do a search and you'll be amazed and INSPIRED by everything she's accomplished!

READING SUGGESTIONS

I hope you'll want to learn more about:

THE GADIGAL PEOPLE OF THE EORA NATION &

INDIGENOUS AUSTRALIA

WOMEN SCIENTISTS

WOMEN MATHEMATICIANS

LEONARDO FIBONACCI

ALBERT EINSTEIN.

Do a search and **BE INSPIRED!**

NOTE FROM THE AUTHOR:

Dear readers,

Thank you for choosing to read the story about Grace and Vincente. I hope you enjoyed reading it, as much as I enjoyed writing it!

I was born in Ontario, Canada, but lived in Sydney, Australia for over fifteen years with my family.

During that time, I discovered the works of Mary Gilmore. The poem included in this novel inspired me greatly, and I wanted others to discover it, too.

When the characters of Grace and Vincente first came to me, I wasn't certain I was prepared for the task set before me. She was a mathematical protege and he was a cricket player - neither of which I had

any great knowledge. It took a lot of
ruminating, researching, building - before
I even sat down to write the first draft.

I was busily finally working on the first
draft, when I attended a Writer's Retreat
with the Society of Women's Writers NSW
Inc., and during one of their seminar
exercises opened up, and gave myself
permission to write it. The story flowed
naturally after that revelation. I hope
you enjoy reading it, as much as I enjoyed
writing it.

These days I'm back home in Ontario,
Canada, with my husband, son, cat, and dog.

Thank you! As always HAPPY READING!

Cathy

ALSO BY:

YA FICTION

E-Z Dickens Superhero Book 1 and 2: TATTOO ANGEL; THE THREE

E-Z Dickens Superhero Book 3: RED ROOM

E-Z Dickens Superhero Book 4: ON ICE

NON-FICTION

103 Fundraising Ideas For Parent Volunteers With Schools and Teams (3RD PLACE BEST REFERENCE 2016 METAMORPH PUBLISHING

+ Children's Books

www.ingramcontent.com/pod-product-compliance
Lightning Source LLC
Chambersburg PA
CBHW031152310726
48969CB00001B/52